Hartwood Creek

wood you knot

J.C. HANNIGAN

Editors: Brooklyn Marie (Brazen Hearts Author Services), Karen Hrdlicka (Barren Acres Editing)

Cover Designer: Mignon Mykel (Oh So Novel)

Formatting: Heritage Creek Formatting

ISBN 978-1-989124-19-2 (paperback)

ISBN 978-1-989124-20-8 (ebook)

http://jchannigan.com

DEDICATION

This book is dedicated to Granny Good Witch.
I love you, always and forever.
You created an entire legacy of love and laughter for us.
I am forever grateful for your magical light.

CHAPTER ONE

Sage

The closer I got to Hartwood Creek, the farther away my problems seemed, and the easier it was to breathe again. Perhaps it was the fresh, woodsy air from the forest and the heady scent of Hartwood Lake that helped revive me.

Putting the miles between me and my ex-fiancé, Warren Davidson, was certainly helping ease my fractured heart—and confidence. With each town I drove through, I felt more and more myself and less like the person I'd slipped into when with him.

The pang of bitterness grasped firmly around my heart at the very thought of Warren, and I did my best to push it away, opting to draw in a breath of the crisp air coming through my open car windows. But try as I might, escaping my failings was still a challenge.

I had the worst luck when it came to men. My biological father died before I was born, so I never knew him, and my daughter's father hadn't stuck around. He'd never wanted to be a part of Daphne's life and had tried to insist I "get rid of the problem." Daphne's father had a hockey scholarship and no desire to be a father.

But from the moment I found out about her, I wanted to keep her. I wanted to raise her with all the love and affection I didn't get, regardless of whether her bio dad wanted to participate.

I didn't harbor any resentment toward him for it. If anything, I was thankful I didn't have to worry about co-parenting with someone who had the emotional maturity of a squash. If Derrick's escapades since getting drafted were any indication, Daphne and I both dodged a bullet there.

For years, I'd lived the single-mom life happily. Just me and Daphne, no man required. I tolerated living with my mother long enough to find a stable job, daycare, and a place of our own just before Daphne's second birthday. Then, it was just Daphne and me.

Until Warren walked into our lives...

I'd *thought* I had finally gotten it right with him, but what a disaster that turned out to be.

I met Warren when Daphne was three and a half. He worked a block away from the café, and he would always flirt with me when he came in. He tipped well, and he took his time asking me out, but when he finally did...I didn't hesitate.

I couldn't help but think back to the early days, picking them apart with the hindsight of the present time. I'd thought Warren was so charming and magnetic; he'd said and done everything right to win my heart. He really had me fooled, thinking he was a good, genuine guy. A family man.

I thought he was a total catch. He was good-looking and had a great job. He worked upper level in the finance department, wore suits, and styled his hair...I didn't have to remind him to shower or shave. He cared about the image he portrayed to the world, and I thought that meant he cared about me.

I thought we were building something special, but the whole time, the jerk had been micromanaging every aspect of my life while also shacking up with his secretary, and what a cliché he'd turned out to be.

I was *sick* of clichés, and right now, it was hard not to feel like one myself. Single mom, on her own—again.

"How much longer?" my six-year-old daughter asked, raising her voice to be heard over the music. I turned it down before replying. According to my GPS, we were less than ten minutes out from crossing the town border.

"We're almost there," I said, making eye contact with Daphne in the rear-view mirror. I found a smile for my daughter. She truly was the one good thing in my life—my sole purpose for trying to do and *be* better. I didn't want her to feel like she had to settle for a man who didn't love her and tried to control every aspect of her, just so she wouldn't be alone. "About ten more minutes, then we'll be at our new home."

Daphne's big green eyes seemed to see straight into my soul. She wasn't happy about all the changes. In fact, she was downright angry about them. She didn't understand why the relationship between Warren and I had dissipated so quickly because I refused to go into detail on what actually happened. A six-year-old wouldn't understand such a thing as cheating. All Daphne knew was it was over, and we were moving on.

Daphne wanted to stay in Guelph, but I couldn't find an affordable place for us on my barista job wages. Daphne's solution was for me to forgive Warren so we could keep living with him.

It was bad enough my mother thought I should forgive Warren; I didn't need my daughter echoing that sentiment. The way my mother saw it, Warren had proven he'd take care of me and Daphne. Men were dogs, but Warren was rich. She thought I ought to forgive Warren's "extracurricular activities" for the security he could provide us. My mother was superficial, and that was putting it kindly.

Even worse, *Warren* had believed I'd forgive him. That I'd overlook his indiscretions because "he really loved me, and we had a good life together."

I would rather be on my own and broke as a joke than be tied to a man who couldn't be faithful to me.

This opportunity to work at my aunt and uncle's hardware store and live in the apartments above was a well-timed miracle because, after two weeks of staying with my mother, I was ready to burst with frustration. I couldn't handle her superficial, materialistic nature any longer, and the thinly veiled insults were not something I wanted my daughter to continue to overhear.

Small doses of my mother were key to maintaining a distant and slightly healthier relationship. Elouise Whitaker was used to living on her own selfish terms, and I'd long since learned she wouldn't be the kind of mother to wipe my tears or help me heal a broken heart.

No, she'd just look me dead in the eyes and tell me the ways *I'd* messed up. By not quitting my barista job when Warren heavily suggested it because it made him feel "less manly" that I wanted to keep my paying job. By not "doing enough" in the bedroom to keep his attention. The list was endless, and she'd said it all with little regard to the small ears listening in.

"I don't want it to be our new home. I miss my school and my friends." Daphne crossed her arms and pouted, glaring out the window at the scenery as if it were to blame. "Why can't we live with Warren anymore?"

It wasn't the first time Daphne asked that question, and I knew it wouldn't be the last. I chewed on my bottom lip, deliberating. "Remember how I'm always talking about how important it is to be honest?" I asked, glancing in the rear-view mirror at my daughter. Daphne reluctantly nodded. "Warren was dishonest, Daph. He broke my trust."

"Well, you can forgive him, can't you? Mimi says you should. Forgiveness is important," Daphne said with all the stubborn willfulness she possessed. She took after me in that regard.

"I bet she does," I muttered, my attention returning to the road. My mother had forgiven many cheating men over the years, especially her latest husband, because she was accustomed to the certain lifestyle they provided. "Listen, kiddo. Forgiveness is important, but so is honesty. Warren turned out to be a dishonest person, and I know I deserve better than that. We both do."

It wasn't much, but I hoped it would tide my daughter's curiosity over the matter. Daphne fell silent, staring out at the passing scenery somberly.

We passed the sign that read *Welcome to Hartwood Creek*, and I let my GPS guide me to the downtown core. Eyeing the beautiful green and white gazebo in the center of Hartley Park where a musician—a young guitarist—stood playing and singing into a microphone, I smiled. He didn't have much of an audience, but those that were passing by stopped to listen.

It had been several years since I'd made the trip out to visit Auntie Em and Uncle Ed. As a child and a young teen, I'd spend weeks every summer in this charming, historic town, located on the southern tip of Hartwood Lake, to spend time with my cousins and give my mother a "break."

Funny, those were my fondest memories of growing up—escaping the indifference of my mother.

I was able to score a parking spot out front of the hardware store and peered up at the old brick building. Alcott Hardware had been in my uncle's family since the early days of Hartwood Creek, passed down from generation to generation. My cousins were all married or busy with their careers now, and none of them were interested in taking over the hardware store. Neither was I, really, but I'd happily accepted the position to get the hell out of Dodge.

I'd made it clear to Uncle Ed and Auntie Em that I had no desire to take over the business either. I just needed a job. They both seemed okay with that and were happy to employ me as a cashier.

"Please get out on the sidewalk side," I instructed, and Daphne rolled her eyes in response, sliding across the seat to do as I asked. Not that the streets were overly busy—and as a bonus, the hardware store was sandwiched between the police station and a bistro, making it one of the safest places in town, but one could never be too careful.

I got out of the car, too, stretching the kinks out of my back. As I did so, my aunt and uncle walked out of the hardware store. Aunt Emelia's curly brunette hair was peppered with more gray, and her laugh lines were more pronounced, but I instantly felt at home when she embraced me.

"Sage! It's been way too long," Auntie Em said, squeezing me tight. I closed my eyes, trying to will away the tears that welled at her maternal touch.

Auntie Em was the polar opposite of my shallow, self-centered mother, who didn't seem to have a maternal bone in her body and never had. From her dark hair to her positive, nurturing nature, Emelia was the mother I often wished mine could be.

Auntie Em hadn't tried to convince me to settle for less than my worth, and she'd given me an opportunity for a new beginning.

Moving on to Daphne, Auntie Em hugged her. "Ooh! The last time I saw you, you were in diapers," she crooned, and Daphne looked at me pleadingly.

Uncle Ed caught her distress, and chuckling, moved forward to put his hands on Auntie Em's shoulders. He had also aged over the years, his face more wrinkled and weathered. His light brown hair was longer than I remembered and graying along with the scruff on his chin. "Now, Em, let them have some breathin' room. How was the drive, girls?"

"Long," Daphne complained, peering around them to the hardware store. "Is that the store Mommy's going to work at?"

"Sure is. And those windows right there—that's your new apartment," Uncle Ed said, pointing to the windows above. "Parking is around back for customers and residents, but you're fine there for now," Uncle Ed said this second bit to me, and I nodded.

"Wanna go check it out, Squirt?" I ruffled Daphne's hair. Despite her efforts, the smile Daphne tried to hold back burst through. Uncle Ed flipped the sign to "closed" and locked the hardware store up.

"We'll give you the grand tour," Auntie Em said, her eyes shining with excitement. I followed my aunt and uncle to the door to the right of the hardware store.

Uncle Ed typed in a code to unlock the door. "The code is easy to remember; it's 0-0-0-0," he told us with a bemused grin. "Never got around to changing it, and Mrs. Durand wouldn't be able to remember now if we did."

"Who's Mrs. Durand?" Daphne asked, peering up at her great-uncle.

"She lives in the apartment beside you. Elderly lady, she mostly keeps to herself," he replied, answering her question with a smile my daughter couldn't help but return.

We stepped into a narrow foyer with a set of stairs and a hallway that led to another door at the back of the building. "That's the door you'll use when you park in the parking lot.

The same code that opens the front will open the back," Uncle Ed explained.

He led us up the stairs to the second level, where a secondary door opened to a long corridor. Uncle Ed walked down the hall until he reached the second door, apartment 2B. He unlocked it, then held it open for us to walk through.

The apartment opened into a beautiful open-concept kitchen and living room area with high ceilings and exposed brick. It was way nicer than any place I had ever rented on my own. To my left, I could make out a hallway that probably led to the bedrooms and bathroom—Daphne immediately ran down it to investigate.

"Wow," I exhaled, my eyes widening as I took in every detail with astonishment. I walked into the apartment, instantly feeling at home. The open-concept kitchen was divided by an island. The refrigerator, stove, and a long counter were on the interior wall, with pine cabinets above and below.

The double kitchen sink on the island overlooked the living room, so if I was washing dishes, I wouldn't be staring at a wall, but rather at the living room and the two large windows.

Strolling over to the windows, I peered outside at the view of Hartley Park and beyond that—Hartwood Lake.

Everything was within walking distance, which meant I'd save a ton on gas when we were out exploring the town.

I turned around to face my aunt and uncle. "This is perfect, thank you so much. How much is the rent?"

Uncle Ed and Auntie Em glanced at each other, wordlessly communicating with a single look. "Six hundred dollars, all-inclusive," Uncle Ed replied.

"That seems extremely low." I frowned, glancing around. The apartment was dated and the appliances on the older side, but surely a two-bedroom apartment in the downtown core of a touristy historical town would be a little more? One as beautiful as this one should be well outside my budget.

"It's the family rate," Auntie Em insisted. "You're helping us out. Saving us from having to try and find a suitable tenant."

"You've already given me a job. I can't accept this as well," I tried to insist, my cheeks heating with embarrassment. It was hard not to feel like a charity case.

"You'll work for the job." Uncle Ed smiled. "We own the building, and it has long since paid itself off. We can afford to be generous with the rent."

"We want to help you get on your feet again," Auntie Em added kindly. She knew the gist of what had happened with Warren—and the motherly advice I'd received from her younger sister. She'd been disappointed but unsurprised by my mother's stance. She just so happened to side with me on the matter.

If a man wasn't loyal, there was no sense in loving him. It'd only lead to a lifetime of heartache.

My eyes began to itch with the urge to cry at their kindness and generosity, but before I could succumb to tears, my daughter pulled me back.

"Mommy! Look at my room." Daphne's little voice came from down the hallway, where she stood peering into one of the bedrooms. I cast a suspicious look at my aunt and uncle, who were both looking everywhere but directly at me, and went to join my daughter.

The bedroom that was to be Daphne's had furniture in it already—a white captain's bed and a matching dresser and desk. I recognized the bedroom set from my aunt and uncle's house; it'd been in their middle daughter Livia's bedroom. The entire room smelt like fresh paint, and the walls were a soft purple colour.

"I love it," Daphne declared, unable to mask her excitement

over her new bedroom.

When I peered into the other bedroom—*my* bedroom—I found it was also freshly painted and furnished with a white queen-size sleigh bed, a dresser, and a matching night table. It was the bedroom set that had been in their oldest daughter Madeline's bedroom.

"It's just some extra pieces of furniture we had kicking around from the girls," Auntie Em explained from the living room. "You mentioned you'd left everything behind."

I nodded. Aside from our clothes and worldly possessions, all the furniture had belonged to Warren. He'd insisted I didn't need to bring anything of ours when we moved in, so I had sold everything or donated it. It made sense at the time. Warren's things were newer and nicer, and so was his place.

Now we were starting over, once again. I had a small amount of money saved up, enough to get a few pieces of secondhand furniture and the necessities, but it wouldn't stretch very far. Luckily, I would start at the hardware store Monday after dropping Daphne off at school, so I wouldn't be going *too* long in between paychecks.

I was just thankful I never listened to Warren about quitting my job at the café.

Warren hadn't seen the point in me keeping my job as a barista. Not when *his* job covered all the expenses and more. But I hadn't wanted to part with the job. The hours were great, and I worked alongside some awesome people—one of them being my only close friend, Nellie. I knew I'd go stir-crazy without the distraction.

Plus, I hadn't been complacent with the idea of having him pay for *everything*. I wanted to contribute, and I certainly didn't expect him to cover all my daughter's expenses. She was my responsibility, after all.

Warren had praised me for my independent nature, but

over time that appreciation must have turned to resentment. My mother certainly thought it was a contributing factor.

"Men like to provide, and you've robbed him of doing that by not quitting your silly little job," she'd said with authority, as if she truly had a great grasp on the opposite sex and how they thought. Funny, considering she was on husband number four.

Leaving my job and life in Guelph was harder than leaving Warren. Something had shifted in me when I watched my fiancé's hands explore his secretary's body. The chains tethering me to Warren snapped as though they'd been cut. But leaving my job, my friend, and the life I'd had before him? That was hard.

Oh well, no time to dwell on the past, I reminded myself, glancing around our new apartment. I really was lucky—lucky to have family like Auntie Em and Uncle Ed. Lucky to have this place to live in. Lucky we *could* have this fresh start. I wouldn't squander it.

"Thank you, seriously. You have no idea how grateful I am to you both," I said, hugging my aunt and uncle each in turn. I tried not to let the tears fall, but the relief I felt was immense. My plan for the night was to see if the hardware store sold air mattresses, but now we'd have real beds to sleep in. It was one less thing to worry about.

The weight my aunt and uncle had taken off my shoulders was notable, and I was so thankful for them both.

"It's no problem at all. We have way too much furniture. We can stand to part with a few pieces," Auntie Em said with a laugh.

"You've got a couch and a coffee table coming too," Uncle Ed added. "The Hutchinson brothers said they'd swing by tomorrow morning with it."

I froze, recognizing the last name from my many visits to Hartwood Creek as a little girl and young teen.

Keith and Laurel Hutchinson were family friends of my aunt and uncle. They owned and operated the lumberyard near the marsh. They had four sons, all of them tall, dark, and handsome. I would find myself utterly tongue-tied around each of them, especially one in particular.

I wondered which of the four Hutchinson brothers would show up but quickly pushed the thought from my mind.

"Thank you, truly. I don't know what I'd do without you two."

"We're happy to help. Now let's get that car of yours unloaded," Auntie Em said, her eyes sparkling.

IT TOOK a couple of loads to run everything packed tightly in my car up to the apartment. Once the task was finished, I moved my car around back to the parking lot behind the building. I returned just as Uncle Ed was leaving to head back down to the hardware store. Auntie Em lingered longer, making sure we were settled.

"Mommy, I'm hungry," Daphne said, tugging on the hem of my T-shirt, her soulful green eyes the mirror image of mine. I looked at my watch, wincing at the time. It was nearly six o'clock, and the last thing I felt like doing was cooking. Plus, we'd have to go grocery shopping first as there wasn't any food in the apartment.

Not happening, I thought, the exhaustion hitting me hard. "Let's order a pizza."

"Oh! You'll love Pizza Picasso. They have the best pizza," Auntie Em suggested with a smile. I nodded thankfully, pulling my cell phone out of my purse. I googled the pizzeria's phone number and dialed, lifting the phone to my ear.

"Pizza Picasso. What can I get for you?" a friendly feminine voice asked.

"Hi, I'd like to order an extra-large cheese and pepperoni pizza for delivery," I said, turning to look at my aunt. "We're, um, apartment 2B, above the hardware store?"

"Okay, that will be $26.25. It'll be about forty minutes," the voice replied cheerfully.

"Thank you," I said, hanging up the phone. All I wanted to do was curl up in bed and sleep.

"Oh, by the way, the buzzer is right here." Auntie Em went over to the strange-looking box beside the apartment door. "When someone buzzes up, you can talk to them with that button and let them in by hitting this button." She pointed to the two different buttons.

"That's so cool," Daphne exclaimed, peering up at the door buzzer with interest. She'd never seen one before. The old apartment we lived in before moving in with Warren didn't have one. Warren's apartment had been in a newer building, with a doorman and everything.

Auntie Em smiled at Daphne.

"Uncle Ed's probably closing the shop now, so I better get skedaddling. I hope you ladies enjoy your first night in your new home." Auntie Em scooped Daphne up for a hug, squeezing her tight.

"Thanks again for everything, Auntie Em."

"Of course, Sage. That's what family's for."

Her tender words and maternal warmth made my heart ache, especially when my thoughts drifted to my own mother. Maternal warmth and tender words were *not* her forte, so I'd spent the last couple of weeks hearing her *opinions* on what I should do, rather than being comforted for my broken heart.

I hadn't realized until that moment just how much that sucked.

CHAPTER TWO

Nix

"Don't forget to lift with your knees, fellas," Edward Alcott shouted as he oversaw us struggling to get the large couch out through his front door. I grunted, my fingers catching on the doorframe. I would have sworn if the older man wasn't standing right there watching.

"Got it, Nix?" my older brother, Parker, asked.

"Yeah, I've got it," I replied, shifting my hold on the couch so I had a better grip on it and ignoring the pain from my scraped knuckles. It took us a few tries, but eventually, we figured out how to tilt it to get it outside.

We carried the couch down the patio steps and to my brother's truck. We loaded it in the bed, tying it and the coffee table down securely.

"I appreciate you boys doing this. My back's not what it used to be," Ed remarked, putting his hand on the side of the truck.

"We're happy to help," Parker replied easily, exchanging a look with me.

"Yeah, it's no problem at all, Ed," I added breezily.

"Well, thank you again. I know you boys probably had better things to do with your Saturday."

"We don't mind taking a couple of hours out of our day to help out an old friend," Parker replied for us both.

I'd had plans to meet up and go fishing with a couple of my buddies. Of course, those plans went out the window when our parents asked us to help the Alcotts move a couch from their house to the apartment above the hardware store. They didn't ask often, so I never refused a request from my parents.

The Alcotts were close family friends of ours, with a friendship spanning generations. My brothers and I had grown up alongside their four daughters. We'd all gone to school together, and our families would often gather for cookouts and go on camping trips together.

"Well, again, I appreciate it. I know Sage will too."

I felt my ears perk up with the mention of Sage. She was *kind of* the real reason I agreed to help out, despite my plans. I hadn't seen Sage Whitaker in *years*, but she used to spend a lot of the summer here in Hartwood Creek. I'd always thought she was beautiful, with her long blond hair, sparkling green eyes, and infectious smile.

Emelia, Ed's wife, had told our mother their niece would be moving to Hartwood Creek and renting the apartment above the hardware store. I was looking forward to seeing her again; I used to have a crush on her when we were younger. Making her laugh had always been my main objective, although my secret desire was to make her mine. I could never seem to get past the hurdle of asking her out, though.

Not that I had planned on doing that today, but my curiosity had gotten the better of me, that was for sure. I couldn't wait to see what she looked like now.

We said our goodbyes and climbed into the truck. Parker twisted the keys in the ignition, and the truck roared to life.

"Don't think I didn't notice you perk up at the mention of Sage Whitaker," Parker teased, shooting me a bemused look. I furrowed my brow.

I could deny it—pretend I hadn't perked up at the sound of her name, but what was the point? "So what? I'm looking forward to seeing an old friend again."

"Sure, sure." Parker shook his head, that bemused smile still on his face. All of us Hutchinson boys had dark hair and brown eyes, just like our father.

Parker pulled away from the curb, driving from the suburbs to the downtown core, turning onto Main Street. In no time at all, we'd reached our destination. We parked in front of the hardware store, and I opened the door, stepping out onto the sidewalk.

Three old ladies were making their way down the street in a Can-Am Commander decked out in purple, squabbling amongst themselves. I nodded at the three of them as they were about to pass. "Morning, ladies."

The purple Commander came to a sudden stop.

"Phoenix Hutchinson, is that you?" the first lady, Alice, asked as she backed up a little to address me. Calling attention to the Hartley sisters as they passed probably wasn't my best bet, but if I hadn't said a thing, they'd have stopped anyway. Those three busybodies never missed an opportunity to chat us up.

Plus, Gran would have my hide if she found out I'd snubbed them in public.

"Sure is, ma'am."

"Well, good morning," Alice said, exchanging a mischievous smile with the other two old women. "How's your gran doing?"

"Very well, thank you. I'll tell her you said hi."

"Yes, please do that." Alice nodded with a smile and adjusted her hat.

"What brings you to town?" Dorothy inquired. She was sitting up front, and she was the only one not wearing a hat.

"Just helping out the Alcotts," I answered, gesturing to the bed of the truck where Parker was standing, waiting for me to help. He caught sight of the Hartley sisters and waved tentatively at the older women. They *kind of* freaked him out a little, not that he'd admit that.

"Oh, right! Their niece just moved into the apartments above the hardware store," Betty said with a knowing grin from the back of the purple Commander.

"That she did."

"It's so kind of you boys to help out." Betty smiled.

"Yeah." I lifted my hand to the back of my neck and rested it there, feeling uncomfortable. It was evident the Hartley sisters had something up their sleeve. I hoped they weren't getting any ideas—the sisters had earned a reputable reputation matchmaking for a reason.

They called themselves the messengers. They liked to meddle and trick couples into drinking the infamous love elixir their ancestor Morgana Hartley created. In The Name of Love Latte, a latte from their local coffee shop, was said to possess magical powers that made the couples who drank it fall undeniably in love.

In fact, they were able to trick Parker and his wife, Tabitha, into drinking it. Now they liked to take credit for their relationship.

"How's business?" Alice questioned.

"Business is good. We've been keeping busy with a few restoration projects," I answered. "I hope you ladies are doing well."

"Of course we're doing well. Why...what did you hear?" Betty demanded.

"He's heard nothing, he's just checking in, you nitwit, no need to get all defensive," Dorothy scolded.

"Send our love to your families," Alice said over her squabbling sisters.

I chuckled as the three women started driving their purple Commander in the direction of Tout de Sweets, still bickering all the while.

Dorothy, Alice, and Betty owned these streets. They were the busiest bodies in town, and they always seemed to know everything about everyone. It was a common occurrence, seeing their purple all-terrain vehicle zooming around town.

I strolled over to the doorway to the right of the hardware store and buzzed up, waiting a few minutes before a sleepy voice came on over the intercom.

"Hello?"

"Hey, Sage. It's Nix Hutchinson. We've got a couch here for ya."

"Oh, right. Thank you so much," she said, sounding more awake and buzzing us up. I pushed open the door and used the doorstopper to prop it open; then I walked back to the truck to find Parker untying the straps.

I released the straps on the other side before I grabbed the side of the couch, maneuvering it down off the truck and onto the road for a moment while Parker jumped out beside it. We picked it up, carrying it across the sidewalk and through the open door.

It was a bit of a process, but we got it up the stairwell and down the hallway. As we were moving past the first apartment door, it opened, and Mrs. Durand scowled at us as if we'd greatly inconvenienced her. I sent her an apologetic smile as we passed, and she slammed her door shut in response.

Mrs. Durand had lived in that apartment for almost four decades now. My mom told me she used to be a famous painter, with her paintings featured in galleries all over the world. Now she was a crotchety old lady who seemed to hate everyone she encountered.

I still made it a point to smile at her, even if that seemed to anger her more.

The second door was propped open, and I walked through it first.

"Just against that wall is fine, thank you," a voice said, and my eyes were pulled immediately to its source in the kitchen.

Sage Whitaker was just as breathtaking as she'd always been. She tucked a strand of long blond hair behind her ear, her captivating green eyes moving from me to Parker as she smiled timidly.

I nodded—my throat suddenly as dry as the Sahara Desert. As I walked backward into the apartment, my fingers began to sweat, and my grip on the couch started to slip. We set the couch down where Sage directed. I straightened and wiped my hands on my jeans, my gaze going to the kitchen—back to her.

She looked as if she'd just gotten out of bed. She was dressed in a pair of baggy pajama bottoms and an old band T-shirt. Even still, she took the very breath from my lungs.

It was the strangest thing, but I'd always found it a little difficult to breathe around her. It was like my body forgot how to do basic functions, like bring oxygen into my lungs. Or speak. Anything I did manage to say was usually ridiculous. I hadn't expected to *still* have that problem years later.

"Thank you so much," Sage said, her gaze going from me to Parker.

"It's no problem at all," I responded, grinning at Sage. I couldn't seem to tear my gaze away from her.

"There's a coffee table too," Parker said, looking at me. But I seemed to be stuck in some sort of trance, my eyes completely unwilling to tear away from Sage. "I'll go grab it." I barely registered my brother leaving; I was too busy searching for something witty to say.

"So I guess you're an official resident now. Welcome to Hartwood Creek," I said, instantly kicking myself. What a lame thing to say.

But she smiled, so it must have done the trick. "Thank you. I'm excited to be back. I've always loved it here."

I was glad she was back too. Though it'd been years since I'd seen her, the moment I'd heard her name, I remembered every feeling I'd had in my adolescence over this girl. The sweaty palms, the lame jokes to make her laugh, the galloping heart rate.

I'd been curious more than anything—curious to see if any of those old feelings lingered. Apparently, they had. I still found her gorgeous and still wanted to make her laugh and smile. I took that as a good sign.

"If you feel like getting out tonight, a bunch of us are meeting up at The Quarter Lounge. You're welcome to join." I hoped she'd be up for it, even if it meant sharing her attention with my friends.

"Thanks, but—" Sage started to reply when she was cut off.

"Mommy?" a tiny, sleepy voice said. I turned to see a little girl standing in the hallway. She was carrying a well-loved stuffed elephant in one hand.

My gaze swiveled back to Sage. I had no idea she had a kid; my mother had failed to mention that part.

"Morning, Squirt," Sage affectionately said to the little girl.

"Who are you?" the little girl asked, eyeing me with suspicion. She was the spitting image of her mother.

I cracked a smile. Although I didn't have kids of my own, I

was pretty good with my nieces and nephew. "I'm Phoenix Hutchinson, but you can call me Nix. What's your name?"

"Daphne," the little girl answered, her wide green eyes probing. "What are you doing here?"

"Nix and his brother were just bringing us our new couch," Sage explained. Daphne seemed to notice the couch for the first time.

"Where's your brother?" she demanded with a frown, looking around. A moment later, Parker returned carrying the coffee table as if summoned. He walked inside, not missing a step, and put the coffee table down in front of the couch.

"That'd be me," he said, grinning. "My name's Parker. What's yours?" He must have overheard her question.

"I'm Daphne."

"How old are you, Daphne?"

"Six," the little girl answered, her eyes going to her mother. Sage smiled encouragingly.

"I've got twin girls your age—Bella and Brielle. Are you starting school on Monday?"

Daphne frowned with concern. "Yes. I'll be in Mr. Robertson's class." She didn't sound too excited about it.

"That's my girls' teacher. You'll love Mr. Robertson; he's nice," Parker told her before he looked at Sage. That seemed to perk Daphne up a little, though she still looked uncertain.

"Oh, isn't that wonderful," Sage said, smiling at her daughter.

"Why don't you and Daphne come over for lunch tomorrow? That way the girls can meet each other before Monday," he suggested, and Sage lit up at the idea.

"We'd love to! Wouldn't we, Daph?"

"Yeah, I guess so," Daphne replied, sounding unconvinced.

"All right, cool. Do you have a piece of paper? I'll write down the address," Parker said.

"I think I do, somewhere…" Sage went to her purse on the counter, rooting through it. She found a pen and an old envelope. Parker walked over to the other side of the counter and took the pen, scratching out his address and directions to his house.

He lived in a century home in one of the original subdivisions. I lived there, too, in the bachelor apartment above the detached garage. "Bella and Brielle would love to meet you; they love making new friends."

I kind of just watched this play out, shifting from foot to foot. Once he'd given Sage his address, we said our goodbyes and left. Neither one of us said a word until we'd climbed into the cab of the truck.

"Still got the hots for Sage, huh?" Parker finally broke the silence, a huge grin on his face. I punched him in the arm.

"Shut up." I frowned, trying to process the last twenty minutes and how tongue-tied I'd felt over seeing her again.

"I did this for you, you know," Parker told me, putting the truck in park. "Now you have an excuse to see her again."

I could find a million excuses to see her again, but I kept that thought to myself. "Gee, thanks. But I think you did it more for Daphne," I pointed out.

"You're not wrong." He nodded. "I can't imagine having to uproot my kids and move them to a new town. It's gotta be hard on the kid." Parker had three kids—twin girls, ages six, and one boy, who was less than a year old.

"Yeah," I trailed off, thinking about Sage's green eyes and hesitant smile, and wondering what brought her here.

CHAPTER THREE

Sage

From the large windows in the living room, we watched the black truck pull away from the curb and drive away. I placed my hand on Daphne's shoulder, and she shrugged it off.

"I don't want to go on a playdate with some kids I've never met before," Daphne sulked.

"Oh, stop. You'll be meeting a lot of new kids. It might make you feel better to know two friendly faces when you start on Monday."

"I hate that I have to go to a new school and make new friends and meet new people. I like my old friends." Daphne's bottom lip trembled, and a wave of intense guilt hit me. It was difficult to breathe through, but I focused on drawing in a stabilizing breath before I crouched down so I was at face level with my daughter.

"I know it's hard, Squirt. I miss my friends too. I know it's not what either of us wanted...but I promise we're both going to love it here just as much. Maybe even more than Guelph."

"I doubt that." Daphne frowned.

I gently pressed a finger to her nose. "Don't doubt it; it's true. Now get dressed, we've got a lot to do today."

"Like what?"

"Well for starters, we're going to go grocery shopping. We've got no food here except cold pizza," I answered.

"I like cold pizza," Daphne said smartly, following me as I walked through the living room and down the hall toward my bedroom to look for something to wear.

Nix and Parker had shown up before I'd even had a moment to change out of my pajamas. I'd just pulled myself out of bed and was using the bathroom when the apartment buzzer went off.

I hadn't even had time to brush my hair. And yet...Nix's eyes had roamed over every inch of me as if I *had* been wearing something irresistible, and not just my baggy pajama bottoms and an old band T-shirt.

In fact, he'd asked me out—or, at least, I think he had. He'd invited me to The Quarter Lounge.

Nix was probably just being polite, wanting to welcome me to town with an invitation to the bar everyone probably hung out at most weekends. Not that I would have been able to say yes.

When Daphne came out, Nix had seemed surprised by her existence. Of course, the last—and only—time I'd brought Daphne to town had been a quick visit over Christmas when she was an infant, and I hadn't seen any of the Hutchinsons during our brief stay.

My clothes were in a bunch of garbage bags, and I dumped them out one by one on my bed and rooted through the pile until I found a sundress. It was a little wrinkled from being in the bag, but it'd have to do.

Daphne's clothes were also in garbage bags. It was the easiest way we could fit everything into my car. I found a cute sundress for her too. While I applied a light layer of makeup, I had her write out a shopping list. Daphne *loved* making lists—a little trait she might have gotten from me.

With our shopping list in hand, we locked up the apartment and headed down to the car. I drove forty minutes out of town to the nearest Walmart, knowing I could get most of the things on our list there.

A FEW HOURS LATER, we returned, our arms loaded with bags from our shopping excursion and my bank account several hundred dollars emptier. Daphne's mood had improved greatly as I let her pick out decorations for her new room and a brand-new outfit for her first day of school.

It took us several loads to get everything out of the car, including the forty-five-inch television I bought for the living room and the console table it would sit on. At 6 p.m., I was still attempting to put the console table together. It took me several tries, but eventually, I figured it out.

When the new TV was finally hooked up, we had our first official movie night in our new place. Daphne picked *Inside Out*, and as I snuggled my daughter on the couch in our new apartment, I couldn't help but feel happier than I'd felt in months. Years, even.

But when Daphne was tucked in bed and sleeping soundly, I was left alone in the apartment with a host of emotions and feelings I knew I'd have to process sooner rather than later.

I hated my relationship mistakes had affected my daughter. I'd had to uproot her from a pretty good life in Guelph, but I knew I could build a better one for us *here*. One where I didn't have to rely on a man for my happiness.

I'd always loved Hartwood Creek. Always felt the happiest while here. Not that I was unhappy elsewhere, but...something about this place had always felt more like a home to me than any of the homes I'd had. Even the one I'd tried making with Warren.

Things had been good, leading up to me accepting his proposal. That's when the dynamic between us really changed. It was as if he expected that by me saying yes to his marriage proposal, I would start agreeing to all the things he wanted to do that I wasn't so keen on—like quitting my job. He thought I'd do that the moment the ring was on my finger.

I wandered around the apartment with a glass of white wine, taking it all in. The apartment was looking more like *us* and less empty. Although we'd been here for just over twenty-four hours, it felt more like home than Warren's place ever had.

From the masculine, contemporary furniture to the decor, it was Warren's place. He hadn't liked clutter—and Warren's definition of clutter was different from mine. I loved hanging Daphne's artwork up on the refrigerator, but he hadn't liked magnets or artwork on it, considering it clutter. I'd had to show-case Daphne's art on a wire in her bedroom.

Most of Daphne's toys had been kept in her bedroom, while the rest of the place looked like a showroom for a lifestyle magazine. Daphne's bedroom was large enough to accommo-date all her toys and more, but now that I'd removed us both from that situation, I was beginning to realize how controlling and unhealthy it'd been.

Never again would I let a man tell me how to live or how to raise my daughter. Daphne and I had been fine on our own without Warren before, and I knew we'd be fine without him. Never again would I let my foolish heart try to appease some-thing that wasn't right for me, simply because it looked good on paper.

My phone rang, and I had to search around to find it. "Hello?" I asked a little breathlessly after scrambling around and finding it wedged between the arm of the couch and the cushion.

"Hey, girl! How's the new place?" My friend Nellie's voice was a welcome distraction to the previous silence.

"It's really nice—exposed brick, beautiful high ceilings. I think we'll be happy here," I replied, making my way to the sofa to sit down. "Speaking of, when are you going to come visit?"

"Soon. I put in a request for some time off a couple weekends from now." Sal, my former boss at the coffee shop, relied heavily on Nellie to run things. "When do you start at your new job?"

"Monday," I replied, topping off my glass of wine. I put the bottle back in the refrigerator and headed over to the couch, curling up against the armrest.

"I can't really picture it, you working in a hardware store." Nellie chuckled.

"Thanks for the vote of confidence," I deadpanned, trying to ignore the nervous swirling in my gut. I *was* anxious, but I knew my uncle would show me the ropes. I'd be more self-conscious if I didn't know my boss.

But I'd always had fun with Uncle Ed. He was the closest thing to a father figure I had. Growing up, my mother had dated *a lot* of men and even married a few of them, but none of them were worthy of the title "stepdad." Not even her most recent husband, who we'd seen very little of during our forced stay with her.

"I'm sure you'll do great; you're a fast learner. Plus, it's not like you're starting over in a totally new-to-you place. You know people in Hartwood Creek."

"Yeah..." I replied, my traitorous thoughts straying to a certain Hutchinson brother.

"Well, one thing's for sure. It's not the same here without you." Nellie sighed. "It's boring. And guess who walked in the other day for a coffee?"

"Ugh. Let me guess...Warren."

"Yup, and *she* was with him. I tell you, Sage, I was *this close* to putting something disgusting in their cups. I would have, too...if Sal weren't peering over my shoulder."

It stung a little to know how quickly Warren had moved on with the woman he cheated on me with. After I caught him red-handed, he tried to convince me to stay for all of five minutes. He must have realized my mind was set, and *nothing* could change it. Then he made it *my fault*. I'd been too distracted, too focused on my daughter and myself, too focused on my one friend and my silly minimum wage job—on every-thing that *wasn't* Warren.

I had no insight into how selfish he was until I caught him in his web of lies, and the good-guy mask fell to the ground, shattering the illusion.

"I wish I could say I'm over it, but I'm still mad as all hell." I sighed, wishing that wasn't the case. Anger and bitterness would get me nowhere, but I was just so angry that Warren had made me believe he was someone he wasn't. Though I was mostly angry at myself for not seeing through the guise.

"I don't blame you. You were going to marry that guy," Nellie exclaimed.

"Don't remind me," I groaned, massaging my temple. Marrying him had felt like the next step at the time, and I thought he'd wanted it too. And maybe he did. Maybe Warren just wanted to have his cake and eat it too. Be married to me with his side piece.

"Honestly? I never liked the guy. He was too pretentious and boring," Nellie insisted. I smiled, although she couldn't see it. Nellie had always been honest about her feelings for

Warren. She hadn't understood the appeal. "He was *so* not your type."

I think I'd been drawn to Warren in his crisp suits because he looked the part of a responsible man. In high school and in college, I'd gone for the jock types and had been repeatedly disappointed by their lack of maturity and loyalty.

Turns out men in suits were just as disloyal as men in sports jerseys.

"Well, it's time to leave him in the past, where he belongs." I sighed, pausing to take another sip of wine.

"Hear, hear," Nellie cheered. "I can't wait to come visit. Not going to lie, I googled the town. It looks adorable. I could use a vacation!"

"It really is, and there really is so much to do here." I smiled, my excitement rising. I loved visiting when I was a kid, and I used to daydream about moving in permanently with my aunt and uncle. At least that way, I'd get to be a part of a functioning family.

Raising Daphne in this town was going to be amazing; I could feel it in my bones. I just had to get her more excited about it. Hopefully, the playdate at Parker Hutchinson's tomorrow would do the trick.

"I DON'T WANT TO GO," Daphne pouted from the back seat. I peeked at her in the rear-view mirror, catching her with her arms crossed and a worried crease in her brow.

My sweet child needed routine and familiarity, and I'd seriously shaken that up by moving us four hours away. But I knew in my heart this change was exactly what we needed. I'd always felt the most support from my aunt and her family, and I loved the small town they resided in.

We just had to get used to the changes, that was all.

"Daph, it's going to be fun. I promise," I assured her. "And then you'll have two new friends when you start on Monday."

"What if they don't like me?"

"Impossible," I told her. "You're the most likable kid I've ever met."

"You have to say that; you're my mom," Daphne retorted, unconvinced.

Parker's address came into view. He lived in one of the older subdivisions, in a beautiful blue Victorian-style home. There was a detached garage that somehow looked brand new while built to match with Gothic influences. It had a pitched roof and intricately designed woodwork.

There was a minivan and two trucks parked in the driveway—the black truck from yesterday and a white one that said Hutchinson's Lumber & Construction. I pulled in and parked behind the Hutchinson's Lumber & Construction truck.

"I don't have to say that. If you were an unlikeable kid, I'd tell you," I assured her with a wink. "Try to find a smile, sweetheart," I pleaded, and Daphne forced a smile that didn't reach her eyes.

We got out of the car and walked up the front steps to the beautiful wraparound porch. I rang the doorbell, and Daphne hid behind me, peering out from around my legs when the door opened.

"Hello! You must be Sage and Daphne. I'm Tabitha. I've heard so much about you both. Come in." She stood aside to make room for us, and we walked into the foyer.

"Hi, Tabitha. It's a pleasure to meet you," I said, holding out the white dessert box from Tout de Sweets. I hadn't wanted to show up empty-handed, so we made a quick stop to pick up some fresh donuts and pastries.

She took the box from me with a wide, friendly smile. Tabitha was beautiful with long brown hair, thick bangs, and cornflower-blue eyes framed by dark lashes. "Thank you so much. Everyone's out in the backyard; follow me."

Tabitha led the way through their beautiful home and out through the patio doors off the open-concept dining room and kitchen at the back of the house. She set the box of baked goods down on the counter before opening the sliding door. We stepped out onto a large deck, and my eyes immediately went to Nix.

He was standing beside Parker in front of the barbecue, holding a baby boy in his arms. Both men turned at the sound of the sliding door opening, and the grin that appeared instantly on Nix's face made hundreds of butterflies explode in my belly.

Seeing him holding a baby did weird things to my lady bits, but I tried to push away my initial reaction. An attractive man holding a baby would make any warm-blooded woman's womb ache. It was basically a biological response.

"Hey, Sage," Nix said, his eyes traveling from my head to my toes and back up again, a slow grin finding his lips.

"Hi, Nix. Parker." I nodded, trying to appear unaffected.

The sweet baby in Nix's arms caught sight of Tabitha and held his hands out, whimpering for her. She took him off Nix and proceeded to walk to the railing overlooking the beautifully landscaped backyard. There were lush gardens and what looked like a miniature version of their house, painted the same shade of blue.

"Bella! Brielle! Come say hello to Daphne," Tabitha called out.

The door to the playhouse opened, and two little girls

poked their heads out. "Hi. Come play with us," they cheered in unison. They were mirror images of each other and resembled their mother with their long dark hair and big blue eyes.

Daphne looked at me for help, and I smiled encouragingly at her. "Go on, go say hi." Begrudgingly, my daughter walked slowly toward the playhouse, as if she was about to face the firing squad.

But the girls must have had the Hutchinson charm, because within minutes, Daphne was relaxing and even smiling a little as the girls chatted her up and showed off their beautiful playhouse.

"That's a lovely playhouse," I said to Tabitha.

"Thanks. Parker and his brothers built it a few years ago for the girls' third birthday," Tabitha said, adjusting her hold on the baby. She pressed a kiss to his forehead and smiled when he giggled at her.

"And what's this little cutie's name?" I asked, smiling at him. He had the Hutchinson brown eyes, like melted dark chocolate.

"Bryson. He'll be turning one next month. He's a handful," she said with a chuckle.

"Hello, Bryson." I waved at him, and he waved back, a big, toothy grin on his face.

"Can I get you anything to drink? Fresh lemonade? Iced tea?" Tabitha asked, playing the part of hostess.

"Lemonade sounds refreshing."

"I'll get you a glass," Nix offered, his husky tone sending an unexpected shiver down my spine. "Anybody else need anything?"

"I could use another beer," Parker replied, holding up his nearly finished bottle. Nix looked at Tabitha next, cocking a brow at her.

"I'm okay for now," Tabitha said. He nodded and disappeared into the house. "Let's sit down, shall we?" she suggested. I nodded, and we walked over to the patio table. It was set for lunch, with condiments and salads. I sat down beside Tabitha, facing the yard so I could keep half an eye on Daphne.

"You have a lovely home," I remarked, glancing around and taking it all in. I didn't want to acknowledge to myself that I felt a little envious. But Tabitha's smile reached her eyes, and I found that envy slipping away. Her genuine kindness and welcoming nature could be felt from across the table, and it put me at ease.

"Thank you. You should have seen it when we bought it. It was a serious fixer-upper. We've lived here for what...seven years now?" she asked, looking to Parker for confirmation.

"Almost eight," Parker corrected with a wry grin. "Been working on restoring it ever since. Nix has been a great help there."

At that moment, Nix returned with a glass of lemonade for me and two beers. He handed Parker his beer before passing me my glass. Our fingertips brushed, and a little tingle of awareness shot up my spine.

Nix gave me a cheeky grin as I took it, then he twisted the top off his beer bottle and took a sip, sitting down across from me at the table. I tried to ignore the way a simple brush of his fingertips against mine set my heart rate galloping in my chest.

"Parker tells me Daphne will be in Mr. Robertson's class. That's exciting. You'll love him. He's a great teacher. He's awesome with the kids. And he's single." Tabitha waggled her eyebrows at me.

Nix frowned darkly at her commentary.

"Ah, well, good for him." I shifted uncomfortably, trying to avoid the heat of Nix's gaze when his eyes moved to me. I wasn't sure why Tabitha was telling me about Mr. Robertson's relationship status, but if I had to guess...it was probably because the word had already gotten out about my failed engagement and bachelorette status.

In a town as small and cozy as Hartwood Creek, everybody knew everybody else's business, and everyone had an opinion about it. Given the fact this town had an odd obsession with playing matchmaker to its inhabitants, I figured it'd only be a matter of time.

"Nix, go grab me a plate, would you? The burgers are almost done," Parker called out. Nix looked as if the last thing he wanted to do was get up, but he did so, disappearing inside and leaving Tabitha and me alone to chat.

"Is Daphne nervous about tomorrow?" Tabitha questioned, bouncing Bryson on her lap. He giggled, reaching for the utensils on the table.

"A little bit," I replied, my eyes straying to the playhouse. The girls were still inside, and I could distantly hear them talking but couldn't quite make out what they were saying. "I'm hoping that after today, she'll be more excited about it. She's not exactly happy about the move."

"Aww, I bet. Kids are resilient, though." Tabitha smiled kindly at me. "Hartwood Creek Elementary is a wonderful school. She'll love it here eventually; it's impossible not to fall in love with this town."

I nodded, completely in agreement with her. "I loved visiting when I was younger. I wanted to move in with my aunt and uncle, just so I could live here all the time. I think the pace will be better for Daphne. It's so different from Guelph, where we used to live."

"Oh! That's quite the change. Hartwood Creek is less crowded, for sure. It's a beautiful place to raise a family," Tabitha said, pressing a kiss to Bryson's forehead. He giggled and tried to pull away from her kiss attack. I smiled, reminiscing about when Daph was that tiny.

I felt the familiar ache in my empty womb. I'd always wanted more than one child. I'd wanted to have at least three of them, close in age. Growing up as an only child had been isolating, and I'd always been slightly envious of my cousins for having each other.

I think it's why I was in such a rush to accept what Warren offered. I wanted to get married and have a few more babies. That desire had blinded me to a lot of Warren's faults.

"It really is." I nodded in agreement, sipping my drink.

"Although everybody seems to know everybody else's business," Tabitha remarked—or was it a polite warning? I couldn't tell.

"Yeah. That's going to take some getting used to." I laughed. I was used to big cities; to disappearing in a crowd. To nobody knowing my name unless they read it on my name tag at work.

The small-town vibe was an entirely different ball game. Things just seemed to move at a slower pace here, while everyone seemed overly invested in what everybody else was doing.

Nix returned with an empty plate and brought it to Parker before rejoining us at the table. Parker loaded the cooked burgers and hot dogs onto it, then turned off the grill. He brought the plate of food over to the table and set it down beside the buns.

"Come on, girls, lunch is ready," Tabitha called over her shoulder. Half a second later, the playhouse door opened, and the three girls raced up to the deck, giggling.

Daphne had a smile on her face when she reached the table. "Do you want a hot dog or a burger?" Parker asked her.

"A hot dog, please," Daphne replied politely.

"I can get it," I said, leaning forward to grab a plate and a bun. Parker used the tongs to put the hot dog in the bun for me.

I poured some ketchup and mustard on it—her favourite toppings—then I loaded Daphne's plate with salad.

Once everyone had food in front of them, we dove in. Conversation was relaxed and easy, mostly about the work the Hutchinsons did now.

Nix ran a construction crew that worked on historical renovations and framing. He had even seen to the reconstruction of the lawyer's office after a fire tore through the buildings.

"Looks like before, only better," Parker boasted, giving his brother a proud grin. "Nix has earned quite the reputation around here."

"Not the only one, Brother," Nix insisted with a grin. "Parker and a friend of his started their own portable sawmill service and unique custom wood projects."

"I tend to do a lot of custom cabinet work for Nix's builds," Parker explained. "And custom furniture builds too. Usually dining room table sets, but we've built a few dressers too."

"Is your dad still running the lumberyard?" I asked, remembering that all the boys had worked there when they were teens.

"He sure is. I don't think he'll ever give up the reins." Parker chuckled. The lumberyard had been in their family for generations.

"That's awesome," I said, inspired and nostalgic for that kind of history. My grandparents passed away when I was little, and I had no siblings. No shared history somewhere.

During coffee and dessert, Nix shifted the conversation to me.

"Last time we saw you, you were heading off to college in the fall," Nix recalled. "What did you end up taking?"

"I took a photography course. I didn't end up graduating, though. I had Daphne."

I'd wanted to finish my program, but my mother hadn't

been willing to watch Daphne for me while I was in class; especially not for photography, which she insisted was a hobby and not a real career. I couldn't find a sitter who would take a baby under a year old, so I'd had to withdraw from the program halfway through the second semester. I still had and used my camera, but it was pretty much obsolete now.

The camera came in handy documenting my daughter's life, but aside from bringing it out to take photos of Daphne or occasionally taking photos for Nellie, I'd let that dream gather dust—figuratively and literally. I had no idea how to set up a business, and I'd needed a job that would pay the bills.

When Daphne was old enough to attend day care, I jumped right into the workforce. A year of living with my mother and putting up with her comments was enough. I needed out. I took the first job offer I got—at the café—and worked my butt off to save up enough money to finally move out.

For two years, it was just Daph and me in a tiny one-bedroom basement apartment. Then Warren walked into my life, and I let him shake everything up. I practically handed him the keys to my life and let him take control.

"Do you still take photos?" Nix asked, his smile putting me at ease.

I hesitated, realizing we were monopolizing the conversation. I glanced at Tabitha and Parker, finding them watching the two of us with matching secret smiles on their faces, as if they'd fully intended for this to happen.

"As a hobby more than anything." I blushed.

CHAPTER FOUR

Nix

Talking to Sage was just as effortless as I remembered. It was easy to fall into the conversation and forget we weren't the only ones in the room. Sage being back in Hartwood Creek again—for good this time—seemed a little like fate to me.

I could feel Parker and Tabitha watching us, and so could Sage, by the way she just clammed up and started blushing beneath their gaze. I didn't mind the audience, but I'd give anything for a minute alone with her.

"If you're into sunset pictures, the beach still has the best views." She blushed even deeper at that, and I could tell by the slight lift of her lips she was resisting smiling.

Maybe it wasn't fair to hint at the time we'd almost shared a kiss. But I couldn't help but flirt with her.

"I'll keep that in mind," she said, sipping her coffee to hide her smile.

For the remainder of their visit, Sage was careful to not pay too much attention to me. She shifted her attention to Tabitha, asking her questions about school drop-off and pick-up times.

"I always go forty minutes early to get good parking, unless we walk," Tabitha confessed with a giggle. "I pick up a coffee and bring a book. I can usually get in some reading while Bryson naps."

"That sounds awesome," Sage said, a genuine smile on her face. "My uncle Ed has me working until 3:00 p.m. every day this week so I can get Daph to and from school, but eventually I'm going to need to find after-school care so I can work the full shift. Do you know anyone?"

"There's a really nice day care with a before and after-school program," Tabitha said after a moment of thought. "But I'm not sure if they have any spots available. Maybe I could help you out for a bit? I don't mind picking Daphne up with the girls and bringing her back here. What's one extra kid?"

"That would be great. I'll pay you, of course," Sage said, looking relieved.

It was almost four o'clock when Sage and Daphne left. Daphne seemed to really hit it off with Bella and Brielle, not that that was surprising. My nieces were kind and inclusive kids. Tabitha and Parker had seen to that.

Sage and Tabitha seemed to hit it off, too, and I'd tried not to perk up *too* much at the thought of Sage coming around more. More opportunities to talk and flirt with her.

"Well, that was fun," Tabitha declared, adjusting her hold on Bryson. She was attempting to clear the table with her free hand, piling plates on top of one another. I stepped forward to help, taking the plates off her and collecting the condiments.

"Yeah, it was." I nodded with agreement, carrying everything into the house.

I helped my brother and his wife tidy up before making my way across the yard to the apartment above the detached garage.

I'd helped Parker build the garage when he first moved

here. He wanted somewhere he could work on his projects, but he wanted to keep the historic look. He'd also wanted to include an income property—an apartment above the garage they could rent out for a bit of extra money.

After my relationship with my ex, Lori, ended abruptly almost two years ago, I'd had nowhere to go and hadn't been willing to move back home with my parents. Noah Wood—Parker's best friend and Tabitha's cousin—had been renting the apartment above the garage. He ended up purchasing his own house closer to the resort his family owned and moved out around the time I caught Lori cheating.

I ended up in the apartment above the garage. It wasn't huge, but it was perfect for a single guy...perfect for now. I had a five-year plan. I'd purchased my own plot of land on the outskirts of town and was planning on building. Eventually. I'd been sidetracked by the growing demands of my business.

It was hard to focus on building my own house when we had so many projects on the go, but next summer, I had plans to break ground and start building. For now, I didn't mind my living arrangements. I got to see my nieces and nephew almost every day, and I spent a lot of my evenings helping Parker with renovations or the various woodworking projects he had on the go in the garage.

Carpentry was in our blood, and we bonded over the projects we did. My brothers and I used to spend hours helping our grandpa build furniture as kids, and though Grandpa had long since passed on, we felt closer to him in those moments.

I'd decided I wanted to build on a bigger scale and had started my own construction business after going to trade school. It was an umbrella of Hutchinson Lumber, but I got all the contracts and used supplies and roofing tresses from the lumberyard.

Two of my buddies, Kaleb and Gus, worked with me, and we took on all sorts of projects around town, from historical reconstruction to framing and renovations. Preserving our town's history while keeping it alive and thriving was important to me.

I climbed the stairs on the side of the garage, heading to the door. We'd built a small deck off the side of the garage, large enough for a barbecue and a bistro table and two chairs.

Since I'd just been in the backyard, I hadn't bothered to lock up. I twisted the handle and walked into the open floor plan. A short hallway across the room led to the single bedroom and bathroom.

It was quiet, too quiet, especially after a lively afternoon. The silence tended to drive me mad with boredom. I put on the TV just for some background noise and crossed over to the refrigerator to grab a beer. Sunday nights were always bittersweet, the end of the weekend signaling the beginning of the busy workweek.

I loved my job and loved the distraction it provided during the week, but I'd be lying if I said there wasn't something missing from my life.

Seeing Sage yesterday morning, still mused with sleep and wearing pajamas, had made me long to wake up with her looking just like that in my arms. After spending the afternoon talking to her, it only made me want a million more just like that.

THE NEXT MORNING, I stopped off at Tout de Sweets for coffee before heading out to the lumberyard to pick up materials. As usual, the lineup was nearly out the door—the café and bakery's popularity amongst townsfolk and tourists alike was unrivaled.

I didn't mind the wait. I'd left early to make sure I had time for it. Expected it, even. What I wasn't expecting was to run into the Hartley sisters again. It was a little too early for them to be out and about.

Coffees for myself and my dad in hand, I was just about to head for the door when Alice waved me over. "Good morning, Nix."

Betty simpered. "I heard our newest residents stopped in for a playdate yesterday. How *is* Ms. Whitaker doing these days?"

"How'd you hear that?" I asked, surprised at how much these ladies were in the know. You couldn't pass wind in this town without them knowing. "And she's fine...I guess."

"People talk," Dorothy replied evasively with a wave of her hand.

"You know, I always thought you two looked sweet together," Alice remarked, a mischievous glint in her eyes. I tried not to grin; I really didn't want to add fuel to their fire—but it was futile. The grin came out full force.

I couldn't even help myself. It had entertained me to the ends of the earth when the sisters had set their sights on Parker. Now they had their attention on me, only I found I didn't mind. The Hartley sisters were a lot like my grandmother—I was used to her meddling in my love life.

"*I* used to say that. Remember the Summer Vibes Festival ten years ago? At least, I think it was ten years ago..." Dorothy frowned thoughtfully. "Anyway, the two of you partnered up to do the scavenger hunt."

"Yeah, I remember that," I replied. I'd come close to kissing

Sage that day, but I'd chickened out at the last second. Back then, I had no game. I've since learned how to talk to girls, how to flirt, and how to seduce them. But at that point in my life, I was gangly and awkward. Plus, the beach was *way* too crowded for a first kiss.

"Now that she's back in Hartwood Creek, for good this time, you should make your move before someone else snatches her up."

"We'll see." The sisters weren't wrong; a beautiful girl like Sage wouldn't stay single for long, and I intended to make my move eventually. But for now, I had a to-do list a mile long, and I was already running late enough as it was.

"Don't pressure the boy," Dorothy scolded the other women. "I'm sure he'll make a move in his own time."

"Well, ladies, this was fun, but I better be going. Gotta pick up materials and get to the jobsite." I lifted a hand, waving goodbye to the three meddlesome women, and continued on to the door, chuckling to myself.

The drive to the lumberyard didn't take long. Before I knew it, I was pulling up to the steel gates.

The lumberyard had been in my family for generations, having been started in the 1850s by my great-great-grandfather. Since then, it's been passed down from son to son. My father still ran it, and I didn't see him relinquishing it anytime soon. He was probably dreading the day he had to decide which one of his four sons to pass it on to.

I parked out near the main building and climbed out of my truck, making my way into the office. I spotted my old man sitting at a desk, going over paperwork. "Hey, Dad," I said, setting the coffee I'd brought him down on his desk.

He looked up and boomed, "Nix. It's good to see ya. How was your weekend?"

"Can't complain." I shrugged, stepping back to lean against the doorway. "How was yours? What'd you and Mom get up to?"

"I took her on a little date to Springwood," Dad answered, picking up his coffee. "We caught a movie and had dinner."

I beamed at that. My parents had been married for thirty years now, and they were just as in love as they were the day they wed. "Sounds awesome. Glad you guys were able to get out for a bit."

"Me too. How did helping the Alcotts go?"

"Good. Ed says hello," I replied, and Dad nodded, leaning back in his chair and stretching a little. There was a mischievous glint in his eyes.

"And how's Sage doing these days?" Judging by the look on his face, my father had an inkling of my attraction to the beautiful blonde.

"Good, I guess." I shrugged, opting to change the subject instead of indulging in another conversation about my blatantly obvious crush. "I'm here for business, though."

"Yeah, I know. We've got your materials ready to go. Jerry will help you load up. How's the latest renovation project going?"

"So far, so good. We're on track. It helps I don't have to wait ages for materials," I said with a grin. It wasn't just the perk of being family. We made sure we processed orders quickly and efficiently so our customers didn't have ridiculous wait times. And yeah, maybe I got a *little* special treatment on that end. I considered it a perk to being a Hutchinson. "Thanks, Dad. I'll be back later this week to pick up that other order."

"Don't forget we've got a pile of scrap wood to donate to the high school. I need you or one of your brothers to drop it off."

"I can do it," I replied with a nod. "I'm off early on Friday, so I'll come back that afternoon and pick it up."

"Sounds good. And your mother wants you all to come over for dinner Sunday night."

"Okay. I'll be there," I said, rapping my knuckles against the wooden doorframe before taking my leave.

CHAPTER FIVE

Sage

I found a parking spot at Hartwood Creek Elementary School and pulled in. Putting the car in park, I turned off the engine and twisted to look at Daphne. "Ready?" I asked brightly, a smile on my face.

Daphne was too busy worrying her bottom lip to reply, but she nodded, apprehension clouding those pretty green eyes. She'd been nervous all morning, to the point her appetite had been affected. She hadn't eaten much at breakfast.

"Look! There's Bella and Brielle," I said, pointing in the direction of the Hutchinson twins. They were standing with their mother by the schoolyard gate. I opened the door and stepped outside, waiting a moment for Daphne to follow suit.

She unceremoniously dragged herself and her bag out of the car, sending a wary look to the red brick building. I closed the door for her and held out my hand. She took it, still young enough to want to hold my hand when she was scared. I dreaded the day she wouldn't reach for me, but for now, I'd cherish it.

"Good morning," Tabitha said with a grin when we approached. She had Bryson in a stroller in front of her and was feeding him Cheerios to distract him. "Are you ready for your first day?" She directed her question at Daphne.

"I guess." Daphne nodded, looking a little pale. I squeezed her hand reassuringly.

"Mr. Robertson is awesome! He lets us do classes outside if the weather's nice," Bella told Daphne. Now that I'd spent some time with the girls, I was able to tell them apart. Bella's hair was longer, and Brielle had a dimple in her right cheek when she smiled.

"Come on, we'll take you to meet him," Brielle told her. Daphne let go of my hand and took the twins' hands, walking through the gate with them.

"I'll pick you up after school, okay, Daph?" I called out. She looked over her shoulder at me and nodded, still worrying her lip. Bella said something to distract her, pulling her attention forward again.

"She'll be fine. The girls will show her around," Tabitha assured me. I nodded, still watching the three little girls as they approached a tall man in the schoolyard. He had dark hair and a bit of scruff, and Tabitha was right—he was cute.

The twins said something to him, and he held out his hand for Daphne to shake. She did so, and he said something along the lines of *welcome to Hartwood Creek*, if my lip-reading skills were to be trusted.

"Well, I better get to the hardware store," I said, though moving my feet was difficult to do. "Have a good day, Tabitha. I'll see you later."

"You have a good day too," Tabitha said with a smile. "Good luck!"

I got in my car and drove to the hardware store, parking

around back in my spot. I rushed into the store a few minutes later than I should have been.

Uncle Ed was behind the counter, already ringing a customer out. I waited until the customer paid for their purchases and grabbed their bags before approaching. "Sorry I'm late, Uncle Ed."

"No worries, Sage. How did Daphne do with drop-off?"

"She seemed a little nervous, but the Hutchinson twins took her under their wings, so I'm sure she'll be fine."

"Those girls are sweet," he said with a tone of approval. "Now, are you ready to get started?"

"Yes, absolutely." I nodded eagerly, and Uncle Ed handed me a green apron. "Thank you again for this."

"Don't thank me yet—your training is about to begin." He winked. "First thing I'm going to train you on is cash. This is the product binder; it has the SKU codes for everything in the store." He lifted a hefty old binder from underneath the cash register and set it on the countertop.

"You don't have a computer system?" I asked, unable to hide the surprise from my voice.

"A dated one," he said, gesturing to the small monitor by the register. "But we also keep records in the product binder."

Uncle Ed spent the next several hours showing me the ropes. He gave me random lists of products to find, and I had to walk up and down the aisles and find them.

Before I knew it, it was lunchtime. I ran up to the apartment to grab a bite to eat, loving the convenience of being able to do just that. If I could only manage to avoid the bistro next door, I'd save a lot of money by not eating out.

On my return, I ran into three almost identical old ladies leaving the hardware store. "Oh, there she is! We were just talking to Ed about you," the one with dyed hair said. Betty, was it?

Recognizing the three of them as the infamous Hartley triplets, I smiled. In my youth, when visiting Hartwood Creek, it was common to run into these three ladies at events and around town. They always made a point to come up and talk to Uncle Ed and Auntie Em. They also took credit for some of my cousins' matches in the love department.

The Hartley sisters owned the Tout de Sweets café and bakery in town, and they were known for their In The Name of Love Latte. It was said to be enchanted with magic, that any couple who drank that particular latte would fall undeniably in love.

"Good things, I hope?" I laughed, feeling a little awkward and put on the spot.

"Of course. We wanted to officially welcome you to Hartwood Creek," Dorothy explained.

"We have a welcome basket for you. Just some homey things, a candle, some incense, a body scrub that we *swear* by—just look at our youthful complexions—and hand soap," Alice added, handing me a basket wrapped in cellophane.

"Oh, well, thank you for the warm welcome." I took the woven basket and returned their smiles with a warm one of my own.

"Hartwood Creek is happy to have you as a permanent resident," Alice told me before her face transformed with a secretive smile. "Have you run into any old friends yet?"

This encounter was beginning to feel an awful lot like a trap. "Just Nix and Parker, actually. Daphne's in the same class as Parker's twins, so we got them together for a bit of a playdate yesterday."

"Ah yes, we heard about that," Alice declared, and Dorothy elbowed her gently, giving her a scolding look.

"I really should be getting back to work now..." I trailed off, trying to mask my uneasiness. "It was nice seeing you ladies."

"Yes, dear. It was good seeing you too. Don't be a stranger," Dorothy said before the three sisters crossed the sidewalk and climbed into the purple all-terrain vehicle parked in front of Alcott's Hardware.

AT THREE O'CLOCK, Uncle Ed let me head out early so I could pick Daphne up. I couldn't seem to find parking close enough, so I parked down the street and walked up to the school.

Tabitha was already there, pushing the stroller back and forth while she stood in place and chatted with another woman. She caught sight of me walking and waved me over.

"Lilah, this is Sage Whitaker. She's new in town. Sage, this is Lilah Willard. Lilah's kind of an old resident of Hartwood Creek who moved away for a spell and has come back to us," Tabitha explained, and I gave Lilah a warm smile. "Lilah's little girl, Riley, is also in Mr. Robertson's class."

"That's awesome! It's nice to meet you, Lilah." I held out my hand, and she shook it.

"Hi, Sage. It's nice to meet you too," Lilah responded, smiling. She had dark curly hair and beautiful brown skin.

We made small talk for a couple of minutes, and I found out Lilah had relocated back to Hartwood Creek to open a spa.

"No way! We'll have to come check it out. Do you have any availability this weekend?"

"I do, actually." Lilah's entire face lit up.

"I could use some post-breakup pampering. Can you book Daphne and me for Saturday morning?"

"Of course!" Lilah replied eagerly.

The bell rang, and the three of us waited for the girls. Mr.

Robertson's class was the third wave to come out of the school. One by one, he let the kids run to their parents when he saw them waiting.

Daphne was standing toward the rear of the group with Bella, Brielle, and another little girl who looked a lot like Lilah.

"Riley," Lilah called out when she caught sight of her daughter. The little girl, Riley, looked up and spotted her mother in the crowd, then she tapped on Mr. Robertson's elbow to get his attention.

Mr. Robertson looked over and saw the three of us. He smiled and said something to the girls, then they all started walking over. Daphne caught sight of me and started to run, looping around Mr. Robertson to get to the gate.

She was through it and wrapping her arms around me before Mr. Robertson had even reached the gate. He had a relaxed smile on his face until he caught sight of Lilah. He swallowed hard, like he hadn't expected to see her, but quickly regained his composure.

"I take it you ladies are Daphne's and Riley's moms," Mr. Robertson said, looking at us each in turn with a welcoming smile.

"Yes, I'm Sage Whitaker. It's nice to meet you," I replied, holding out my hand to shake his.

"It's nice to meet you too, Sage." Mr. Robertson shook my hand and smiled at me before he looked at Lilah, and something passed between the two of them as he reached out and took her hand to shake it too.

"We've already met. Lilah, wasn't it?" Mr. Robertson asked. Lilah nodded, seemingly at a loss for words. "Well, I just wanted to let you both know the girls did amazing today. They were both a little shy at first, but by the end of the day, they were engaging and playing with their peers."

"Glad to hear it," I said, smiling down at Daphne. She returned the smile, peering up at me with her wide green eyes.

"I also wanted to mention...in a few weeks' time, we'll be doing the Fall Fun Fundraiser here at the school. The goal is to raise money for extracurricular activities and new books. We rely heavily on volunteers to run it. I sent the students home with newsletters about it. We are still looking for volunteers to run some of the tables."

"What tables?" Lilah asked. Mr. Robertson's gaze went to her.

"Face painting, mainly." He smiled. "I'm hopeless with a paintbrush, and the lady who usually does it just had wrist surgery."

"Mommy, you can face paint," Riley interjected, tugging on the hem of her mother's shirt. "Remember when you did it for my birthday?"

"Can you?" Mr. Robertson asked, looking at Lilah with hopeful eyes.

"Uh, sure. I could do that," she replied.

"We'll also need someone to run the photo booth, and Daphne mentioned you were a photographer, Sage?" Mr. Robertson turned his attention to me.

Now it was my turn to feel a little put on the spot. I could feel Tabitha's eyes on me, urging me on.

I took a breath. I didn't exactly like putting myself on the spot—I'd had a not-so-great experience with Daphne's last school's Parent Teacher Association, but I wanted to embrace our new life in Hartwood Creek. I knew what Auntie Em would say. She'd tell me to do it for Daphne.

"I'm not really a professional, but I could do that."

"That would help us out so much. We already have the booth and props from last year. Hartwood Creek Flowers is donating fresh flowers. We won't charge, but families are asked to donate what they can, and the images will be shared digitally."

"That sounds good." I nodded.

"Phenomenal!" Mr. Robertson grinned. "Thank you both so much. There's a form along with the newsletter. If you could fill it out and send it back with the girls tomorrow, that would be awesome. You don't have to attend planning committee meetings, but it's greatly appreciated if you do. Either way, I'll be keeping volunteers informed via email."

"Okay, sounds good," Lilah said while I nodded along in agreement.

"Great. Welcome to Hartwood Creek, ladies," Mr. Robertson said warmly, smiling once more before he headed off to talk to the other parents waiting for his attention.

"I'm on the planning committee too. You guys should come to the meetings, they're actually pretty fun." Tabitha smiled.

"Yeah, sure." I nodded in agreement, even though I was dreading the very idea of it.

We said our goodbyes and headed to the car.

"Did you have a good day?" I asked Daph as I unlocked the car and held the back driver's door open for her.

"Yeah." Daphne sighed, climbing in. She still seemed a little somber. I knew it was going to take some time for her to adjust, but I couldn't stand seeing my usually chipper little girl even a little sad.

"Do you feel up to going on an adventure tonight?" I asked.

"Where?" she perked up at that.

"Out for dinner to celebrate our first day at a new school and a new job. We did good, Squirt. And after, we could go check out the park and the beach."

"Okay!"

CHAPTER SIX

Sage

We stopped off at home so I could change out of my work clothes and into something more...me. I chose a blue sundress with a white floral pattern and buttons on the front. We were just about to leave when I saw my camera out of the corner of my eye and hesitated.

It had been some time since I'd picked my camera up. My recent heartache and the chaos of my life turning upside down had prevented me from doing, well, anything that formerly brought me joy.

Especially photography, which Warren had always viewed as a *"cutesy little hobby of mine."* The few times I'd talked about maybe starting my own photography business, he'd laugh and say, "Everyone thinks they're a photographer nowadays. Besides, everyone has cell phones and takes their own photos."

That shut me up quickly, even though I disagreed with him. It's hard to chase your dreams when you don't have support, though, and Warren wasn't the first to fail in that department.

But if I was planning on running the photo booth at a fundraising event for the school, I was going to have to dust off my camera and get myself reacquainted with it. Plus, I really did want to capture the sunset.

I grabbed my camera bag and checked that the battery pack still had a charge—miraculously, it did. I slipped my wallet into the front pocket and slung my bag over my shoulders.

"Ready, Daph?" I called out.

"Yes," she shouted, coming out from her bedroom. She'd changed, too, into a pair of shorts and a tank top. I could see the straps of her swimsuit underneath. "If the water's warm, I wanna go swimming." Although it was September, the weather was warm and balmy, as if summer was lingering to welcome us.

"Okay." I was happy my daughter didn't seem to be so upset anymore.

"Mommy! Are you going to take pictures?" she asked, her eyes widening at the camera bag.

"Well, you volunteered my services. I feel like I should practice a little. It's been a while," I told her, gently bopping her nose with my finger.

"Yeah, you do need practice," Daphne agreed solemnly. Shaking my head, I locked up the apartment and took my daughter's hand.

We walked around Main Street and did a little more exploring, checking out a few of the beautiful historic shops before we ended up at a diner called The Hungry Hub. I held the door open for Daphne, and she walked in, peering around the bustling restaurant.

"Feel free to seat yourselves. Anywhere's fine," a woman with blond hair pulled back in a high ponytail said, sounding a little out of breath. She had her hands full of dirty dishes she was carrying back into the kitchen.

Daphne and I walked over to one of the free booths and sat down. Not long after that, the blond waitress came over with her order pad and a couple menus.

"Good evening. I'm Emily, and I'll be your server this evening. Can I get you ladies something to drink?" she asked, setting the menus down in front of us.

"Two iced teas, please," I replied, earning a smile from Daphne. She loved ordering iced tea; it made her feel grown up.

Warren hadn't thought it was a good idea to let her drink caffeine. He thought it made her too hyper. I didn't mind the surge in energy—especially when we were going to the beach after. She'd crash eventually. But Warren was steadfast that it wasn't good for her.

Suddenly, it dawned on me. I didn't have to worry about what Warren thought anymore. Screw him.

"You ladies have a look at our menu, and I'll grab those iced teas for you," Emily said, disappearing toward the counter.

"What do you think, Daph? They've got cheeseburgers, chicken tenders, pasta dishes..." I trailed off, my eyes scanning the menu.

"I want a cheeseburger and fries," Daphne decided. I nodded, liking the sound of that.

When Emily returned with our drinks, I handed back the menus. "She'll have a cheeseburger and fries, and I'll have a cheeseburger with onion rings."

I *never* would have ordered that when I was with Warren. He was the kind of man who cared *a lot* about appearances and eating healthy, so I'd always end up ordering a salad when out with him.

"Coming right up!" Emily announced, taking the menus before heading to the kitchen to put in our order.

"Here's to a successful first day for the both of us," I cheered with a grin, lifting my glass toward Daphne. She picked hers up, and we clinked our glasses together before we each took a sip. I hadn't realized how thirsty I was until the cold liquid hit my tongue.

Daphne sipped at her tea, her green eyes taking in the busy restaurant and all the patrons. Conversations were buzzing all around us, with patrons calling out to one another in recognition, trading bits of gossip and news. A group of girls close to Daphne's age sat a few tables over, dressed in matching soccer uniforms.

My daughter sent a longing glance at them, and I knew she was thinking about her old soccer team in Guelph. I made a mental note to investigate local teams.

"I want to hear all about your day. Did it help to know Bella and Brielle ahead of time?"

"I guess so. I had them to play with, at least. And Riley," Daphne replied, her little shoulder lifting in a shrug. "I still miss my old friends and my old school."

"That's okay; you can miss your old friends and enjoy getting to know your new ones," I assured her, a gentle smile playing on my lips.

Daphne looked as if she hadn't considered that. "Okay."

"Mr. Robertson seems nice," I commented, trying to press her for more details and discreetly change the subject from her old school and friends to the new one.

I didn't want to ignore that she missed our old home, but I knew there wasn't much we could do about it. Guelph was four hours away, and although Zoey and Chloe's mothers both promised to keep in touch for the sake of the girls, we'd never been particularly close.

"He is," Daphne replied.

"It was Riley's first day at a new school too. I bet she was thankful to meet you. It probably made starting at a new school a little easier for you both."

"Yeah, Mr. Robertson paired us together since everyone else already had partners."

"Is she nice?"

"Yes, and quiet," Daphne answered. "Bella and Brielle talk a lot; sometimes it's hard to keep up with them."

I smiled. If they were anything like their uncles, I believed that. The Hutchinsons were a boisterous group. Their antics had always fascinated me.

Before I could drill her some more, Emily returned with two plates. The cheeseburger was the size of Daphne's face. Her eyes went wide when the waitress placed it in front of her.

"One cheeseburger with fries and one cheeseburger with onion rings," Emily said with a flourish, a huge grin on her face. She grabbed a bottle of ketchup and mustard out of her apron and set them down on the table between us. "Let me know if you ladies need anything else."

"Thank you." I smiled. Emily walked off to deal with another table, and I got Daphne situated, cutting her burger into quarters. We both dug into our meals, and I had to stop myself from moaning when the delicious flavours hit my tongue.

"This is the best cheeseburger ever," Daphne declared after taking several bites. I beamed at her, finding mine every bit as good.

We were halfway through our meals when the door chimed, and in walked Nix Hutchinson. He was by himself and dressed in his work clothes. He made his way over to the service counter and exchanged a few friendly words with Emily while she rang his order in and handed him a takeout bag.

He spotted us on his way out, and his face broke into a huge grin as he made his way over to our table. "Good evening, ladies." His warm brown eyes went to me first, then settled on my daughter as he gave her his full attention. "How was your first day at school, Daph?"

"It was good," Daphne replied, eyeing Nix with equal parts suspicion and interest.

Nix nodded, his gaze moving back to me. Daphne watched with hawk-like intensity. "And how about you, Sage? How was your first day at the hardware store?"

The way the corner of his lip kicked up in a half smile sent a tingle of awareness down my spine.

"Good," I replied, feeling that weird swooping sensation of attraction as he looked at me. I pushed that feeling away, rejecting it on principle.

I wasn't here to get myself into another relationship with a man. I was here to get back on my own two feet again. To build a life for my daughter that nothing could uproot.

I didn't have time for the swooping butterflies in my belly or the racing heart. Nix was just extending kindness to us, making us feel welcome in a new town. I appreciated him for it, but I was angry at myself for my reaction to his attention.

"That's good to hear. Any special plans to celebrate?"

"We're going to the beach," Daphne supplied, a smile coming to her lips. "You should come with us!"

"Maybe another time, Daph. I'm sure Nix wants to get home and unwind," I said quickly.

"Another time, for sure," Nix said, his eyes sparkling as he looked at me. There was a promise in his brown irises that confused me. "You ladies have a good night, now," he added, dipping his chin in farewell before he left the diner.

I watched him go, appreciating the view of his muscular back and how he filled out those Carhartts.

Unfortunately for me, Emily picked that very moment to

stop by our table and check in on us, and she caught me ogling Nix's retreating form.

"How is everything?" she asked, pulling my gaze from Nix. She gave me a knowing smile.

"Great," I managed, my cheeks heating with embarrassment at being caught.

"Awesome. Let me know if I can get you anything else." I nodded, and Emily went off to check on her other tables.

HALF AN HOUR LATER, we left The Hungry Hub and walked toward the beach, the musty, earthy scent of the lake enveloping us. Our stomachs were so stuffed that we were moving at a snail's pace as we explored the beach, but that didn't matter.

The wind was a little chilly, but that didn't stop Daphne from playing in the water and looking for stones. I got my camera out and snapped a few photos of Daph playing on the shoreline before the sun started to set over the water.

I snapped picture after picture of the sun slowly sinking. I'd forgotten how breathtaking the sunsets were in Hartwood Creek, and I was thankful Nix had reminded me to check it out.

Seeing it—and *him*—again reminded me of the summers of my childhood when I'd come here to visit. The last time I'd visited, Nix and I had ended up as partners on the Summer Vibes Festival scavenger hunt.

We'd come so close to winning that summer, but a moment on this very beach had cost us our win. Paxton and Preston ended up reaching it before we could.

Still, I wouldn't exchange that moment for the win, even if

nothing had come of it then. I still remember the way I felt with Nix's soulful brown eyes on me. I'd thought for sure he was going to kiss me. He'd even moved in a little closer, but the kiss never came.

The disappointment had, though. The whimsical romantic in me had wanted that kiss so badly, but Nix wanted the win more. He'd spotted his brothers getting closer to the treasure and grabbed my hand, tugging me along.

Seeing him again today made me realize I had to get a hold of myself. Sure, he'd gotten even *hotter* with the scruff along his jawline, but I refused to let my attraction to him matter in any capacity. I wasn't here to immediately fall into a new relationship. I was here to rebuild our lives.

Shaking my head, I forced myself back to the present. "Time to go, Daph," I called out.

"Aww!" Her cry of disappointment could be heard over the waves crashing onto the shore.

"Don't worry; we'll come back. We live here now, remember?"

"Oh, yeah!" At the reminder, Daphne collected all the cool rocks she'd found and joined me on the beach. She picked up her sandals, carrying them as we walked back to the apartment.

CHAPTER SEVEN

My muscles were aching something fierce. I'd been on-site all day, working hard to keep this job on track since we were down a couple of men. Kaleb's wife was in labor at Springwood Hospital, so he understandably wouldn't be coming in this week, and Gus was out with a bout of the flu, leaving our usual five-man crew down to three.

I loved building, and I loved creating something out of lumber. This project was a beautiful one—a historic two-bedroom, year-round cottage on the lake that had sustained some damage after a particularly nasty summer storm. We'd had to reframe the main area of the cottage after an ancient silver maple tree crushed half of it.

I didn't feel like cooking dinner, so I grabbed some takeout from The Hungry Hub. Luck seemed to favour me, and I ran into Sage and Daphne. The little girl was a carbon copy of her mother, down to her hopeful green eyes when she'd invited me to join them.

I'd wanted to say yes, but I hadn't gotten the vibe that Sage wanted me there. Her eyes had widened with shock, and she'd rushed to answer before I could. *"Maybe another time, Daph. I'm sure Nix wants to get home and unwind."*

I hadn't wanted to impose on their evening, but now that I was back in my quiet apartment, I kind of wished I'd said yes.

After a quick hot shower, I put on the game and dove into my dinner. I stared at the television screen, not really seeing it. My thoughts on Sage and how I couldn't really get a read on her. Was she interested in me like I was interested in her? It was hard to tell. Sometimes I got the impression that something more lingered between us, but that could just be my blind hopefulness.

She wasn't cold toward me, but she had her defenses up. I had a feeling it had something to do with the reason she'd moved to Hartwood Creek, alone.

GRAVEL CRUNCHED beneath my tires as I pulled into the lumberyard Friday afternoon. It was a gorgeous day. The sun was shining, and after a week of steady work, we were miraculously ahead of schedule at the jobsite, so I told the crew to take the afternoon off at lunch.

It gave me a chance to drop off the scrap materials at the high school. Maybe I'd get home in time to run into a certain green-eyed blonde. Tabitha had started bringing Daphne home with the girls after school for a couple of hours, but I usually arrived home after Sage had already picked Daphne up.

Since I was off early today, I was hoping for a chance to talk to her before she took off.

I spotted Jerry Mulligan, an old friend of Dad's who frequently helped around the lumberyard, helping customers load up their supplies. He was a regular fixture around here and a good friend of the family.

"Hey, Jerry. Is Dad around?" I asked.

"He's in the office, I think," Jerry replied, scratching the back of his head. "Least, that's where I saw him headed last."

"Thanks, man. How's Shirley?"

"She's doing good. Busy knitting up a storm for the school fundraiser—she's got her own crafts table and everything. She's mighty proud. I've got about ten birdhouses ready to go myself."

"Right on." Hartwood Creek was always doing some kind of festival or fundraiser. The Fall Fun Fundraiser was a newer fundraiser Hartwood Creek Elementary School put on to raise money for extracurriculars and books for the library.

When the girls started school, Tabitha and Mom joined the planning committee, and they'd enlisted our help every year since.

Parker and I were going to man the ring toss table while Dad ran the beanbag toss. Tabitha sold wooden signs and other small wood projects at a vendor table with Mom and Gran. Even my younger twin brothers helped, taking turns at the dunk station.

Folks purchased tickets from the organizers, and those tickets were spent on playing carnival games. There was a silent auction that families and local businesses donated to. A lot of the local vendors set up to sell their products, their table fees counting toward the fundraiser's earnings. They'd often donate a portion of their earnings at the end of the evening too.

"Guess you're here to pick up the scrap material for the high school?"

"Sure am," I replied.

"Ah, I'll get that loaded for you." Jerry tipping his hat.

"Thanks, Jerry. I appreciate it," I said before I took off into the office.

I found Dad sitting behind the desk, looking at his computer screen, his reading glasses perched on the edge of his nose. I rapped my knuckles against the doorway to let him know I was there.

He looked over and smiled. "Hey, Nix, here to pick up the scrap wood?"

"Yes, sir," I said. "And I wanted to check on that order for the MacDonald's cottage. It's still ready for pick up Monday morning?"

"Yup." Dad nodded. "Your mom wants to remind you about dinner Sunday. Have you told Parker about it yet?"

"Not yet; I've been pretty busy. We haven't really seen each other," I admitted.

Even though I lived in the apartment above the garage, I didn't see Parker *all* the time. He had a life of his own with his family, and I tried not to be underfoot too much unless Parker initiated it. This week, he'd been busy clearing trees on a property north of Springwood with his portable sawmill service.

"Be sure to tell him tonight, or your mom will have my hide," Dad said. "I should have called him myself, but we've been swamped here."

"I'll make sure I tell him or Tabitha tonight." Satisfied with my answer, Dad nodded his approval, his gaze returning to his computer screen. "Well, I better get the scrap material dropped off. See you Sunday, Dad."

"See you Sunday, Son," Dad said, looking up at me long enough to smile.

While I was in the office talking to my father, Jerry had loaded my truck up with all the scrap materials for donation. "Thanks, Jerry."

"No problem-o," Jerry replied, tipping his hat at me.

"I don't know what we'd do without you," I said with a grin. It was true, Jerry was a huge help to my dad at the lumberyard. He was nearly half a decade older than Dad and had worked at the lumberyard longer than I'd been alive.

"Don't make me blush," Jerry joked. "See you around, kid."

I saluted him before climbing into my truck.

School was still in session when I pulled up to Hartwood Creek High School. Teenagers were everywhere, hooting and hollering. A group of them huddled near the fence on the edge of the property line, smoking cigarettes. I couldn't help but chuckle at them, remembering my own high school days and that time Parker and I snuck cigarettes off my old man to smoke in that exact spot.

Turns out, smoking wasn't for me. I hacked up a lung and threw up. Haven't touched a cigarette since. Parker, however, picked up the habit and only recently quit after Bella and Brielle started calling him out for it.

I went into the main office to let them know I was there. The receptionist paged the shop teacher, Donavon Ashe, who helped me unload the scrap materials into the woodshop around back. The high school students would be making booths for the fall fundraiser at the public school as part of woodshop class.

"Thanks again, Nix," Donavon said after we'd finished loading the scrap lumber into the woodshop. He ran a hand through his short red hair, shaking his head a little. "I was getting really low on materials."

"No problem," I replied. "You know that we're happy to make the donation to the school." And we were. Not only did it feel good to give back to the community, but it kept our lumberyard looking tidy and organized.

"Will we be seeing you tonight at The Quarter Lounge?" Donavon asked, looking at me expectantly. Donavon was a part of my long-standing friend group. We'd known each other since our days at this very high school. Those of us who hadn't left Hartwood Creek gathered every Friday night for a brew at The Quarter Lounge.

Donavon had also worked at the lumberyard throughout our last two years of high school before he went off to college. He took on summer positions at the lumberyard until he graduated from college, then he worked part time for my old man while he continued to look for a teaching job.

When a position at the local high school came up a few years back, Donavon took it. He taught history and woodshop now, though he still frequently stopped in at the lumberyard to visit my old man and pick up supplies for his various projects.

Donavon had bought his own place on Hartley Way a few years back, and like most of the older houses in this historic town, it needed a lot of work to update it.

"Probably," I shrugged. It was how I typically spent my Friday night unless I had a date, and that hadn't happened in some time. Not since Lori, and that was a thought I didn't want to entertain.

"Awesome, see you then," Donavon said, waving as he headed back into the school through the woodshop door that he'd left propped open so we could bring in the lumber.

I opened the door to my truck and climbed in, making it home just as Tabitha was leaving to go and get the kids. While she was gone, I grabbed a quick shower and got dressed in a white T-shirt and a pair of cargo shorts.

Grabbing my keys and wallet, I shoved them into my pockets before leaving my apartment. Tabitha pulled up and parked in the driveway as I descended the stairs. A moment later, the minivan door slid open, and three little girls tumbled out, carrying their backpacks.

They headed down the pathway between the house and the garage. "Hey, Uncle Nix," Bella said when she spotted me.

"Hey, girls, how was school?" I asked. Sage's little girl, Daphne, shrugged.

"It was *great*! It was art day," Brielle informed me. "I painted a picture of the Hartwood Creek lighthouse. Mr. Robertson said my waves looked real."

"Wicked. I can't wait to see it," I told her, ruffling her hair. Brielle was a little artist and always had been. Tabitha and Parker had to hide all the markers and pens when she was a toddler because if she found one, she'd instantly start creating art on whatever surface was closest. Usually a wall or an appliance, herself, or her sister.

When Brielle got a little older, Tabitha enrolled her in art classes once a week at The Art Cave. It was enough to satisfy her artistic cravings and provided her with a great outlet, and something that was just for her.

"You'll see it at the fundraiser, along with everyone else," Brielle informed me.

I chuckled. "What about you, Bella, what did you make?"

"A lighthouse, too, but mine looks like it's melting." Bella sighed. She preferred books to art. Where Brielle was always creating art, Bella was always reading.

"Did you make a lighthouse?" I asked Daphne, and she nodded.

"Everyone did," Daphne replied with a shrug of her shoulder. "We have to showcase them during the fundraiser."

"That's exciting. I'm looking forward to seeing them all." I smiled, and Daphne sent me an inquisitive look.

"You'll be there?"

"Oh yeah, Uncle Nix comes every year," Bella said proudly. "Uncle Preston and Uncle Paxton will be there too."

"You have *more* uncles?" Daphne gasped, like she couldn't believe it.

"Oh yes—and that's just on Daddy's side. We have a very big family," Bella explained with a toothy smile.

"Let's go to the playhouse," Brielle suggested, and all three little girls ran around the house to the backyard.

"Hey, Nix," Tabitha said as she walked around to get Bryson out of his car seat. Bryson was putting up a fuss at having been left by the girls. He stopped complaining the moment Tabitha picked him up and he spotted me.

"Hey, Tabs."

The little boy stretched his arms out toward me. "Do you want to see Uncle Nix?" Tabitha asked him, and he started bouncing with excitement in her arms.

"Come here, little guy," I said, taking my nephew from her. Bryson put his little hands on either side of my cheeks and pushed, squishing them together. I made a funny sound, letting the air leave my cheeks like a deflating balloon, and Bryson laughed with delight.

Tabitha had a few groceries to take in, so I carried Bryson with one arm and grabbed a couple of bags for her, bringing them into the kitchen. I set them down on the counter.

"The parentals wanted me to let you and Parker know they expect us all for dinner Sunday night," I told her.

"I know," she said, putting groceries away. She sent a wry grin my way. "Laurel called me today."

"Of course she did." I smirked. My mom wouldn't leave it up to my dad to spread the word, even if she tasked him with that very job.

Opening the sliding door, I stepped out onto the patio with Bryson and walked over to the table, sitting in one of the chairs facing the yard and plunking him down on the tabletop.

I could hear the girls in the playhouse. Brielle was giving

instructions for the game. "Okay, you be the daddy, Daphne, and I'll be the mommy, and Bella, you can be our baby."

"I don't want to be the daddy," I overheard Daphne reply. She sounded a little sad. "Can I just be the aunt or something?"

There was a pause, then Bella said, "Okay," and the three girls went about their game.

Tabitha came out about ten minutes later with a plate of cut-up watermelon. She put the plate down on the table. "Girls, come have a snack!" She scooped Bryson off the table and sat down across from me with him in her lap, grabbing one of the finer-cut pieces to offer him.

Bella and Brielle came out of the playhouse and raced across the lawn. Daphne followed behind them looking a little uncertain. I didn't know her very well, but I could tell something was off. Bella and Brielle grabbed their pieces of watermelon.

Daphne waited until the twins had selected their pieces before grabbing one of her own.

"Hey, Daph," I said to her, and she turned to look at me. "How can you tell the ocean is friendly?"

"I don't know," she said, her little brow furrowing.

"It waves."

Daphne blinked at me, then reluctantly smiled. "That's a pretty lame joke," she told me before taking a bite of watermelon.

"Uncle Nix *always* tells lame jokes," Bella warned her. "We're used to it, though. Just laugh politely and he'll stop."

"Hey," I exclaimed, bringing a hand to my heart as if my niece's sassy words had offended me. "I do *not* tell lame jokes."

"Sorry, Nix." Tabitha smirked. "Your jokes *are* pretty lame."

I ignored Tabitha and looked back at Daphne. "Why did the leaf go to the doctor?"

"Why?" Daphne asked skeptically.

"It was feeling green!"

This time, I *almost* got a laugh out of her. But the twins rolled their eyes in unison. They'd had their fill of watermelon and wanted to get back to playing their game.

"Come on, let's go," Bella said, grabbing Daphne's hand. They raced back to the playhouse, leaving Tabitha to grill me.

"So?" she said, looking at me expectantly with a clandestine smile.

"So what?"

"I know you're hanging around with hopes of seeing a certain someone," Tabitha called me out. I frowned.

"That's not true," I tried. Tabitha sent me a pointed look. "Okay, maybe it's a little true."

"Why don't you just ask her out?" Tabitha rolled her eyes.

I opened my mouth, but I couldn't think of a reply. Aside from inviting her to The Quarter Lounge that day Parker and I moved her couch in, I hadn't even tried. When I asked her out then, I hadn't known she had a daughter.

Not that her being a mother was a turnoff—far from it. In fact, in the last week, I found myself thinking about settling down more and more. Kids weren't a deal breaker for me—in fact, I wanted a big family. But I knew I couldn't just invite Sage out at the last minute to go hang out at a bar. I'd have to get a little more creative.

"I plan on it when the time is right. She just moved here. I thought maybe I'd let her get settled first," I answered. "I don't want to rush her or make her feel like she's fresh meat...you know?"

Tabitha's expression softened. "You're a good guy, Nix."

CHAPTER EIGHT

———————

Sage

At six o'clock, I pulled into Parker and Tabitha's driveway. I was exhausted after doing inventory all day with Uncle Ed and couldn't help but feel relieved that the first official workweek was over.

I sat in my car for a minute, just pepping myself up to go knock on the door. I could see the second truck parked in the driveway, the white Hutchinson's Lumber & Construction truck, and I knew exactly which Hutchinson brother it belonged to.

Nix hadn't been around the last few days when I'd picked Daphne up, but he was here now. Of course he was when I looked more haggard than ever. I checked my reflection in the visor mirror, confirming that I looked about as tired as I felt.

Several flyaway hairs had escaped the ponytail I'd tossed my hair up in earlier that morning. I debated tugging the band free, but then I'd have a bump in my hair. Shaking my head, I frowned at my reflection.

Why did I even *care* what I looked like? Of course, the

second *that* thought came into my mind, it was followed with another.

Nix was the reason, naturally. My attraction to him was undeniable, even if I played the game of denying it to myself. Which I fully intended on doing.

Sighing, I flipped the visor back up and climbed out of my car. I could hear the girls playing in the backyard.

Tabitha had been watching Daphne after school every day this week for me, and I could usually find them in the backyard playing. When they were out back, Tabitha wouldn't hear me knocking, so I went around the side of the house and opened the gate, letting myself in.

Daphne just so happened to be looking in my direction when I walked through the gate. Her face split into a grin, and she ran toward me, shouting, "Mommy."

Her arms wrapped around my waist, the momentum of her little body propelling me back two steps. "Hello, Squirt. How was school?"

"Good."

"Just good?" I pressed, and she shrugged.

"I'll tell you later. Are we still going to Auntie Em's tonight?"

"Sure are. Just need to head home and grab a quick shower," I told her before looking around for Tabitha. She was walking down the deck steps to meet me. "Thanks again for watching her, Tabitha."

"It's my pleasure," Tabitha insisted. "We'll see you ladies Monday!"

Despite my efforts, my gaze drifted to Nix. He was leaning against the porch railing, his brown eyes watching me. The corners of his lips lifted in an almost shy, half smile that had my heart rate jumping a little.

I hated I *liked* having Nix watch me. I hated I was so aware of him, of how he had the potential to make me feel dangerous things. Things I had no business feeling. I was healing and here to rebuild my life with my daughter.

The last thing I wanted was for people to think I couldn't stand on my own two feet, but I couldn't be rude about it either. It wasn't Nix's fault my traitorous body responded to him. He was just trying to be nice and welcoming. I was probably reading into things more than I should. I had a tendency of doing that, and it usually resulted in me feeling disappointment when things didn't work out the way I hoped.

LATER THAT EVENING, Daphne and I sat at my aunt and uncle's table, enjoying Auntie Em's chicken alfredo lasagna and homemade garlic bread.

Auntie Em and Uncle Ed lived a few streets away from Tabitha and Parker, in an elegant white house with black shutters on a tranquil lot nestled by tall pines, birch trees, and beautiful landscaping. They'd lived here for as long as I could remember, raising their four daughters in the enchanting five-bedroom home.

Their gourmet kitchen had white sand-coloured cabinets offset by oyster-shell granite counters and glass tile backsplash. It was set up with a five-burner gas stove, a built-in microwave and convection oven, and a huge pantry that made for incredibly fun hide-and-seek games with my cousins as a child.

With just the four of us, we were eating in the kitchen tonight, but they also had a formal dining area that accommodated large family gatherings. I cherished my visits to Hartwood Creek as a child because, for a little while, I got a snippet of what it felt like to be a part of a family.

"How are you girls finding Hartwood Creek?" Auntie Em asked us both, looking at us expectantly.

"I think it's safe to say we're loving it, huh, Daph?" I replied, smiling at my daughter.

She shrugged. "I guess so." She really didn't sound convinced. I knew she was still struggling to adjust, and she missed the familiarity of before.

"Oh, you just wait, little one. This town is full of fun and charm. You'll see," Auntie Em declared. "There's even plenty of local legends about magic."

Daphne's eyes were as wide as saucers as she stared at Auntie Em in wonderment. "What kind of magic?"

"Well, there's a special drink at Tout de Sweets, a latte that is said makes people fall in love with each other," Auntie Em explained, her eyes mischievous. "If the couple in question consumes the In The Name of Love Latte, they'll fall in love with one another."

"Locals believe it, and tourists love it," Uncle Ed added, sending a conspiring wink to Auntie Em.

"Did you guys drink it?" Daphne asked, her eyes as wide as saucers.

"Of course we did. On our second date, didn't we?" Auntie Em looked at Uncle Ed, love in her eyes and affection in her smile.

"I thought it was the third..." Uncle Ed trailed off, his lips twitching with amusement at the look Auntie Em tossed him. He chuckled. "It was the second date," he confirmed.

"Sounds like a tourist trap to me," I replied. There wasn't a magical drink in the world that could make people fall—and stay—in love. Most people were just too selfish for the kind of love Uncle Ed and Auntie Em experienced. They were the lucky few who got to have it.

"It's certainly not. We don't need tourist traps to bring the tourists in," Auntie Em frowned a little, as if my opinion on the matter had wounded her feelings. "Besides, we've been married for thirty-six years now."

Daphne's gaze volleyed back and forth between my aunt and me. She was paying more attention than I would have liked to this conversation.

I forced a smile on my face so my sourness wouldn't shine through, trying to soften the blow my disbelief of the love latte seemed to have on my aunt—and my daughter. She seemed...disappointed.

"I believe you and Uncle Ed have the real deal, I'm just saying I don't think you have it because of the love latte. I think you have it because you're genuinely good for one another."

Auntie Em considered my explanation and nodded slowly. "Give it a little time, watch the magic happen, and then you'll change your mind." She winked at Daphne, and Daphne smiled back.

I didn't want to argue with her—or offend her—so I nodded politely and helped myself to another piece of garlic bread.

"So any exciting plans for this weekend?" Uncle Ed asked, sensing the need for a change in topic.

"Daphne and I have a date at the new spa in town. We're going to get facials and our nails done, aren't we, Daph?"

"Yep." Daphne nodded, all excitement and smiles.

"That sounds fun! I haven't been to a spa in a long time." Auntie Em smiled. "Is this the new one that opened up downtown?"

"It sure is. Do you want to join us?" I asked.

"Thank you for the invite, but I have plans to meet Livia in Springwood for shopping and lunch."

"That will be fun too. How's she doing?"

"She's doing great. She just made partner at the firm." Livia was a lawyer specializing in criminal law.

"That's really awesome," I exclaimed, smiling. Livia and her fiancé didn't have any children, and they weren't planning on it. Livia wanted to focus on growing her career, while her fiancé just seemed pleased to go along with whatever Livia wanted.

I'd met him a few times, and he seemed nice. He was a lawyer, too, so he understood the demands of Livia's job. In fact, they'd both met at the firm Livia had made partner at.

"Tell her I said hi when you see her," I said, pausing to take a sip of wine.

"I will," Auntie Em promised. "We'll have to have the girls come out for a barbecue sometime. I know they want to see you and Daphne."

"Yeah, that sounds good. Let me know when you plan it."

It'd been years since I'd seen my cousins Livia, Madeline, Cate, and Jo-Anna. The last time would have been when I brought Daphne out to meet everyone at Christmas when she was a wee little thing. We stayed in touch on social media, but it just wasn't the same.

It was hard not to feel a little envious of my cousins. They all had incredible careers, their own houses, and Livia and Madeline had men who seemed to support their every move. They'd gone about things the right way and had a lot to show for it, while I...

I'd gone about things ass backward, becoming a single mother before I'd solidified a career for myself. Sure, I worked—and hard, at that—but my paychecks had always been peanuts compared to what my cousins brought home with their careers.

I was thankful for my aunt and uncle, thankful for my new job at the hardware store and the apartment. But it was hard not to feel like a failure when I thought about my life in comparison to my cousins.

Comparison is the thief of joy, I told myself, repeating Theodore Roosevelt's famous quote. It was something I tried to tell myself frequently as an adult, because as a child, I'd spent a lot of time wishing things were different.

Now I knew if I wanted things to be different, I had to make changes. It took finding Warren with another woman and breaking up with him to rediscover myself and realize I'd inadvertently done *exactly* what my mother did. I'd changed myself for a man's love and affection.

Inwardly, I sighed. Outwardly, I smiled and kept the casual conversation going until it was time to head out. Auntie Em loaded us up with leftovers and the rest of the brownies she'd made, then we left.

Daphne was so exhausted she fell asleep on the short drive home, and I had to carry her inside. She didn't wake when I transferred her into bed and took off her shoes.

THE NEXT MORNING, Daphne and I headed over to Lilah's spa for a day of much-needed pampering.

Girls' days were something we used to do frequently in Guelph. Sometimes Nellie would join us, but it was usually just Daphne and me.

I'd been taking her since she was a toddler, mainly because I'd wanted to get manicures and pedicures for myself and didn't have many people who would watch my daughter for me. I figured it was something she could partake in. As it turned out, toddlers can *absolutely* be coaxed into soaking their feet and getting their nails painted pretty colours. Daphne loved it, and she behaved, so the estheticians always loved having her in their chair.

Since I'd walked in on Warren with his secretary, things had been chaotic, and I certainly hadn't made any time to pamper myself—or Daphne. That was about to change.

Lilah's spa was in the downtown core, beside the florist shop.

We found parking out front and went inside to the Serenity Shores Day Spa.

Lilah's face lit up when we walked in. "Hi, girls!"

"Hi, Lilah, thank you so much for squeezing us in," I said, approaching the reception desk with a smile. "You have *no idea* how badly we need this, huh, Daphne?"

"Oh yes, we are overdue." Daphne's eyes widened comically, and Lilah and I both chuckled.

"Why don't we start with the facials, then move on to the manicures and pedicures?" Lilah suggested.

"That sounds perfect."

Lilah's spa was clean, with soft, wispy white sheer curtains allowing privacy from the bustling main street while still letting in plenty of light. The walls were painted an earthy grayish green and were lined with more soft sheer curtains, giving the entire space a wispy, whimsical feeling.

The music selection was soft and instrumental. The moment I stepped inside, I felt the weeks of stress start to melt away.

Lilah led the way past several spa chairs and manicure tables. She walked through an open door into a spacious room with two beds made up in white linens.

"All right, Daphne. I'm going to need you to hop up on this bed. Can you do that?"

"Yup," Daphne said, proudly showing off her skill as she climbed up. I set my purse down and climbed onto the other one.

"Is this your first time getting a facial?"

"Yes. But I've had my nails done lots of times before," Daphne replied.

Lilah smiled patiently and got to work. While she was getting everything set up, she asked me a few questions about any prescriptions or supplements we took, any skin concerns I had, our diet, how much water we drank, and any products I was currently using.

Once the consultation was over, Lilah set to cleansing our faces. First, she wrapped our hair in white wraps to keep the product off it. Then she cleansed our faces using cotton pads.

When Lilah brought out the bright magnifying lamp, Daphne's eyes widened. "What are you doing?" she asked when Lilah started examining my skin.

Lilah smiled patiently at her. "I'm just doing a quick skin analysis on your mom, then I'll do one on you. It helps me figure out what kind of skin type you have—dry, oily, sensitive, a combination. Then I can choose the appropriate products and treatment."

"You can tell all that from a light?" Daphne sounded impressed, and Lilah laughed.

"I sure can." Lilah rolled her chair over to Daphne to examine her skin, careful not to shine the light in her eyes. "You both have great skin types—well balanced. Your T-zone—your forehead, chin, and nose—is a bit oily, but overall sebum and moisture is balanced, and your skin is a healthy mix of not too oily and not too dry."

Lilah used a steam machine, directing a thin vapor of warm steam to my face, and while she did that, she walked Daphne through what she was doing. "If you want, I can give you the steam treatment too. But if you're not sure about it, we can skip that part," she told her. After watching me with the machine, Daphne was all for trying it out on herself. She did a gentle enzyme treatment on both of us throughout the steam.

Next came the extraction—something Daphne didn't need, but I certainly did. Daphne watched with wide eyes as Lilah removed the blackheads and whiteheads. It was a little uncomfortable, but I knew it'd be worth it in the end, so I closed my eyes.

"Time for the best part—I think, anyway," Lilah told us with a grin. "The facial massage."

Lilah worked on Daphne first, and the way she relaxed had me smiling. I did the same when Lilah rolled back to me and started my facial massage.

"Ahh...this is the life," Daphne declared, somehow sounding like an adult despite her childish voice. Lilah caught my eye, and we both tried not to laugh.

"So how did the opportunity to own a spa come about?" I asked, mostly making conversation, but I was also curious. Lilah didn't seem that much older than I was.

"I took an esthetician and spa program in college and worked at a spa for several years. It's always been a dream of mine to open my own spa, but I had trouble finding a suitable place back in the city. I found out from my grandfather there was a space available downtown that would be perfect for my spa, so I rented it. My grandpa started renovations earlier this summer, and here we are."

"That's so cool. Congratulations." I smiled. "It's a beautiful setup you have here."

"Thank you! What about you? What brings you to Hartwood Creek?"

"Mommy dumped her fiancé for being dishonest," Daphne beat me to the punch. My cheeks heated with embarrassment, and I lifted my shoulder in a half shrug when Lilah looked at me.

"He cheated," I mouthed.

"I'm sorry to hear that," Lilah's expression was that of

sympathy and understanding. She gave me a gentle smile and finished up with my facial massage before moving on to the mask part.

Once Lilah was finished applying our facial masks, she stood up. "I'm just going to go prep the stations for your manicures. You girls relax for a few minutes, and I'll be right back."

She slipped out of the room and closed the door, and once she'd gone, I let out a contented sigh. "This is nice, huh, Daph?"

"Mm-hmm. Feels funny, though," Daphne admitted. "Like I've got mud all over my face."

"That's the fun part, I think." I smiled. The calming music enveloped us, and I felt myself thawing, my worries melting away.

Fifteen minutes later, Lilah returned. She cleaned away the masks and applied toner, serums, and moisturizer. When she was through, my face felt brand new.

We ended the day off with manicures and pedicures. Daphne chose a pretty sea blue for her nails, while I went with a French manicure. Something subtle but still feminine and pretty.

"Thank you again, Lilah. This was everything we needed and more," I told her as I paid for our day. I didn't even care that it ate a huge chunk of my savings. In my opinion, it was worth it. Daphne had a megawatt smile on, and she'd spent the afternoon chattering away happily about every subject that came to mind.

Normally, my daughter had a lot to say...but this move had silenced her a bit. She'd made her displeasure with it known, of course, but when she realized her opinion on the matter wouldn't change the outcome, she'd opted for the silent treatment and sulking.

But after a week in Hartwood Creek, Daphne was beginning to settle. She was making friends and having fun exploring the town. I was catching her smiling more and more often, although I knew she still missed her old friends.

I'd given her my phone last night so she could message both Zoey and Chloe's moms about potentially having a video call this weekend. Unfortunately, both had replied with they were sorry, but they were busy, and the video call would have to happen another time.

I was a little annoyed, but I'd expected no different from their mothers. They hadn't exactly been welcoming to me in the past.

Daphne, however, had been deeply disappointed, and I was worried that disappointment would linger the rest of the weekend. But the spa trip was exactly what we needed to perk her up.

"It's my absolute pleasure," Lilah insisted, her smile thankful and wide. "And hey, if you guys are free later when I'm off work, I'm taking Riley to the beach."

Daphne whirled on me. "Can we go?" she pleaded.

"I don't see why not," I replied, then I gave Lilah my cell phone number so she could text me when they were heading to the beach.

Once we finished at Lilah's spa, we grabbed some lunch at The Hungry Hub before we went shopping at a few of the stores in town, just to explore a little more of our new home while supporting local. Daphne was especially excited about the toy store in town. I was impressed too. It carried the same small-town vibe a lot of the downtown core had—including the hardware store.

Later that afternoon, we walked into the apartment loaded down with shopping bags from our excursion. Daphne had picked out some new outfits from Two Sisters Clothing and toys from The Knickknack Shack, and I had picked up a few more decorations for the apartment from a beautiful home décor shop called Décor My Way. We had enough time to drop everything off before Lilah's text came through that they were heading to the beach.

I tried not to feel guilty about all the money I'd spent as I waited for Daphne to change into her swimsuit.

I used to spend money on myself and Daphne without blinking, but when I started seeing Warren, I had someone to question my spending habits—and question them, he did. *All the time.* If I went on a shopping trip and spent money frivolously, I'd hear about it. Warren thought it was better to save and invest than spend money on things "we don't really need." He believed in a minimalistic existence.

The silence that greeted me in our apartment carried only my guilt, not his judgments, but I told myself I could afford to splurge a little with the deal I was getting on rent. Nevertheless, I made a silent promise to myself that this was the last frivolous thing we'd be doing for a while.

CHAPTER NINE

Nix

Sunday evening, I was sitting around the old harvest table at my parents' house, surrounded by the entire family. The comfortable hum of conversations happening all around me made me feel at ease and relaxed.

Family dinners were a semiregular thing that we did. It was a little difficult to do them weekly now that we all had our own jobs and lives, but every other week, we tried to gather and share a meal at my parents' house.

Gatherings were always a little chaotic with the four of us rowdy boys, but now that the twins and Bryson had joined the ranks, the chaos had only grown in the best way possible.

It was hard to get a word in edgewise with so many people around the table, but I didn't mind just sitting back and listening to it all unfold. My nieces had spent the first half of dinner excitedly chatting about how the school year had been so far for them. No sooner had they wrapped up their stories, did my younger brothers launch into filling us in on the latest stuff happening with their YouTube channel and other endeavors.

My younger twin brothers, Preston and Paxton, were creative entrepreneurs. The summer of their twentieth birthday, my brothers bought a center console boat together and named it "Bass to Mouth."

In addition to carpentry, our family was big on fishing. Grandpa had spent a lot of time showing us the best spots to fish.

The twins were never really into carpentry the way Parker and I were, although it ran in their blood too. They took more of an interest in their creative pursuits and figured out a way to make a living off their love of fishing, although they also worked at the lumberyard.

About four years ago, they started a YouTube channel to showcase their fishing adventures and homemade lures. Despite our family's skepticism, the whole thing really took off, and they were doing quite well for themselves with over 555,000 subscribers. Their homemade lures were available for purchase online, and they had stock in a couple of shops in town.

A few times, they'd done odd work for me too—which they filmed for their various channels. They also occasionally made my older brother participate by showcasing some projects they collaborated with him on whenever he enlisted their help.

According to Paxton, "everything was content." I had to admit, the twins knew how to work social media, and I'd garnered more than a few jobs from the videos they posted, and so had Parker.

"We recently got a new collaboration opportunity," Preston was saying. "With *My Life Is Crappie*."

Mom choked on the bite of food she'd been eating, her eyes

widening. "What kind of business name is that? It's no better than yours!"

"I think they're both pretty witty," Tabitha remarked.

"You just love the innuendos," Parker teased her, and she smirked.

"How exactly are you collaborating with them?" Mom pressed, ignoring Tabitha and Parker. She still wasn't sold on whatever the twins were up to.

"We'll be doing a lure-making competition," Preston started.

"And a fishing challenge with the lures we make," Paxton finished with a grin. "We get to travel to Lake of the Woods to do it."

Preston and Paxton had done well for themselves with their homemade fishing lures and social media-based business, and with very limited overhead costs with them both still living at home with our parents, they were raking in the dough.

"When will you be doing that?" Dad asked, his eyes bright and proud. Though he'd been the most doubtful about the twins' plans, he'd really come around when he realized how much joy and success it brought them.

"Not until sometime this summer," Preston assured him. "We'll let you know for sure when we iron out the details with Shawn."

Gran was watching everything happening with a smile on her face. Although she was nearly completely deaf now, she'd spent years learning how to lip-read and could mostly follow along with conversations. Not that she was following along now, she just seemed happy everyone was together.

She must have felt my eyes on her because she turned her head and smiled at me.

"Anything new happening in that love life of yours, Nix?"

she asked a little too loudly, garnering the attention of everyone else at the table. Gran was just as meddlesome as the Hartley sisters when it came to us. I think she'd been more heartbroken than I'd been when I called things off with Lori. At least, until she found out the reason.

"Nope, still just committed to my job," I joked.

"Well, that's not *entirely* true," Parker teased from across the table. Of course he'd zero in on that question. I shot him a look.

"Is this about Sage Whitaker moving to town?" Mom demanded, her eyes brightening with excitement. She was just as bad as Gran, if not worse. If Mom had it her way, we'd all be married off with kids by now. Even the twins.

"Who?" Gran looked notably confused.

"You remember Ed and Emelia's niece who would come out for the summers?" Mom reminded her. "The little blonde Nix had a crush on for years."

"Oh yes, I remember now. So when are you going to make your move?" Gran sent me a knowing look.

My cheeks heated with embarrassment. Yeah, my entire family knew about the massive crush I'd harbored on Sage as a kid and teen. I wasn't exactly the greatest liar, and I'd never been able to mask my feelings. Generally, I'm a happy, charismatic, easygoing guy, but I always acted like such an awkward doofus around her, so it'd been obvious to them all back then.

"Hey! Why aren't we grilling the twins about their love life?" I demanded, shooting a look at my younger brothers.

Preston and Paxton both raised their hands at the same time. "Hey now, we're not pushing thirty," Preston, the traitor, said.

"Yeah, we still have plenty of time to settle down. You, on the other hand..." Paxton sent me a judgmental look. "You better get thinking about your next move. That receding hair-line of yours is going to do you no favours."

I scowled. "I do not have a receding hairline."

"Yet. It's genetic," Paxton pointed out, gesturing to our father's lack of hair. It was Dad's turn to frown.

"He's letting her get settled first, which I think is sweet," Tabitha cut in, coming to the rescue. "She just got out of a rela-tionship, so I'm sure she's not even thinking about that yet."

"Well, she won't stay single long in Hartwood Creek. The Hartley sisters will get to her," Gran predicted.

"Oh, there's your answer," Preston declared with a shit-eating grin. "Give her the love latte, and she'll be unable to resist your nonexistent charm."

Bella and Brielle exchanged scheming looks with one another—looks I trusted about as much as I trusted my twin brothers.

"I'm not going to give her the love latte." I shook my head. "And I really don't need dating advice from the likes of you two. You wouldn't know how to date a woman if you got slapped with an instruction manual."

"Is that a challenge?" Paxton arched a brow, exchanging a cunning look with Preston. "Because that sounds like a challenge."

"It sure did sound like a challenge." Preston nodded in agreement. "I bet we could find dates before you even work up the courage to ask Sage out."

I exhaled, trying not to let the irritation and frustration at my brothers' antics sour my mood. Easier said than done—they knew exactly how to pick at me.

"Boys, you do *not* date women just to win a challenge with your brother, and you don't place bets on love," Mom lectured sternly, eyeing both Preston and Paxton with her no-bullshit stare to convey how serious she was about this.

Preston and Parker had the sense to look chided, but I could still see their brains whirling with the prospect of a challenge.

CHAPTER TEN

Sage

The next week seemed to fly by. I was so absorbed with learning the ropes at the hardware store and getting Daphne adjusted to our new routine that I'd had little time to mentally prepare for the Fall Fun Fundraiser planning committee meeting.

I'd forgotten all about it until Tabitha asked me Friday when I went to pick Daphne up if I'd be attending the planning committee meeting at the school later that evening.

"Um...I don't know. I forgot all about it..." I trailed off.

"Oh, that's okay." Was it just my imagination, or did Tabitha seem a little disappointed? "It's a quick meeting, won't be longer than an hour, and they always have snacks and coffee."

"I'll see if Daphne can hang with Auntie Em and Uncle Ed for a bit tonight. If they're okay with it, then I can come."

Tabitha's smile brightened. "Okay, text me and let me know what they say. Maybe we'll go out for drinks after."

I warred with myself the entire drive home. Part of me was

super exhausted from my workweek, but another part of me didn't want to let Tabitha down. Plus, I felt wildly unprepared for the role I'd agree to take on. Maybe going to one of the planning committee meetings would help me get more comfortable with what was expected of me.

Once we got inside, I tossed an easy dinner together for Daph before sneaking into my bedroom to give my aunt a call. It rang once, and Auntie Em picked up. "Hello, Sage. I was just going to call you."

"Oh really?" I asked, surprised.

"Yes, I wanted to remind you about your cousins coming to town tomorrow. Are you and Daphne able to make it to the barbecue? The girls would love to see you."

"Oh, right. Yeah, we'll be there," I said, a little too chipper. Suddenly, asking for a favour felt wrong. I hated asking for help, especially when I felt like I'd be an inconvenience.

"Perfect." Auntie Em paused. I drew in a breath, trying to work up the courage to ask. "Is everything all right?"

"Yeah, everything's great. Well, kind of...I forgot about the Fall Fun Fundraiser planning committee meeting tonight."

"Oh, right, Laurel mentioned that was happening. Did you need me to watch Daphne?"

"Could you?" I bite my bottom lip, peering down the hallway to look at my daughter as she sits at the island counter eating her dinner. I braced myself, expecting her to tell me she was too busy like my mother would have had I asked her.

"Of course! Why doesn't she come over for a sleepover?" Auntie Em suggested. "We'll watch a movie, eat some junk food, and stay up late. You could go to the meeting, maybe go out with Tabitha after, maybe even sleep in tomorrow. I can only imagine how long it's been since you had a night to yourself."

"Really, you'd do that?" I couldn't keep the skepticism from my voice.

"Absolutely, I'd love to," Auntie Em insisted. "Bring her over; we'll see you soon." She hung up, and I stared at my phone in dumbfounded shock.

My mom would have *never* responded that way. In all the years I'd been a parent, she'd taken very little initiative to be a part of Daphne's life. She insisted on being called "Mimi" because "Nana" and "Grandma" made her feel old. I could count on one hand the number of times she held Daphne as a baby, and she'd *never* offered to take my daughter overnight.

She'd made it perfectly clear from the very beginning that Daphne was my child and my responsibility, and she'd done her time raising me and had no interest in repeating the process.

"Hey, Daph?" I said tentatively as I rejoined my daughter. She looked up from her half-eaten bowl of mac and cheese.

"Yes, Mommy?"

"Do you feel like going to Auntie Em's for a sleepover tonight?"

Daphne's face lit up. She'd only ever experienced a sleepover *with* me—after we left Warren's and ended up on Nellie's couch for a couple of days before her roommate got angry and demanded we leave. Then I had to run with my tail tucked between my legs back to my mother's.

"Okay! Are you coming too?"

"No, not this time. Auntie Em wants to have just you over. I'll be going to the school for a planning committee meeting for the fundraiser."

"That sounds boring." Daphne's little nose wrinkled with disdain. "I'd rather go to Auntie Em's."

"Well, you are. Finish eating. I'll go pack your pajamas and a change of clothes."

AN HOUR AND A HALF LATER, I found myself walking into Mr. Robertson's class. There was a bunch of other parent volunteers waiting for Mr. Robertson, who wasn't there yet. The parents were all chatting with one another, sipping coffee or eating from the snacks provided.

I spotted Lilah, Tabitha, and Tabitha's mother-in-law—Nix's mom, Laurel—all standing by the refreshment table set up on the far side of the classroom. I made my way over to their familiar faces.

I tried to act confident, like I belonged there, but memories of my previous attempts at the PTA at Daphne's old school resurfaced.

The parents at the old school hadn't exactly been friendly toward me. I think a lot of it had to do with my age: I was a lot younger than they were. I was also single, or at least...I had been when Daphne started school. The other moms at the school had made me feel as if I was too young and naïve, too inexperienced to have a say.

Worse than being treated like a pariah was after things got serious with Warren, their attitudes toward me became a little more inclusive and a lot less frosty.

I wasn't looking forward to being the single mom again. Not that I minded being alone—I was kind of used to that. I had spent a lot of my childhood alone. I just wasn't looking forward to the way people treated me, like I was either out to steal their man or in desperate need of their help landing a date.

"Sage! You've *got* to try the pumpkin spice latte," Tabitha insisted, grabbing a paper cup and filling it from one of the coffee urns.

"What kind of latte?" I frowned mistrustfully at the coffee she was holding.

"Pumpkin." Tabitha laughed.

"There's no love latte here if you're worried about that," the woman standing beside Tabitha said, giving me the same smile I often saw on Nix.

I'd met Laurel Hutchinson many times before, but I hadn't seen her in several years. She was just as warm and friendly as I remember her being, but the secretive smile she exchanged with Tabitha when I walked in made me feel uneasy.

"Oh, thanks...but I'm not a big fan of pumpkin." I smiled apologetically.

"I'll get you a regular coffee, then," Tabitha amended, setting the cup down and grabbing another. She went about filling it up with the secondary urn.

Nix's mom caught my eye. "It's so good to see you again. I'd like to officially welcome you back to Hartwood Creek." Laurel's tone was welcoming and warm, and she surprised me when she leaned forward and hugged me.

Her hug threw me off—to say I wasn't used to such blatant displays of affection was an understatement. I couldn't remember the last time my mother had hugged me, and although Auntie Em gave out an abundance of hugs, I was only really used to *her* hugging me. So I froze.

"Uh, thanks, Mrs. Hutchinson."

"Oh please, call me Laurel," she insisted with a chuckle, pulling back. "We're all adults here, and Mrs. Hutchinson makes me feel like my mother-in-law."

I didn't have time to respond, as Mr. Robertson walked in, and everyone scurried to sit down. I chose a desk between Lilah and Tabitha, and Laurel sat down on Tabitha's right, still watching me with a peculiar look in her eyes. Not a bad look, per se, but...an inquisitive one.

"Good evening, everyone. Thank you all so much for coming out tonight. We've got a lot to go over," Mr. Robertson said with his signature grin as he leaned against his desk, facing the rest of us. His clipboard in hand, he started going over the itinerary.

"So first off, the food and beverages. The Hartley sisters have offered up to supply baked goods and coffee from Tout de Sweets, although we'll need volunteers to man the table."

Two women raised their hands, and Mr. Robertson glanced at them. "We can do it," the one offered. Mr. Robertson wrote their names down on the clipboard he held.

"Thank you, ladies. And Pizza Picasso donated fifty large pizzas, which we'll be selling at three dollars per slice. We'll need someone to collect money and someone else to serve the pizza."

Another woman eagerly raised her hand, and when Mr. Robertson nodded at her, she said, "Damien and I could run the pizza table." The man sitting beside her nodded with confirmation.

Mr. Robertson smiled at them each in turn before writing their names down too. "Perfect, thanks so much."

"That's my cousin, Damien Wood, and his fiancée, Charlotte Gauthier. Damien has twins, too, Aria and Ronan. They're also in Mr. Robertson's class," Tabitha whispered.

"What's with all the twins in this town?" I whispered back.

"Must be something in the water," Tabitha giggled.

"Or maybe it's the love latte," Laurel interjected with a wink before raising her own hand.

Mr. Robertson nodded at her to speak. "I've enlisted the help of all my boys again. Preston and Paxton will run the dunk tank. Parker and Nix will man the ring toss, and Keith said he would do the bag toss."

"Excellent. Are you guys still doing a vendor table?" Mr. Robertson asked.

"Yup! Tabitha and I will run that, along with Gran, if she feels up to going. We'll have small wood projects available and some of Jerry's beautiful birdhouses."

"Perfect! Lilah, are you still able to do face painting?" Mr. Robertson's eyes drifted to Lilah. She stilled as if surprised he'd remembered her name and was addressing her.

"Yes, I am. I can also donate a gift basket with some goodies and a gift card to my spa for the silent auction."

"That's perfect," Mr. Robertson said animatedly before writing a note down on his handy clipboard. Lilah seemed to blush under his attention. He beamed at her for a beat longer before turning to address me. "And Sage. You're still interested in running the photo booth?"

It felt like every eye in the room turned to look at me, the new girl. I swallowed, then forced a smile. "Yeah."

"Okay, great. You won't have to worry about setting anything up. We have a group of student volunteers from the high school who will be helping set up the booths as a part of their required volunteer hours, so everything *should* be set up before you arrive."

"Sounds good," I replied.

"Also, you're more than welcome to bring business cards to give away to help promote your photography business," he added.

"Oh, I don't have an official business...not yet, anyway." My face heated. It suddenly felt like it was a hundred degrees inside, probably because everyone was still staring at me.

"That's okay." Mr. Robertson gave me an easy smile. "No pressure to promote yourself, but we absolutely don't mind the vendors and volunteers making connections. After all, that's what community is—making connections."

CHAPTER ELEVEN

Nix

It was Friday night, which meant I was headed to The Quarter Lounge to meet up with the guys. Since Parker and I had been so close in age, we had a lot of mutual friends and tended to kick it with the same crowd. Normally, he'd be joining us, but since Tabitha was at the fundraiser planning committee meeting, he was on kid duty at home.

Not that he minded in the slightest. When I left his place, he was making an epic blanket fort with the girls. I think he was more excited about it than they were.

The bar was already packed, typical for a Friday night. I spotted the guys sitting at our usual table by the pool tables and made my way over, stopping to talk to a few locals along the way.

With Parker on kid duty and Kaleb at home enjoying his babymoon with his wife, that left just Donavon, Noah, and myself. Auston Robertson would show up later, after the planning committee meeting.

There used to be more of us gathering every Friday night,

too, but over the years, they'd gotten married and settled down. We still saw them on occasion, but not as much as before, when we were all bachelors. Now it was down to Donavon, Noah, Auston, and me—the only remaining bachelors of the group.

Donavon lifted his chin in greeting when I joined them. There was a full pitcher of beer already on the table and an empty beer glass waiting for me. I sighed in appreciation as I sat down in a vacant seat across from them and poured myself a drink.

"Tough week?" Donavon joked while Noah just smirked at me.

"Not really, no." I shrugged, unable to explain my mood. I felt like I was in limbo, though, stuck between where I wanted to be and where I was. Not that either Donavon or Noah would get that—they both seemed to enjoy the bachelor life.

"I'm telling you, man, you just need to get laid," Noah said, shaking his head. His long brown hair fell over his shoulders with the movement. His blue eyes twinkled with mirth as he leaned back against the booth and appraised me. "What's it been, a year since the last time?"

I scowled, not liking the direction this conversation was already headed in. Why the hell was everyone suddenly on me about my love life, or lack thereof?

The guys knew I wasn't one to do the whole random hookup thing. Call me old-fashioned, but I liked to wine and dine a woman and get to know her a little more before taking her home. They also knew the *one* time I'd allowed myself to partake in a random hookup, after the whole Lori thing, had ended up with the woman borderline stalking me.

Luckily, that woman had been a tourist, and after three months of dealing with that crazy situation last summer, she returned to her hometown. But it had *seriously* turned me off from casual hookups. Since then, I'd been under a bit of a dry spell. I hadn't met a woman I'd wanted to get to know more on that level.

At least, not until Sage came back to town. Now she was all I could think about, but I sensed she was still nursing a broken heart, and I wasn't the kind of guy to take advantage of that.

"He's not wrong, you know." Donavon shrugged. He chuckled when I turned my scowl on him. "Sex lowers stress and anxiety. Proven fact."

"Yeah, unless sex results in a stalker, which increases stress and anxiety."

"That was one time." Noah laughed. He thought that whole situation was hilarious. Parker hadn't been so impressed, though...considering the woman had shown up several times uninvited to the residence he also lived at with his family.

"I don't know, I could see how that would sour a guy." Donavon chuckled. He was practically the king of casual hookups and had so far never encountered a crazy stalker. Guess he just had more practice and could suss out problematic people. He also had a list of rules a mile long—one of them being *no hooking up with colleagues or parents of students.*

I was too trusting, too new at the game, and I hadn't had any rules at all. I'd just wanted to forget how shitty Lori had made me feel.

Lori had been my college sweetheart. We'd started dating shortly after we met while attending the same community college. Well, I suppose most of us attended Springwood Community College, but still.

I'd thought we were building a life together, but Lori had other plans—plans that involved cheating on me every chance she got, until I caught her red-handed.

I opened my mouth, about to fire off a retort, when Noah's gaze darted to the door. He straightened up immediately, interest flashing in his eyes. "Well, damn. Hello, fresh meat. Who are the gorgeous babes with Tabitha?"

I turned my head, catching Tabitha walking into The Quarter Lounge with two other women—Sage and a woman I didn't know.

"That's Sage Whitaker and...I don't know..." I trailed off, not recognizing her. Not that I was even looking at her—my attention was on the captivating blonde who had the strangest hold on me.

"Sage Whitaker; why is that name so familiar?" Donavon asked with a frown as he tried to work out where he knew her from.

"She's related to the Alcotts," I answered, pausing to take a sip of beer. My throat had suddenly gone dry. Wasn't hard to guess why...not that Sage, or Tabitha, for that matter, had noticed us sitting over in the corner as they made their way inside. "She used to visit during the summer when we were kids."

"Oh, *that* Sage," Noah said, sounding as if everything made complete sense. He exchanged a look with Donavon. "Damn..."

"What's that supposed to mean?" I frowned.

"Means she's even hotter now," Noah explained with a smirk. "If you don't make a move, I just might."

Before I could tell him to back off, Tabitha spotted us and waved, then said something to the others, and they started walking over to our table. Sage and the other woman didn't look too thrilled at the prospect of coming over to chat with us, but they followed Tabitha anyway.

"Hey, guys. I wanted to introduce my new friends. They just moved here," Tabitha said once she was standing beside the table. "Sage Whitaker and Lilah Willard. Sage, you already know Nix—he's my brother-in-law," she said with a grin, introducing me to Lilah.

"Nice to meet you," Lilah said, and I tipped my chin and smiled in greeting.

"This is Donavon Ashe, he's the history and woodshop teacher over at Hartwood Creek High School, and Noah Wood —another cousin of mine who also happens to be my husband's best friend." Tabitha continued making the introductions, pointing to Donavon and Noah each in turn. "You'll probably end up spending some time with Donavon at the Fall Fun Fundraiser, since he wrangles the sophomores that will be helping with setup."

"It's a tough job, but someone's got to do it," Donavon joked. "Nice to meet you ladies, and welcome to Hartwood Creek."

"Thanks. It's nice to meet you too," Sage said, politely smiling, but then her eyes landed on me. "Nix." She nodded at me in greeting.

"Hey, Sage." The two words were all I seemed able to get out, the rest of what I was going to say dying on my tongue when her eyes locked on mine.

I was hypnotized; it was like she was calling out for me—or calling to me. Her gaze alone was a siren's lure. I could get lost in the depths of those green eyes for hours, but then she blinked and looked away, and the spell was broken—although not forgotten.

"Well, enjoy your evening, fellas! It's moms' night out, so we're going to go drink our faces off. It's time to introduce you ladies to my girls," Tabitha told them, a mischievous look on her face.

About once a month or so, Tabitha met up with her girlfriends for drinks at The Quarter Lounge, and when she did... she tended to go a little wild. I'd likely be making my current beer my only beer, just so I could play designated driver later.

I couldn't help but watch as they walked off toward the

table by the stage, where Annalise Galloway, Ophelia Loucks, and Isla Bennett were sitting, a huge pitcher of their go-to drink —sangria—half-finished in front of them. The three girls waved at Tabitha as soon as they spotted her.

Tabitha, Sage, and Lilah had just joined them when Auston Robertson walked in and spotted us.

Auston was the last to join our friend group when he moved to Hartwood Creek as a teen. He and Donavon had gone to college together and both worked on the Fall Fun Fundraiser.

"Sorry I'm late, had to clean up after the meeting," Auston apologized, sliding into the booth beside me and reaching for the last empty beer glass. The pitcher of beer that had previously been full was practically empty now, but the server, Mae, was way ahead of us.

She replaced our nearly empty pitcher with two full ones.

"Ahh, thank you, Mae. You are a godsend," Noah said, grinning with appreciation.

"Just doing my job," she replied before skipping off to serve other patrons.

Auston poured himself a beer and took a long sip. After swallowing, he wiped his mouth. "I'll be glad when this fundraiser is over. So much planning goes into it."

"Yeah, but you're never short on volunteers," I pointed out with a smirk. Seemed like every year, the volunteer participation from parents grew—and it was mainly moms signing up. Some would drag their husbands along, but I knew far too many were there to ogle over the good-looking, dark-haired teacher.

As one of the few eligible bachelors in town, Auston had amassed quite the fan club. He wasn't a player like Noah, nor did he often partake in one-night stands like Donavon. He was more like me, waiting on that right person to take a chance on.

"Ha-ha," Auston said dryly.

"Hell, some of them are gathered over by the stage," Noah pointed out, gesturing by lifting his chin toward the table Tabitha, Lilah, and Sage had joined. Auston looked over his shoulder and grunted. "Think one of them would volunteer to come home with me? That dark-haired one...mmm."

Auston's head turned so fast, I was surprised he didn't injure it, and the unamused look on his face was enough to make even Noah take pause.

"Don't even think about it," he grumbled.

"What, did you both call dibs? That's not fair." Noah sulked.

"Nobody's calling dibs on anyone. They're human beings, Noah." It was my turn to frown.

"So neither one of you would be pissed off if I went over there and offered to buy one of those beautiful specimens a drink?" Noah challenged.

Auston's jaw clenched, but he lifted a shoulder in a half shrug. "Go for it."

I bit my tongue. Pushing away the primitive urge to bang on my chest and stake a claim. "You're free to do what you want," I managed.

Noah tossed back what was left of his beer. "Well, if you'll excuse me...I'm about to shoot my shot." He gave Donavon a pointed look, and Donavon moved aside so he could get out of the booth.

Donavon, Auston, and I watched as Noah sauntered over to the girls' table. He said hello to Ophelia, Annalise, and Isla—who were all used to his antics by now and paid him little attention. Then he turned his blue-eyed gaze on Lilah and started flirting with her. I was pretty sure he asked if he could buy her a drink because he'd gestured to the bar.

Lilah lifted her full glass and shook her head, saying something in response I couldn't make out from where we sat. Noah turned to address Sage with a grin and some smooth words. She immediately started laughing, saying something equally cutting that made Noah return a moment later with his tail tucked between his legs.

"Shoot and a miss twice, huh?" Donavon ribbed when he got back. He stood again, letting Noah slide back into the booth.

"Shut up." Noah scowled.

"What'd they say?" Auston asked, trying to hide his interest in the answer.

"Lilah told me she could afford her own drinks, and Sage told me I might want to wait five minutes before trying to hit on a new girl after facing rejection."

"I mean, she's not wrong. Rookie mistake." I laughed, and Auston just smirked, glancing back over his shoulder at Lilah for half a beat before returning his attention to us.

I could tell, though...he was interested in her. Not that he'd act on it. Auston was just as strict with his rules as Donavon: students' moms were completely off-limits.

CHAPTER TWELVE

Sage

The drinks were going down a little too easy, and I couldn't remember the last time I laughed and smiled so much.

I'd never been a fan of meeting new people. It was intimidating, and half the time I felt like I was being judged and found lacking. That wasn't the case at all with Tabitha and her friends.

Annalise Galloway, Isla Bennett, and Ophelia Loucks were well into their second large pitcher of sangria when we joined them, and I immediately understood why she was friends with them.

Annalise and Isla had grown up in Hartwood Creek with Tabitha, and Ophelia had joined their ranks when the three of them met at college. She now resided on the outskirts of Hartwood Creek. Together, the girls were an unstoppable force of jokes and positive affirmations.

They also took the time to get to know Lilah and me, asking us questions about what brought us to Hartwood Creek.

"I just opened up the Serenity Shores Day Spa downtown," Lilah explained with a smile.

"Ooh, a spa! We'll have to come check it out," Ophelia suggested.

"We haven't done a spa day in so long," Annalise added, nodding with agreement. "I could *so* use a spa day."

"Me too," Tabitha agreed. "Do you do HydraFacials?"

"I do."

"Ooh...in that case, we'll definitely have to plan a girls' day soon." The others nodded in agreement, and then it seemed like everyone was turning to look at me for *my* story.

"What about you, Sage?" Annalise asked kindly. Tabitha sort of knew, and she gave me an encouraging smile.

"I caught my fiancé cheating, left him, and had nowhere else to go. So I'm working at my uncle's hardware store now and living in the apartment above it," I admitted, my nose wrinkling a little at the sad story. It wasn't nearly as motivating as Lilah's relocating to open her business.

"I'm sorry." Ophelia made a face like she knew all too well the heartache of an unfaithful man. Lilah got a look about her, too, as if she knew. There was a sense of comradery even without either one of them divulging their stories.

"It's okay." I shrugged, toying with my drink. "It woke me up. Made me reevaluate my life—a lot. And it made me see him and our entire relationship through a whole new lens. I realize now he wasn't the most supportive person out there, even if he tried to insist on 'taking care' of my daughter and me. He wanted me to fit the mold of what he expected out of a partner. Obedient and complacent, willing to turn a blind eye to his...extracurriculars."

I was worried my lips were a little too loose and the women would judge me for what I was saying, but they all nodded wisely, like they understood exactly what I meant and what I'd been through. Maybe they did, or maybe it was just the sangria —either way, I felt seen, heard, and understood by all of them, and it was such a good feeling.

"It's a good thing that it happened *before* you married him," Ophelia remarked, taking a hefty sip of her sangria. "I've seen some crazy stuff in my job..."

Ophelia was a destination wedding consultant and ended up sharing a horrifying story of a wedding that didn't go quite according to plan, which launched Annalise into a few recollections of her own. Annalise worked at her family's bed and breakfast and had also witnessed some interesting relationship dramas unfold from guests that stayed at the inn.

Isla had no such stories to share. She was a freelance graphic designer who worked from home so she could be with her two kids, both too young for school. "I miss out on all the fun drama," she pouted.

"Oh! That reminds me, Sage. You should get Isla to help you with a logo and a business card."

"I don't have a photography business, remember?" I pointed out, arching a brow.

"So? Make one. Unless you want to work at the hardware store forever."

I frowned a little. "Nothing against Uncle Ed, I love the hardware store—but yeah. I'd like to not be in retail. It would be cool to do photography full time one day..."

"She's *talented* too," Tabitha interjected, pulling up my Instagram account to show off the photos I'd recently taken at the beach and passing her phone around so the girls could get a good look.

"You're so good," Ophelia exclaimed, her expression impressed as she handed Tabitha her phone back.

"You totally should start your own photography business," Lilah urged. "What's stopping you?"

"I don't know how to run a business, and besides...I don't even know what I'd call it." I laughed awkwardly. I'd never had so many people encouraging me to go for it. Usually, I just heard about how it wasn't lucrative, that so many people were doing it. That I was silly for wanting to try...

These girls looked at me like I was crazy for not already doing it, though.

"Nobody knows exactly how to run a business, even those of us running our own business." Lilah smiled kindly. "It's a learn-as-you-go kind of thing. As for the name..." she paused, thinking, and the rest of the women around the table seemed to be doing the same.

After some quiet thought, the suggestions started pouring out.

"What about 'So Lensational Photography,'" Tabitha tossed out.

"Or 'Flash Me Photography,'" Ophelia added with a cheeky grin, feeding off Tabitha's suggestive name.

"Those names are great, but they may give the impression you only do boudoir photography," Isla said, taking a more thoughtful approach. "What is your niche?"

"I have a lot of practice with babies and kids, since my daughter's pretty much been my only subject for the last several years," I said, pausing to think on it before continuing. "I love landscape photography and capturing candid moments. I always thought it would be cool to do wedding photography—more destination stuff, less indoor venue...but I've never done anything like that. I'm not really big on studio photography; I don't have much experience with it..."

"You could keep it classic and use your full name or initials. What's your last name again?" Isla asked.

"Whitaker..."

"So Sage Whitaker Photography, or SW Photography," Isla suggested with a smile.

"Ooh, yes. I love both those options." Tabitha nodded. "Which one do you prefer?"

"I don't know." I laughed, feeling their genuine excitement and encouragement. It was more intoxicating than the sangria.

"Well, think on it and shoot me a message when you decide. We'll talk about a logo, and I'd be happy to do up some business cards for you," Isla told me, pulling a card of her own out of her purse and handing it to me. Her business logo read *Graphic Sense*, and beneath that was her name and email. When I flipped it over, there was a QR code on the back. "If you scan that with your phone, it'll bring you to all my social media accounts. We can talk about doing that for you too."

Lilah looked impressed as she studied Isla's card over my shoulder. "I wish I'd known about you sooner; I would have hired you to do my logo design and cards. I ended up hiring someone from back home before I left."

She reached into her purse and pulled out a card for the spa. "Oh! I love that, though," Isla exclaimed. "It's neat, clean, and simplistic. The graphic designer did a very good job."

"I'm happy with it." Lilah nodded. "But in the future, I'll make sure I go to you for my graphic design needs."

While Isla and Lilah were talking, Ophelia turned her hazel gaze on me. She reminded me of a grown-up Merida, all that long, curly red hair, porcelain skin, and soft freckles. Her beauty was kind of intimidating, and if I'd judged her off her appearances alone, I would have never spoken to her for fear of thinking her beauty made her mean. But her smile was every bit as friendly as she was.

"If you're interested, I could pass your contact information along to some of the photographers we work with? Sometimes they need second shooters," Ophelia inquired, watching me with keen interest.

"Second shooters?" The sangria was making my brain feel a little fuzzy.

"Yeah. A second shooter is an additional photographer taking photos at the wedding. You'd get paid to take the photos and send the raw files to them, and they'd edit the photos in their style. It would give you a little experience doing weddings."

"That would be perfect for you, Sage," Tabitha squealed, reaching for my hand and squeezing it.

"Okay, sure. That'd be great." I smiled.

"Cool. As soon as Isla does up your business cards, give me a few, and I'll hand them out. Once you've done a few weddings as a second shooter, you can be added to our list of photographers we recommend to brides and grooms...if wedding photography is still something you want to do after you've tried it. Who knows, you might hate it." She laughed, her eyes sparkling with levity.

We spent the next two hours talking about anything and everything. By the end of the night, I knew so much about each of them that I felt like a part of the group too. They didn't just monopolize the conversation to talk about themselves, but shared stories and hyped one another up. They had the kind of friendship I'd always read about and seen depicted in movies but had never had the fortune of being a part of.

"Once a month we try to meet up for drinks. You two should join us again next time," Ophelia said at the end of the night when we were standing at the bar paying our tabs off.

"Yes, join us again next time! It was so good meeting you both." Annalise was very affectionate, and she wrapped Lilah and me both up in her arms at the same time and pressed sloppy kisses to our cheeks. "Welcome to Hartwood Creek, ladies."

Isla's husband was reportedly waiting outside for them, and he'd be driving Annalise and Ophelia home. I hadn't planned on drinking as much as I had, but I was far too tipsy to drive, and I knew that. Unfortunately, I'd been the one to drive. Lilah had walked to the school, and Tabitha had gotten a ride with Laurel to the committee meeting, then talked us both into going to The Quarter Lounge after.

"Huh. Guess we better call a cab? Or walk?" I said before immediately hiccupping. Lilah giggled.

"We could split the cab if you'd like?" she offered.

"No, no, no. No one's taking a cab." Tabitha shook her head back and forth. "Nix will drive us. He only had the one beer three hours ago, so he's good."

At the mention of his name, I looked up and saw Nix was still there, sitting with his friends, only he had a tall, half-full glass in front of him with what I could only assume had soda in it. It certainly wasn't the beer I'd seen him with when we first arrived.

He turned his head, spotting us at the bar and catching me mid-perusal, and the corner of his lip kicked up in a half grin. He said something to his friends, and Auston stood up to let him out.

Auston and Nix both tossed a few bills down on the table. No sooner had they stood up, then two women were sliding into their vacant spots. Neither Donavon nor Noah seemed put out by their arrival, though. Both women were stunning—one of them with long dark hair and an edgy vibe to her, while the other woman had lighter brown hair and an almost hippie vibe to her.

Nix said something to the edgy girl, and she fired off a response that made him grin. The jealousy that surfaced caught me off guard, and I looked away when he and Auston started heading over.

"Ruh-roh, testosterone incoming." Tabitha giggled, waggling her eyebrows at Lilah and me.

"Ugh, better not be that Noah guy again." Lilah frowned, refusing to turn around and look.

"Noah's not that bad, he's just a big flirt," Tabitha explained, rising to her cousin's defense.

Noah had approached Lilah earlier in the evening to ask her if he could buy a drink. When she turned him down, he immediately turned to me with the bluest eyes and a dazzling grin that probably *did* earn him a lot of yeses. He wasn't unattractive, by any means...but he certainly wasn't looking for forever.

I'd turned him down, too—what girl wanted to be the second choice, anyway? He must have been drunk to think I'd say yes. But the look he'd worn when he first walked over was calculating, almost like he *knew* we'd both turn him down but was still doing it.

In fact, Noah was watching both Nix and Auston with a smirk, and I was beginning to think his actions earlier this evening were driven by...something that my tipsy brain struggled to connect.

"Ready to go?" Nix asked Tabitha, and she nodded. Then he looked at Lilah and me. "Anyone else need a ride home?"

"Yes, please." Lilah sighed with relief.

"You only have three seats in your truck, though," Tabitha pointed out sweetly, blinking up at Auston as if waiting for him to chime in. I opened my mouth to suggest taking my car, but Tabitha shot me a look, discreetly shaking her head.

Auston picked up what she was suggesting. "I can give someone a lift home." Was it my imagination, or did he quickly glance at Lilah with hope? Tabitha sent me another look that said, *see?*

Lilah bit her bottom lip. "I'm a little out of the way. I live in the suburbs behind the school."

"That's where Auston lives too," Tabitha exclaimed, clapping with delight. "Okay, so you ride with Auston, and Nix, you can drive Sage and obviously me home." She had a content smile on her face as if she was pleased with herself about this blatant setup.

Neither Lilah nor Auston seemed to mind, though. There was a tension between them that even I'd picked up on in my sangria haze, and I think they both were a little more than thankful for the opportunity.

Once we'd made the arrangements and split off in the parking lot, I noticed Tabitha was beginning to look a little green, her satisfied smile slipping with every wobbly step she took.

When we reached Nix's truck, she started to groan as if in agony. "Ugh, I feel like I'm gonna be sick," she admitted, leaning over and clenching her stomach.

It was almost as if Nix expected it, though. He waved a finger at her. "If you puke in my truck again, I'm going to be mad as hell, and *you're* going to be the one to clean it."

"I did that one time," Tabitha squeaked, her cheeks heating with embarrassment.

Nix looked at me sheepishly. "Sorry, but I'm gonna make her sit in the passenger seat with her head out the window. I don't trust her."

I laughed at the look on Tabitha's face, like she was greatly offended. But she didn't argue with him—she just climbed into the passenger seat while Nix held the driver's door open for me.

I hopped up into the cab, sitting in the small space between

Tabitha and Nix. When Nix climbed in, his thigh pressed against mine unintentionally. Although it was involuntary and a result of me being wedged between them with little space, the sensation of his thigh pressed to mine made desire thrum through my core.

It only got worse when he started driving. I could feel the muscles in his thigh as he worked the gas and brakes. I didn't know if I had the sangria to thank or the lack of intimacy in my life, but my body was *reacting* to his.

"I'm going to drop Tabitha off at home first, if you don't mind? I kind of want to get her home before she starts puking. Wait, you're not a puker, are you?"

"No, and I'm not that drunk. Just...tipsy. My stomach feels fine, though," I replied, glancing at Tabitha. She looked the worse for wear. She had her whole head out the window and was groaning softly.

Nix nodded, driving to old town. He pulled into the driveway of Parker and Tabitha's house, and no sooner had he put the truck in park was his brother stepping out onto the front porch. He jogged over to open the passenger door.

Parker was grinning as he helped Tabitha out, like this was a regular occurrence. He picked her up and tossed her over his shoulder. She let out a little giggle and then groaned, flopping over his shoulder. "Thanks, Nix." He nodded at his brother before shutting the door and carrying Tabitha into the house.

Once he'd shut the door, I slid over, giving myself a little space and distance to try and collect my thoughts. My body was still thrumming on that high of desire Nix's thigh against mine had evoked. Part of me wanted to act on that feeling, but even tipsy, I knew that wasn't a good idea.

Nix tossed me an almost shy smile before reversing out of the driveway to take me home.

CHAPTER THIRTEEN

Nix

As I drove back toward the hardware store, I couldn't help but reminisce about how it had felt to have Sage's leg pressed against mine for the first half of the drive.

I needed to distract myself, otherwise, I was going to have a very apparent reaction to her. Breaking the silence seemed to be the wisest course of action.

"Suffice it to say, my dear sister-in-law doesn't handle her liquor very well," I teased as we headed back toward the main strip.

Sage smiled, glancing at me from across the cab. "At least she didn't throw up."

"The night is still young." I chuckled, shaking my head. "But yeah, at least it didn't happen in my truck this time."

"I'd love to hear that story," Sage told me, the smile reaching her eyes. I took that as a good sign.

"Nothing dramatic, really. Tabitha went out with the girls last month, overindulged like she usually does, and ended up puking on the floor of my truck. She forgets she can't drink like she did in college."

Sage smiled. "I found my alcohol tolerance changed after having Daphne. Probably because I don't drink as often as I did before I got pregnant with her."

"I guess that makes sense. Tabitha doesn't drink as much either. Only when the Quarters get together."

"The Quarters?"

"It's a cutesy nickname Parker gave Tabitha, Ophelia, Isla, and Annalise." I shrugged. "It's easier to say than all of their names."

"That is cute." Sage smiled. "It's great that Tabitha was able to stay in touch with all her friends."

"Weren't you?" I was a little surprised when she shook her head sadly. Sage had one of those energies about her; you just wanted to be in her company.

"When I got pregnant in college, none of those friends stuck around for the next phase of my life. They were too busy finishing the college stage," Sage explained, lifting her shoulder in a delicate shrug. "Prior to college, I didn't have many friends because my mom moved us around a lot."

"Makes sense," I said. It wasn't that I pitied her—Sage was not a woman to pity—but I did feel for her, especially when I looked back in my memories and thought about how alone she must have felt. She'd seemed happy in Hartwood Creek with her cousins, but I'd had no idea what her home life was like. I'd never even met her mother. "I'm sorry you had to deal with that. Moving around a lot as a kid, I mean."

"It's okay," she replied, lifting her shoulder as if dismissing it. "I did make one awesome friend back in Guelph. Nellie. She's pretty much the only thing I miss about that place."

"Well, if Tabitha has her way, I'm sure you'll be a bonified member of the Quarters in no time at all. We might have to start calling you guys a Dollar and Change, though."

Sage let out a laugh, shaking her head. "You're ridiculous."

I parked at the curb out front, close to the door that led to the apartments. Turning off the ignition to my truck, silence filled the cab, but it wasn't an uncomfortable kind—it was the charged kind. Though she was masking it well, I could feel her attraction to me just as acutely as I felt mine to her.

It'd started with the little exhale she'd let out when I'd first climbed into the truck beside her, the pretty little blush that coloured her cheeks, and the way she'd tense any time I happened to move my foot to brake at stoplights, like the feel of me against her was affecting her just as much as it'd affected me.

"Did you have a good time?" I asked at the same time she said, "Thanks for the ride home, Nix."

We both paused, then laughed awkwardly.

"Yeah, I did have a good time," she replied, tucking her hair behind her ear as she stole another glance at me. "I haven't had a night out in...I can't remember how long." She wrinkled her nose a bit, as if struggling to recall the last time.

"Does...Daphne's dad not take her very often?"

"Try never," Sage said, giving me a self-deprecating smile. "He isn't involved in our lives."

"Oh, I thought...never mind." I shook my head.

"If you're referring to my failed engagement, he wasn't Daphne's bio dad." Sage bit her bottom lip, averting her gaze like she was ashamed of that.

"No judgment from me. Both those guys lost out on an amazing woman—and a great kid," I told her. Her eyes shot back to me, and I could tell my words affected her.

She gave me a watery smile. "Thanks, Nix."

"Just speaking the truth," I assured her. Our gazes remained locked, and something potent passed between us. Sage's tongue darted out to lick her lips, and I almost leaned forward to kiss her.

Something held me back, though. I knew it wasn't the right time, not yet. Her eyes went to my lips—like she knew I wanted to kiss her, and maybe wanted to kiss me too. But then, she drew in a solidifying breath before the walls shot up. She shook her head as if clearing it and gave me a small smile.

"I should probably go inside; it's late," Sage said, reaching for the door. She opened it and went to climb out, then paused and looked at me over her shoulder. "Again, thank you for the ride."

"No problem. I'll see you around."

I let her climb out—even though it was the last thing I wanted to do. I watched to make sure she got to the door safely, though I wasn't overly concerned. It was safe in Hartwood Creek, and aside from the occasional issues with tourists, we had a low crime rate. Not to mention, the police station was right next door. Sage was probably in the safest place in town.

Still, I didn't drive away until I saw the light in her apartment come on.

JUST AS I PREDICTED, Tabitha was really feeling her night of overindulgence the next morning. Parker took pity on her, and after setting her up in their room with a large glass of water and some Tylenol, he came downstairs to cook breakfast for the kids.

Bryson hadn't woken up yet, and Bella and Brielle were in

the living room, watching one of their favourite television programs while I sat at the kitchen island, stealing a cup of coffee from my brother.

Sleep had been futile for me. I'd tossed and turned all night, unable to get those green eyes out of my head.

"You didn't take long to drop Sage off last night," Parker remarked, taking a bowl down from the cupboard before grabbing the milk and a carton of eggs from the refrigerator.

"Well, I was only dropping her off, and it's not like she lives far away." I grunted, taking another sip of coffee.

"You didn't ask her out?" Parker tossed me a look over his shoulder, like he couldn't believe I *still* hadn't done so.

"The opportunity didn't exactly come up." I frowned. "All I did was drive her home."

Parker laughed. "Lies, you're just a chickenshit."

"Yeah, maybe." I shrugged, sighing. I pushed my hand through my hair, thinking back to our conversation. It wasn't I was too chicken to ask her out. It was I had realized how difficult it would be for her to just "go out on a date" with me, even before I'd learned that Daphne's dad wasn't involved. Now that I had more clarity on her situation, I knew asking her out was going to be even more challenging.

I was also a little hesitant because she'd just broken off an engagement. While I'd never quite gotten there with Lori, I could only imagine how difficult that would be. To have accepted someone's proposal, only to call things off...something must have happened. Judging by the mistrustful look in her eyes and the walls she'd thrown up, I could take one wild guess on what went wrong there.

Parker shook his head, cracking eggs into the bowl. "Not everything has to be perfect for you to make a move. If you're waiting for the ideal situation, it's never going to happen."

"Gee, thanks for the wise words, bro," I said dryly, watching as he poured the milk in and knowing there was truth in his advice. The look Parker tossed me over his shoulder suggested he sensed I knew he was right.

He started whisking the egg and milk mixture. "All I'm saying is, she's here now, and so are you. You're both single, and there's *obviously* something between you two..."

"I don't know about 'obviously.'" I shook my head, trying to cover the small smile his words brought out with my coffee mug. Still, Parker had a point.

"Uncle Nix, if you need help planning a date, we can help you," Bella said, suddenly appearing at my right elbow. She climbed onto the stool beside me.

"Yeah! We can help you, Uncle Nix," Brielle echoed, climbing up onto the stool on my other side.

Parker arched a brow at his daughters, pointing the whisk at them each in turn. "What did I tell you two about eavesdropping on adult conversations?"

"We weren't eavesdropping. We overheard." Bella rolled her eyes, the sass a carbon copy of her mother.

"Same thing." Parker shook his head, moving to the stove to see if the frying pan had warmed enough.

"All we're saying is, we could help. Maybe we could have Daphne come for a sleepover one night so that her mom can go out," Brielle suggested.

"Yeah. Daphne doesn't have a daddy, so that would work." Bella nodded, and Parker tried to hide his amusement with a cough and his hand.

"The rest is up to you, Uncle Nix. You'll have to ask her mommy out, and I'll be honest, I'm not sure she'll say yes." Brielle shook her head, and Parker couldn't contain himself any longer. He burst out laughing, doubling over.

"Gee, thanks, girls," I said dryly, shooting Parker an unamused look.

"Girls, give your uncle a break and stop worrying yourselves about what the adults are doing. Go be kids. I'll call you when the eggs are ready," Parker told them sternly. The twins let out heavy sighs and jumped off the stools, heading back into the living room. Once they'd left, Parker smirked at me. "You know, it's not a bad idea…"

Sage

The next morning, I awoke around ten o'clock with a pounding headache and the driest mouth. All I wanted to do was pull the covers over my head and sleep away the hangover, but I couldn't. Auntie Em had gone out of her way to plan a barbecue and my cousins were all coming to town for it. Even Cate, who lived in LA and had an insane work schedule would be there.

I hadn't seen my cousins in so long, and I really was looking forward to it.

I dragged myself out of my bed and to the kitchen for a glass of water and some ibuprofen. Then I walked down the hall to the bathroom, hoping a shower would wash away the night of sangrias off me. I alternated between hot and cold water, and by the time I got out, I was feeling almost human again. After blow-drying my hair and applying some makeup, I felt like myself again.

It was nearly noon when I finally arrived at Uncle Ed and Auntie Em's. Two unfamiliar cars, a black BMW and a dark silver Camry, were parked in the driveway, likely belonging to my cousins.

Before I could raise my hand to knock, the front door swung open, and my cousin, Cate, squealed and enveloped me in a hug. "Oh my gosh, Sage! It's been forever!" she exclaimed. "I can't believe how much Daphne's grown, she's so sweet!"

"Thank you." I laughed, hugging her back. "I know, it's been ages. How are you?"

"I'm great!" Cate exclaimed, stepping back. Her blue eyes were shining. "I'm just finishing up a project in Edmonton right now, which is why I'm able to be here. Dad picked me up from the airport late last night, and I've got to be back tomorrow morning."

"That's awesome. What project?" I asked, stepping inside the foyer and closing the door behind me.

"It's an adaptation of a popular thriller book by Clairice Saltzman," she replied, her smile widening as we walked through the house together.

"That's so cool!" I exclaimed, grinning back at her. I think out of all my cousins, I was most impressed by Cate's achievements. She'd gone to school for film and television production and had a bachelor's degree. Shortly after graduating, she started working on-set at a popular teen drama show in Toronto. After that, she landed representation with a big talent agency and ended up moving to LA to work, occasionally taking on projects in Canada.

Cate's accomplishments grew every year. She had directed several incredible films and televisions series and had a bunch of recognitions and awards under her belt already at the age of thirty-two.

A lot of her projects involved bringing disabled stories to the big screen. Cate had a rare skeletal disorder called Ollier's disease, a condition where greater than normal growth of the cartilage in the long bones of the legs and arms causes abnormal growth and makes the outer layer of the bone become thin and more fragile. The masses of cartilage are benign tumors called enchondromas. The enchondromas have a 30% chance of undergoing malignant changes to a cancer called chondrosarcomas, although luckily—Cate hadn't had that issue.

The enchondromas can also cause limb deformities, and Cate had had several surgeries throughout her childhood and youth to correct the deformities of affected limbs, and she did experience aching pain and swelling. But for the most part, she didn't let it slow her down. If anything, her condition fueled her.

"Yeah, it's pretty neat. Clairice has an incredible mind, it's kind of terrifying. Working with her has been a highlight of my career, for sure," Cate laughed lightly, tucking her dark hair behind her ear and sending me a curious look. "What about you, have you decided to pursue photography yet?"

"Kind of," I admitted. "Daphne roped me into doing the photo booth at the Fall Fun Fundraiser."

"Mom told us, that's awesome. I know you'll do great!"

"I hope so," I replied as we walked into the kitchen to find Auntie Em, Madeline, and Livia all gathered around the island. Livia had a glass of wine in hand, while Madeline was preparing a salad and Auntie Em was checking on her oven-roasted potatoes and the steamed green beans on the stove.

Madeline and Livia hugged me, then Livia offered to pour me a glass of wine. "Sure, just a small one, though."

"Morning, Sage!" Auntie Em said, covering the potatoes with a lid to keep them warm. "How did the planning committee meeting go?"

"It went good, we planned things," I answered, feeling a little put on the spot. Thinking about last night made me think about how I'd felt sitting beside Nix in his truck, and I needed to avoid that thought. "Where's Daphne?"

"Outside with Dad and the guys," Madeline replied, tilting

her head toward the sliding door. I could see Daphne by the barbecue with Uncle Ed and two men I recognized from Madeline and Livia's social media posts. "Dad's teaching her how to grill the perfect ribs."

"Excellent, one of us should learn how to barbecue," I took a small sip of wine. "How are you both?"

"Pretty good, we're just about finished with the addition on the house," Madeline said. "And just in time too..." she added, her hand covering her stomach, which was just beginning to show. "I'm due in May. I was *planning* on telling everyone at dinner tonight, but Liv wouldn't lay off about the wine, so I had to spill the beans early."

"Congratulations!" I exclaimed, truly excited for her. Judging by the megawatt smile on Auntie Em's face, she was elated.

"Yeah, I guess that's a justifiable reason not to drink with us." Livia laughed, her eyes shining.

"What about you, Liv? What's new?" I asked, turning to my other cousin.

"I've just been busy with work and planning the wedding," Livia replied, lifting her shoulder in a shrug.

"Oh yeah, that's next September, isn't it?"

"Yup! We'll be getting married in Hartwood Creek, at the Whimsical Woods Resort. Joseph's family rented the whole resort out for the weekend." Livia shook her head like she couldn't believe it. "His mother fell in love with Hartwood Creek when we viewed venue options. Originally, we were going to have it at the golf club in Springwood."

"That's really cool." I smiled, happy for my cousins. Madeline, Livia, and Cate all resembled Auntie Em with their dark hair and light eyes and bone structure. Jo-Anna, the youngest, looked more like Uncle Ed with her light blond hair, although she shared the beautiful bone structure of her sisters and mother. "Where's Jo-Anna?"

"Oh, she should be here soon. She got caught in traffic," Auntie Em replied over her shoulder. She was putting the steamed green beans into a dish. As if I'd summoned her by asking, the front door opened and closed.

"I'm here!" Jo-Anna announced from the front foyer, sweeping into the kitchen a moment later. She sounded out of breath and looked more haggard than I felt. "What did I miss?" she asked, hugging everyone in turn.

"Oh, nothing other than Madeline announcing her pregnancy." Cate grinned as the sliding door opened.

"What!" Jo-Anna exclaimed, whirling on her oldest sister with wide eyes. "No freakin' way. Patrick finally put a bun in the oven?!"

"Patrick did what now?" the man in question, Patrick, asked. Half his body was on the porch while the other half was in the kitchen. He hesitated, looking around at the women gathered in the kitchen before he stepped fully inside.

"Congratulations on the swimmers, Pat." Jo-Anna smirked, giving her brother-in-law a hug. "I'm so excited to be an aunt!"

"Oh, you told them." Patrick laughed, his cheeks heating with embarrassment. "Er, thanks, Jo. Uh, Ed says the ribs are just about done."

"Okay, perfect. Girls, want to help take the dishes out?" Auntie Em asked. Madeline grabbed the salad while Cate slid her hands into the oven mitts and picked up the roasted potatoes. Livia grabbed the bottle of wine and her wine glass, following the others and swiftly side-stepping to avoid Daphne as she barreled into the kitchen.

She'd noticed I was inside and raced over, wrapping her arms around my waist. "Mommy! I helped Uncle Ed make the ribs!"

"Oh, really? I bet they're going to taste delicious." I bopped her gently on the nose and kissed her forehead. "Were you good for Auntie Em and Uncle Ed?"

"Yes." Daphne nodded solemnly. "I was the bestest."

"You really were, sweetheart," Auntie Em said, pressing a kiss to her forehead. "Care to carry out the buns for me?"

"Okay!" Daphne agreed, taking the basket from Auntie Em and darting back outside.

"Thanks again for watching her, Auntie Em," I said. Auntie Em wrapped her arm around my waist.

"Honestly, it was our absolute pleasure. She's a joy to have around, and so are you. I'm glad you're both here."

NIX

When I arrived on the jobsite Monday morning, Gus strolled up to my truck before I'd even had a chance to shut off the engine. He had a long list in hand and a wry grin on his face that instantly made me suspicious.

Kaleb and Gus had been my first official hires after I started the business fresh out of college, and now they helped me run things, wearing almost as many hats as I did. With Kaleb still off on his babymoon, Gus had taken on his role as site foreman, managing the subcontractors we dealt with.

"Everything okay?" I asked him after I'd rolled down the window.

"Yeah, boss man. Everything's golden. But we are running low on a few supplies, and we're extremely short on framing nails. I made a list of the other stuff we're running low on," he said, handing me the sheet. "Think you could make a trip to the hardware store?"

"Yeah, I can do that." I tucked the list into my shirt pocket, trying not to let it show how excited I was to do this task—something I'd done a billion times before.

I'd never felt this much excitement over the prospect of seeing Ed. No, this was because I knew a certain green-eyed blonde would be there.

"And maybe stop for some coffees from Tout de Sweets while you're at it. Apparently, our coffee maker took a shit."

We had a few small appliances that we brought to jobsites, like a coffee maker and a microwave to heat up lunches. The coffee maker was old as hell, so I wasn't surprised it finally kicked it.

"All right, fine. Text me your orders," I said, and Gus nodded before heading back into the cottage we were working on.

On a whim, I decided to stop off at Tout de Sweets and pick up the coffees first, adding an extra one to my order for Sage. I'd been paying attention to how she took her coffee when she was at Tabitha and Parker's, and she liked it sweet—two creams, three sugars. Easy enough to remember.

I would have grabbed one for Ed, too, but I knew he was off caffeine. A few years back, he'd had a heart attack, and Emelia had forced him to change up his entire diet—including cutting out caffeine—so I didn't feel bad at all for walking in with just a coffee for Sage.

Not that Ed was even in the store. When I walked in, it was just Sage behind the counter, helping a customer and ringing up their order.

It was Dan Truman, another contractor in town. Technically, he was a competitor of mine. I couldn't begrudge him, though. Dan was an awesome guy and a talented contractor whom I respected a lot. We'd even worked on a few bigger jobs together.

While she was preoccupied with ringing up Dan's purchases, I took my time to glance around the hardware store. Alcott's Hardware had been in Ed's family for generations, the same way the lumberyard had been in mine.

Ed kept it looking the same as his father and grandfather before him, so when you stepped inside, it was like stepping backward in time.

Only, Ed made sure he stocked the best and latest tools. He had more than enough supplies to ensure he could meet the needs of the townspeople of Hartwood Creek without them having to go all the way to the big box hardware store in Springwood.

Dan grabbed his supplies, thanked Sage, and went to leave. He paused when he saw me. "Nix! How's it going? Hope business is good."

"Yeah, it's decent. Hope things are good for you too. Keeping busy?" I asked.

"Sure am. Been at that new subdivision on the north end," Dan replied.

"That'll keep you busy for sure." I chuckled. I didn't mind new builds, but I tended to avoid the cookie-cutter subdivisions. I preferred to work on restoration projects.

"Yup. Well, hope to see you around—gotta get back to it," he said before resuming his exit for the door.

When I looked back at Sage, she was watching me with suspicion. "What brings you in?"

"We need supplies, and I figured I'd bring you a coffee while I was at it," I said, approaching the counter to put down the drink I'd grabbed for her. She eyed it with even more distrust than when she'd looked at me. "It's just a regular coffee —two creams, three sugars. I watched Evelyn make it myself. No love latte. Not that I'd need that to get a girl to say yes to a date with me."

Her gaze lifted from the coffee, landing on my face, a sweet smile tilting her lips. "You sure about that?"

I put my hand over my heart as if her words had wounded me. "Ouch, that hurt."

"I'm sure you'll get over it." Her smile grew a little more. "What supplies did you need?"

I grabbed the piece of paper I'd tucked inside my shirt pocket and handed it to her. She read the list, somehow deciphering Gus's scrawling handwriting. I could barely read it. She nodded to herself and walked around the counter to go about collecting the supplies.

I followed her, helping grab the items off the list. She passed me a new air hose before heading to the nail aisle.

"What do trees say when they are in a really good mood?" I asked her. She glanced over her shoulder and arched a brow at me, waiting for me to continue. "I feel tree-mendous!"

"That's so corny," she said, but I caught a smile before she turned her head.

"Huh, your daughter thinks my jokes are lame too," I remarked as we reached the aisle with all the nails.

"Well, she's not wrong. They are kind of lame." Sage reached for the framing nail boxes and handed them to me. When our fingers brushed, she looked down at the contact as if surprised.

She withdrew her hand quickly, tucking her blond hair behind her ear.

"I've got another one for you..." I started.

"What is it?" She arched her brow.

"Are you a cat? Because I'm totally fe-line this connection between us." I waggled my eyebrows at her, and although she fought it, the smile betrayed her amusement.

"You're ridiculous." She laughed lightly, shaking her head at my antics. She looked back down at the list, reading the next item. Moving on to bracings, she grabbed several before thrusting them in my arms.

She referred to the list again, and her brow furrowed a little as if she was having trouble deciphering an item.

"For real, though...I really would like to take you out on a date sometime. Maybe Saturday night?"

CHAPTER FOURTEEN

Sage

I looked up from the list, unsure if I'd heard him correctly. "Pardon?"

"I said," he repeated, his smile growing a touch nervous, the playful banter gone and replaced with something genuine and meaningful. "I'd like to take you out on a date sometime... maybe this Saturday?"

For a moment, all I could do was stare at him—at those expressive brown eyes that seemed to see straight into my soul, stirring desires in me I thought I didn't have time for...and yet...

My eyes dropped to the list, at the last thing on it. _Say yes. Trust me. You won't regret it._

Looking back up at him, I bit my bottom lip, trying to remember all the reasons it was a bad idea. He waited, letting me mull it over, and I got the sense he'd wait for as long as I needed.

"I..." I trailed off, my head buzzing with conflicting thoughts and feelings. The exhilaration I'd felt zinging through my fingertips when our hands touched resurfaced, and I swallowed, finding a shy smile for him. "I think...I'd like that."

He seemed almost as surprised by my answer as I was, but the nervousness slipped away, replaced with an enamored grin that made the butterflies take flight in my belly.

"Great, I'll pick you up at six thirty?"

"Sounds good." I smiled. We stared at each other for a few minutes, both of us smiling like fools before I laughed awkwardly and looked away. "Well, let's get you rung up. I'm sure you need to get back to the site."

"Yeah." He laughed, and we made our way back to the cash register.

I rang his purchases through, trying not to grin like an idiot the whole time. When he left, I picked up the coffee he'd brought me and took a distracted sip, my thoughts on the hope budding in my chest.

AFTER NIX LEFT the hardware store, my mind wouldn't quit whirling with its insecurities and reservations. I went from hopeful to anxious about the whole thing. It wasn't I regretted saying yes to Nix's date. It was I regretted saying yes so soon.

Maybe I should have waited a little longer. I hadn't even been in town for a whole month, and I'd already said yes to a date. So much for getting on my own two feet again and forging a new life for my daughter and myself that *didn't* involve a man.

I couldn't help but fret about what my aunt might say if I asked her to watch Daphne so I could go on a date. I knew she'd probably be supportive and receptive to the idea since she seemed to really believe in love and magic and all those fuzzy feelings, but a small part of me still worried she'd *also* think it was too soon.

When I pulled into Tabitha and Parker's driveway later that evening to pick up Daphne, I was *somewhat* disappointed Nix's truck wasn't there. But I was also a little relieved.

I walked up to the front porch and knocked on the beautiful hardwood door, waiting until Tabitha opened it. She had Bryson on her hip and smiled when she saw me.

"Hey," she greeted, stepping aside to let me in. She moved to the bottom of the classic Victorian staircase. "Daphne! Your mom's here," she hollered before turning back to me.

"Aww, can't we have ten more minutes?" Bella demanded, appearing at the top of the stairs. She was dressed in a princess dress—Belle, from *Beauty and the Beast*. Daphne and Brielle appeared beside her, also wearing princess dresses. Daphne was dressed in a *Sleeping Beauty* dress, and Brielle was wearing a *Snow White* one. They looked so adorable; it brought an instant smile to my face and lightened my worrisome mood.

"Yeah, Mommy! Please? We're having a tea party," Daphne said.

"All right, fine. You have..." I checked my watch. I wanted to be out of there before Nix got back. "Twenty minutes. Okay?" Daphne nodded in agreement, and the three girls took off.

"Do you want a coffee? I just put some on," Tabitha offered.

"Okay." I nodded, following Tabitha into her kitchen. "Did you want me to hold Bryson?" I offered, and she smiled her thanks.

"That would be great," she said, passing him off to me so she could go about getting our coffees. I sat down at the central island, positioning Bryson on my lap. He seemed content enough to be there, especially when I passed him an apple from the fruit bowl in front of me. He brought it to his mouth and started gumming on it.

"He's teething," Tabitha apologized.

I shrugged. "It's not a big deal, I don't mind," I told her, snuggling a little closer to him. Bryson was such a cuddly baby, and it made me feel a little nostalgic for days that had long since passed with Daphne. I could handle a little drool from a teething baby.

Tabitha smiled and went back to preparing our coffees, doctoring the mugs with sugar and cream. I lost count of how many sugars she put in her own cup, but by now, she'd learned how I liked it—which only reminded me of Nix popping by with coffee earlier, then asking me out.

I still had the supply list in my pocket. I'd stared at it so much today that the words at the bottom of the list seemed imprinted in my brain at this point. *Say yes. Trust me. You won't regret it.*

I looked away, forcing the thought from my head. To distract myself, I focused on my surroundings.

The kitchen was one of my favourite parts of Tabitha and Parker's house, and I loved being in it. Tabitha had told me during one of my earlier visits that it was one of the first rooms they'd renovated after they moved in. She showed me pictures of how dark and dreary it'd been before.

It was an entirely different kitchen now, so bright and beautiful. They'd redone it in an eclectic British Edwardian style, with gently arched openings and the refrigerator, sink, and range forming a work triangle that was organized around the central island.

The green-painted cabinets added a depth and were highly responsive to light. In neutral light, it was a subtle mint colour, with the indoor lighting warming it. The stile-and-rail paneling that covered wall surfaces complimented the lawn and hedges seen through the windows on three sides of the expansive room.

The room was further brightened by light reflected off the marble countertops. Each of the three windows was framed by casework that extended to the countertop. Recessed downlights were concealed behind the beautiful arches over the sink, highlighting the windows over the cabinets.

They'd built a shallow nook just outside the busy work triangle, with a built-in desk that overlooked the backyard and was flanked by shelves for cookbooks. A large opening next to the desk connected the kitchen to the family room.

Everything about Tabitha and Parker's home was bright and inviting, but this kitchen...it was the hub of the home, where all the activity seemed to happen.

I'd always dreamed of having a kitchen like this, somewhere that truly felt like the heart of the home. Maybe because I'd always lacked that. My mother was never into cooking meals or hosting family functions.

Tabitha smiled and placed the mug of coffee she'd made for me in front of me, just out of Bryson's reach. "So how was work?"

"Pretty good," I replied, unsure whether I should confess Nix had been in and asked me out, or that I'd said yes but was now having regrets. I decided not to just blurt it out and instead returned her smile. "How was your day?"

"It was good," Tabitha said, pausing to take a sip of her coffee. "I did some running around for the fundraiser. I can't believe it's in two weeks. Did you have a chance to talk to Isla yet, or figure out your business name?"

"Oh, right...that's coming up fast. No, I haven't. I'll send her a message when I get home tonight. I think I'm going to go with SW Photography for the business name, but I really don't know what I want for a logo."

"Isla is great at figuring that out," Tabitha assured me. "She did Parker's logo for his portable sawmill service and custom wood projects, as well as Nix's logo for Hutchinson's Lumber & Construction. She also did the twins' logo for Bass to Mouth and their social media channels, and she even talked their dad into refreshing the logo for the lumberyard. It still has the original feel, though. Just modernized."

Bryson dropped the apple and let out a squeal when it bounced off the counter and rolled away. Tabitha caught it, returning it to his little outstretched hands, and he gave her a drooly grin, bringing the apple back to his mouth.

"I appreciate you introducing me to her. And the others too. Your friends are so kind," I remarked.

"It's my pleasure, really," Tabitha insisted. "And they liked you a lot too."

I smiled, appreciating her kindness. "I really am grateful for you. You've made this whole situation a lot more bearable for both Daphne and me."

Tabitha's expression softened. "I'm glad I can help."

"I'd like to thank you somehow, so...if you're up for it, I'd like to do a family session for you guys."

"That would be awesome! I don't think we've had family photos done since Bryson was a newborn. It's time for some updated ones."

"I'm free pretty much every weekend, so whenever works best for you guys. I know Parker sometimes works on the weekend."

"He's got a job on Saturday, but we could do it this Sunday if you're up for it?" she suggested.

"Okay." I nodded. "We could meet up at the beach on Sunday during golden hour."

"Golden hour?" Tabitha looked confused at the term.

"It's the period of daytime shortly after sunrise and before sunset, when daylight is redder and softer than when the sun is higher in the sky. I love taking photos at that time; to me, it's the ultimate magic hour." I couldn't help but get excited about the prospect of doing their photos, and it came out in my voice and expression. Bryson twisted to grin up at me, like he could sense my elation.

"That sounds perfect," Tabitha replied. Then she shook her head as if remembering something important. "Oh! That reminds me...the girls have been asking if Daphne and Riley can come over for a sleepover this Saturday night. Would you be okay with that?"

I studied Tabitha for a beat, trying to suss out if she was doing this intentionally. I narrowed my eyes with suspicion. "Are you doing this because Nix asked me out Saturday night?"

"What? Did he really? That's awesome!" Tabitha exclaimed, her eyes widening with excitement. She did seem genuinely surprised when I nodded. "I had no idea. The girls just really wanted to do a sleepover, but that works out, doesn't it?"

"Yeah, I guess..." I trailed off, conflicted. "Daphne can sleep over, but..." I sighed, bringing a hand up to massage my temple. I'd developed a bit of a stress headache, worrying about every-thing. Tabitha could sense my discord, and she leaned forward against the counter.

"What's wrong?" she asked gently, her blue eyes prodding.

"I called off my engagement a few months ago. I feel like it might be too soon to be dating again."

Tabitha nodded thoughtfully as she continued studying me, working over what I'd said in her mind. "Honest question... do you really *feel* like it might be too soon, or are you just worried about what other people *might* say?"

"I don't know," I admitted, lifting my shoulder in a shrug.

"Are you over your ex?"

"Yes," I said firmly. There wasn't a question in my mind about that. Aside from the initial sadness of realizing everything we had was a farce, I'd realized early on that I didn't miss *him*, I just missed the idea of what I thought he was, and what we could have. When Warren showed his true colours, it'd given me the serious ick.

If he were to come here and beg for me back, I'd slam the door in his face without even considering it for a moment.

"And are you...interested in Nix in that way?" she prompted, raising her eyebrows.

I was quiet, thinking about it. I'd always felt a deep attraction to him, and I knew him well enough to know he was kind and good. "I am, but..."

I was unsure how to explain my churning thoughts to Tabitha. She was his sister-in-law, and I knew she cared deeply for him. But I'd been burned before by the "good guy," and although I truly didn't think Nix was putting on a show, I was still hesitant.

What if it didn't work out between us? What if that changed the dynamic of my new friendship with Tabitha? What if it made things awkward for us both around town?

"You're scared of being hurt again?" Tabitha surmised, and I nodded.

"I came here to build a life for myself and my daughter, not get tangled up with another man who I'd have to change everything for."

Tabitha straightened and exhaled, nodding as if she understood what I was saying.

"I get it, I do," she said gently. "But I don't think Nix would ask you to change anything about yourself or your situation. He isn't that kind of guy. You can still build that life for yourself and your daughter, and date Nix...or someone new. It doesn't have to be one or the other."

"I guess you're right..."

"I know I am." She smirked cheekily before growing serious. "But as for the whole timeline thing, the 'when is too soon?'...I think that answer is different for everyone. I think the time is right when you're strong, when you've learned more about yourself from the situations you've had to overcome. When you can listen to your *own* judgment and intuition."

I nodded, my fingers curling around the mug in my hand.

CHAPTER FIFTEEN

Sage

Halfway through my workday on Wednesday, my cell phone rang. Uncle Ed had a check-up appointment with his cardiologist, so it was just me manning the store again. It wasn't busy at all—in fact, we'd only had a few customers earlier on in the day.

For a moment, I debated letting it go to voicemail. Talking to my mother was not my favourite pastime, but I hadn't spoken to her since we left her house for Hartwood Creek. I'd texted her to let her know we'd arrived safely, but aside from a thumbs-up, I hadn't heard back.

My mother kept a busy social calendar, so she didn't have time to sit around and think about the fact her fourth husband was never around and likely off having extramarital affairs. So long as she still had access to his credit cards, she didn't care.

But I knew if I avoided her call, she would only try again with more persistence, or worse...call Auntie Em.

On the fourth ring, I answered, "Hey, Mom."

"Hello, darling. I'm just calling to check in and see how

things are going there in Hartwood Creek, since you haven't bothered to call me and tell me yourself."

I rolled my eyes and swallowed a sigh. "I know, I'm sorry. Things have been crazy busy. I started my new job, and I've been focused on getting Daphne adjusted."

"Daphne's not adjusting well? I told you that would happen. You should have stayed with Warren and avoided all this unnecessary confusion." My mother's voice could be very grating, especially when she was saying stuff like that.

"I really don't think it's 'unnecessary confusion,' Mom. I left Warren, and we had to move."

"You didn't *have* to leave Warren, and if you hadn't left him, you wouldn't have had to move," my mom pointed out.

This time, I let her hear my sigh. "Mom, we're not getting into that again. It's over between Warren and me, forever. Now moving on—yes, she's had a little trouble adjusting. She misses her old friends, but she's made plenty of new ones already and seems to really enjoy living here."

"Oh, well. That's good to hear. I'm glad she's making friends. And how are you liking working at Ed's...quaint little hardware store?" The way she'd said quaint made it sound bad.

"I love it," I answered honestly. I loved the small-town, almost antique-y feel of it, and the customers were all so kind and patient. If I had trouble finding a product right away, they were all too happy to point me in the right direction—without making me feel bad for not knowing.

"Oh, that's good, I guess," Mom said, sounding surprised and almost disappointed by my answer. It was as if she wanted me to realize I'd made a big mistake in moving and taking this job, but honestly, I felt like moving to Hartwood Creek was the best thing I could have done—for myself *and* for Daphne.

"Yeah. And I've made friends, too, quite a few of them. I'm

even volunteering at Daphne's school fundraiser. They'll have a photo booth set up, and I'll be taking the photos," I told her.

"Oh, how *lovely*," Mom said, but I could detect the complacent note in her voice.

"Yeah, I'm excited about it. But anyway, how have you been?" I asked, changing the subject to my mother's favourite topic—herself.

"I've been very well, thank you. Went on a little holiday with Bridgette. We flew down to Vegas for a weekend, gambled away some money. It was wonderful. And you'll never believe what happened when I got home."

"Oh really? What happened?" I asked, half paying attention while I stocked shelves with the shipment that arrived earlier.

"Warren came looking for you. He showed up with the most beautiful bouquet of roses. He wanted to apologize again for...what happened between the two of you. He was surprised you weren't here."

"Did you tell him I've moved on, literally and figuratively? Because I have," I replied, my tone as cold and dead as my feelings toward my former fiancé. His little ploy of bringing me flowers fell flat, especially considering I'd told him on more than one occasion that roses were my *least* favourite flower.

"Well, I did tell him you moved, yes. But I think he really regrets it, and I think you should hear him out—"

"No, Mom," I said, cutting her off midsentence. "I'm not going to 'hear him out' because I no longer care what he has to say about it. I'm over it, I'm done with him, and I'm not revisiting this subject again with you. Please respect that."

"No need to get your back up, darling. I'm just trying to help you." My mother sounded offended and wounded, but in that moment, I didn't care. She didn't care how I felt about the matter after *months* of the same discourse, so I wasn't about to coddle her feelings.

"If you wanted to help me, you would accept my decisions and support them—and me," I told her. I heard her sniffle on the other end of the line, and I sighed again. "Look, I'm happier than I've ever been, and I won't be taking him back. Not now, not ever. Okay?"

"Fine, but I think you're making a foolish mistake." The door chimed, alerting me to the fact that Uncle Ed had just walked in.

"I'm at work, Mom, so I need to go. I'll call you later. Love you, bye," I said, hanging up before she could say anything else.

"Everything okay?" Uncle Ed asked as he walked over to me. He'd overheard the tail end of my conversation, judging by the concerned look in his eyes. He knew how my mother was.

"Yeah, everything's great. How was your appointment?"

"Good. Doc says my ticker's doing just fine, and I got out of there with enough time to meet your aunt at Candlelight Bistro for lunch. How were things here?"

"That's awesome. It hasn't been too busy since you left, so I've just been stocking shelves and doing inventory," I replied as cheerfully as I could muster. There was no doubt about it, though, talking to my mother always brought my mood down several notches.

Uncle Ed nodded, studying me for a moment as if he could sense the shift in my aura. I'd been in such a good mood the last few days, high off the excitement of talking to Isla and nailing down my logo for my newly launched photography business. I'd even changed my Instagram handle to match, and I was looking forward to getting a little more practice under my belt before the Fall Fun Fundraiser.

But one brief phone conversation with my mother had taken the wind out of my sails, and as much as I tried to hide it,

Uncle Ed could plainly see. "Why don't you take off early today? I can finish up and handle things around here."

"I don't mind staying until my shift ends," I assured him.

"If it's been as quiet as you said it's been, you might as well head out early and enjoy some of this beautiful weather," Uncle Ed said kindly.

"Are you sure?"

"I'm as sure as I'm standing here," he replied. When he smiled, his eyes smiled too.

"Go on, enjoy the rest of the day. Take a walk along the harbour, you'll love the view. Maybe bring your camera and take some pictures."

I debated on arguing, but honestly, a little fresh air might do me good, and Uncle Ed's idea didn't sound so bad.

After hanging up my apron and grabbing my purse from the office, I said goodbye to my uncle and headed up to my apartment to change out of the jeans and the green button-up. Uncle Ed didn't have an official uniform for the hardware store, but I'd picked up on his preference of wearing button-ups and purchased a few I could wear. I gathered my equipment and tucked my wallet into my camera bag before heading back outside.

Uncle Ed was right—it was a beautiful day. The sun was shining, the weather was warm without being overly hot, with just enough of a breeze to keep me comfortable as I walked down to the harbour.

People meandered around the harbour, sightseeing and admiring all the boats docked. I felt like a tourist with my camera in hand, but Uncle Ed had also been right about the view of the lake from the docks. The water was murky, and parasailers out in the lake were an arresting visual that I just had to capture.

After I'd taken over two hundred or so photos, I checked

my watch. It was almost two thirty, so I made my way over to Tout de Sweets to grab a salted caramel iced coffee before I headed to pick Daphne up.

The coffee shop was almost as busy as the waterfront. I waited my turn, ordering a drink from the dark-haired woman behind the till. She looked familiar, and I realized with a start she'd been one of the women to sit across from Noah and Donovan at The Quarter Lounge.

"You're Sage Whitaker, Emelia and Ed's niece, aren't you?" the woman asked as she handed me my order.

"I am." I smiled in greeting as I passed her the money for my drink. "It's nice to meet you..."

"Evelyn. Evelyn Hartley," the woman answered, her tawny eyes sparkling.

"Otherwise known as boss lady—she's the manager of Tout de Sweets," the second person working behind the counter said. He'd been listening in to our conversation.

"My mother and aunts own it, but I manage it for them now that they've all retired," Evelyn explained with a smile.

"Though they still try to run things," the man added with a cheeky grin. He was tall with beautiful dark dreadlocks wrapped up on top of his head. He had a pleasant smile, and although he hadn't said much, I could tell he had a dazzling personality. "I'm Jayden, by the way. Welcome to our idyllic little town."

"Hi, Jayden and Evelyn. Thank you for the warm welcome, and the iced coffee," I beamed.

"It's our pleasure to fulfill your caffeinating needs." Jayden winked. I laughed, moving out of the way of the customer behind me.

"I'll see you around," I said, turning to leave.

The moment I turned around, I was accosted by a whirlwind of bangles, pastel pantsuits, and perfume. The Hartley sisters had officially caught up with me. I'd been dreading this moment, although I knew it was only a matter of time.

"Sage! We were just talking about you," Alice preened, taking a hold of my right elbow. Betty flanked my other side, and Dorothy stood beside her. All three of the women wore similar scheming smiles.

"Oh really?" I asked, eyeing the three busybodies with suspicion as they led me deeper into the café. "What about?"

"We heard Nix asked you out," Dorothy said, cutting straight to the chase.

"Nothing gets past you three, huh?" I remarked dryly.

"Nothing at all," Betty returned my dry remark with an equally dry one of her own. Her dyed red hair was brighter than the last time I'd seen her, so she must have recently coloured it. "Come and sit with us for a spell."

"Oh, I have to pick up my daughter soon."

"We won't take up much of your time, just a few moments for a couple old broads?" Alice said, peering at me almost pleadingly.

There was something grandmotherly about her, and I couldn't refuse. I'd never had a grandmother—my mother's parents had both passed away before I was born, and I'd never known my father or his side of the family.

I found myself ill-equipped to deal with the elderlies' not-so-subtle demands, so I allowed the Hartley sisters to lead me to an empty table in the café. Dorothy pulled a chair out for me.

"So tell us. Are you excited for your date with Nix? He's such a sweet boy. I've always liked him," Alice said as she all but guided me into the chair.

I sat heavily, my gaze bouncing from Alice to Betty, and then to Dorothy as the three women sat down in their own chairs, expectant eyes on me. The sisters had a striking resemblance to one another, although they weren't identical. Dorothy wore her white hair long and braided over her shoulder and Betty had short, dyed red hair. Alice kept her hair short too, but it was snow white like Dorothy's.

"Um. Yes?"

"You don't sound so sure, dear." Dorothy frowned.

"No, I am...I'm just...not used to everyone knowing my business, I guess."

"Oh, well. You'll have to get used to that." Alice laughed richly, her two sisters joining in.

"It's true, we're a bit nosey, but we mean well. We just want to see Nix happy—and you too, of course. But our Nix deserves to settle down with a good, loyal girl. He's got so much love in him to give, and after what happened with Lori..."

"Who's Lori?" The question left my lips before I could call it back. Alice, Dorothy, and Betty exchanged looks with one another, and Betty arched a brow. Alice nodded, and Dorothy seemed to shrug.

"His ex, dear," Dorothy replied. "He was ready to propose to her, but he caught her...engaging with someone else, if you know what I mean."

"Cheating," Betty cut in.

Alice's usually joyful expression twisted into one of disapproval. She clicked her tongue and shook her head ruefully.

"Ah. I see." I could relate to that, and gauging by the knowing looks the sisters gave me, they knew it too.

"Such a shame, but really it was all for the better. I always knew that Lori wasn't it for him," Alice remarked, giving me an insightful look.

CHAPTER SIXTEEN

Nix

The workweek flew by, keeping me busy and distracted. It was a good thing too; I was so exhausted by the time I got home at night that I had very little opportunity to stress about Saturday night's date with the girl of my dreams.

I still couldn't believe she said yes. I hadn't planned on asking her when I walked into the hardware store Monday morning, but...I don't know. Maybe it was the way she'd reacted when our fingers had touched. Or maybe it was Parker's grand speech about there never being an opportune time to make a move.

In that moment, it felt right, so I went with it.

Word had spread like wildfire that I'd asked Sage out, and she'd said yes. The whole town seemed invested in it. Even the Hartley sisters had caught up with me to congratulate me on growing some balls and making a move. Well, they didn't exactly say it like that, but the pointed look Dorothy gave me said it all.

Now that it was Friday night, I was beginning to panic a

little. I had a small idea on what I wanted to do, but I'd need Noah's help to pull it off.

"So tell me again what you need from me?" Noah asked, leaning back in the booth and acting like his usual cocky self. Donavon and Parker were there, too, and I'd already endured the razzing from them about how great it was I finally worked up the courage to ask her out. *They'd* had no qualms using the phrase "grew a set."

"Permission to use the private beach at the resort," I replied.

"What for?" he poked, grinning wider. He was taking great pleasure out of this. Parker smirked, just as amused, while Donavon had the decency to look a little sympathetic.

"I was thinking a tailgate dinner while we watched the sunset, and the private beach is...more private." The guys seemed impressed by my plan, exchanging looks of approval with one another and nodding like they thought it was a good idea.

I'd wanted to recreate that first *missed kiss* opportunity as well as I could, minus the Summer Vibes Festival. Unfortunately, the main beach was far too busy to pull this idea off, and I couldn't very well drive my truck out onto it.

I could with the private beach at the Whimsical Woods Resort, though. Providing Noah felt charitable enough to loan me the keys to the gate.

Sometimes residents and tourists trespassed on the private beach, but they always waited for it to get dark so they wouldn't get caught. Noah's older brother, Damien Wood, didn't exactly *approve* of people trespassing on their private beach. Not that he'd call the authorities, but he's been known to chase people off himself in the past. That would put a damper on a first date...

The goal was to arrive an hour or so before sunset and set

up blankets and pillows in the bed of my truck. Then we'd eat dinner—probably take-away, because I wasn't the greatest cook, and I didn't want to give her food poisoning—and just...hang out and talk.

I mean, sure. I wanted to kiss her and all that fun stuff too. But I was willing to take it as slow as she needed. But I certainly didn't want an audience for our first date, and I was positive she didn't either. It seemed like the townsfolk were all overly invested in us already, so I wanted to do something low-key and quiet...something for just the two of us.

I followed her on Instagram after she moved back to town, and she posted a lot of beautiful sunset and sunrise photos that she'd captured. She was talented with a camera—she had an eye for capturing the beauty around her, and I already knew how much she loved sunsets.

"Hmm. All right. I suppose I could help you out. I'll give you the keys, but you better make sure the Hartley sisters don't get a hold of them. They'll make copies, and then it'll be game over. Damien will *kill* me if that happens."

"I promise, I won't let the keys fall into anybody else's hands—especially not the sisters," I promised. Turned out the biggest trespassers were the meddlesome Hartley sisters. They were always sneaking onto the private beach with their purple Commander.

I was certain, even *if* the Hartley sisters attempted to sneak onto the private beach, they'd see us and give us a wide berth. Or spy from afar. Either way, I didn't think Noah had any real reason to worry about them getting a hold of the gate keys.

Noah dug into his pocket for his keys, pulling one off the key chain. "Okay, here you go," he said, handing it to me.

"Thanks, Noah. I appreciate it." I put the key on my own key chain so I wouldn't lose it, aware that if *that* happened, Noah would kick my ass too.

"No problem. I'm happy to help you break your dry spell," he teased, raising his beer glass toward me before taking a sip.

Before I could think of a witty response, my brother started talking. "You should pick up a bottle of the chocolate stout from the brewery. Tabitha *loves* it. She swears it's the best chocolate stout she's ever tasted. Plus, it made her really...frisky, if you know what I'm saying." Parker wiggled his eyebrows at me, and I shuddered.

"Unfortunately, I do. Thanks for that disgusting visual," I deadpanned. My brother threw his head back and laughed.

"Parker's right, though, it's damn good brew. We offer it in our couples retreat packages and they love it," Noah chimed in. "Klaus makes batches especially for us."

I DIDN'T END up staying out too late at The Quarter Lounge. I was home and in bed by eleven thirty, but my anticipation for the next day kept me from falling asleep until well past two o'clock in the morning.

After I woke up, I stopped off at the Brewery and picked up a bottle of Choco Temptation before my appointment at the Get Buzzed barber shop for a fresh cut. I came home to shower and change before I took the tools out of my truck bed storage drawers and loaded them with pillows and blankets, tucking the bottle of Choco Temptation in an ice bucket and securing it with the blankets.

Before picking Sage up, I grabbed take-away from The Hungry Hub, remembering she had ordered a burger and onion rings that time we ran into each other. I figured it'd be a safe bet to stick with a couple of cheeseburgers, a side order of onion rings, and a side order of fries.

At six thirty on the dot, I parked in front of the hardware store and grabbed the bouquet of flowers I'd picked up from Hartwood Creek Flowers. I wasn't sure what to go with at first. I wanted something beautiful and unique to Sage. I felt like roses were too common and didn't evoke her soft, almost angelic beauty.

After coaxing me to share a little about my date, Ezra Reynolds, the owner, put together a special bouquet—a stunning collection of pink dahlias, purple asters, and goldenrod with pink and peach zinnias, light pink snapdragons, maroon cosmos, purple ageratum, and pink carnations. He'd tossed in a beautiful purple glass-blown vase because I wasn't sure if Sage had one.

Tucking the vase into the crook of my arm, I left everything else in the cab of my truck and walked up to the access door for Sage's apartment. I buzzed up, and a moment later, Sage's voice came over the buzzer. "Hello?"

"Hey, I'm here for our date."

"Great! Come on up." She hit the button to unlock the door, and I opened it, stepping into the hallway.

I paused for a moment at the bottom of the stairs and drew in a breath. I couldn't remember the last time I'd been so nervous—certainly not when I'd asked Lori out.

If I was being completely honest with myself, the last time I felt *this* level of nervousness was when I almost kissed Sage on the beach during the Summer Vibes Festival all those years ago.

I lifted my hand and rapped my knuckles against the door. A moment later, it swung open to reveal Sage.

She was wearing a black sleeveless tank top tucked into a pair of distressed blue jeans. Her blond hair was down around her shoulders, and she'd taken the time to curl it into soft ringlets. I didn't know exactly what she'd done differently for her makeup, but her green eyes seemed even more dazzling.

"Whoa, you look beautiful," I managed when I finally found my voice.

"Thank you, you look really good too." Sage gave me a soft smile as she took in my fresh haircut and wardrobe. I'd worn a pair of my best dark wash jeans and a white fitted Henley T-shirt. Her gaze dropped to the bouquet in my hand, her eyes widening with surprise. "You brought me flowers?"

"Of course I did," I said, unable to hide my grin as I held them out for her to take. Her eyes seemed to shimmer as she lifted the bouquet to her nose and sniffed.

"They're beautiful, thank you so much," she said, looking at me, her green eyes still sparkling. "You can come in while I find something to put these in," she added.

"I also grabbed a vase because I wasn't sure if you had one," I said, stepping into the apartment and handing it to her. She took it from me with an appreciative smile.

As she moved into the kitchen to fill the vase, I glanced around. It had been barren the last time I'd set foot inside, but since then, Sage had worked hard to transform the apartment into a beautiful, lively space.

I joined her in the kitchen, staying about a foot away from her, and watched as she arranged the bouquet in the vase. She touched a petal, her expression suddenly contemplative.

"I hope you like them. I wasn't sure what your favourite flower was..." She turned her head the moment I spoke.

"I love them. They're beautiful, truly," Sage assured me, her smile tender before she returned her attention to arranging the flowers in the vase.

CHAPTER SEVENTEEN

Sage

For a moment, all I could do was stare in wonderment at the beautiful arrangement of flowers Nix brought. I didn't know the names of all the different flowers, but they were *stunning*. An enchanting assemblage of various shades of purples and pinks, with light peach, green, and yellow throughout.

The date hadn't even officially begun yet, and I was already a goner—already completely free falling. With this one action, Nix had shown me he was thoughtful and considerate—and romantic.

It wasn't like it was the first time a man had brought me flowers, so I shouldn't be so affected by the action. But none had come close to this dazzling selection. None had put the thought into getting me an arrangement that was unique and beautiful.

In the past, Warren had bought me flowers. Always roses. Usually for my birthday, Valentine's Day, or as an apology after he said or did something that upset me. I hadn't liked roses before I'd met Warren, but throughout my time with him, I'd really grown to hate them and what they symbolized.

But *this*? This was...something completely different.

This is precisely why I'd spent the greater part of the day panicking while talking to Nellie. After I'd dropped Daphne off, I was left alone with my thoughts and almost canceled on Nix fifty times before Nellie talked sense into me.

I'd been worried because I felt it was too soon to be feeling these kinds of feelings. Nix was no stranger to me, but...I wasn't sure my heart could handle another disappointment.

Nellie had done her best to assure me *one date* wouldn't make or break me, that it was *good* to get out there and start seeing other people, but I was already a puddle at his feet over flowers.

"I'm glad you love them," Nix said, his voice coaxing me back from my ruminating. He was standing with his hands in his pockets. "I can't take any credit for it, I won't lie. Ezra, the owner of Hartwood Creek Flowers, picked them all out."

"Well, they're lovely. Thank you." I smiled again before moving to grab my sweater and purse off the island.

"You ready to go?" Nix asked, arching a brow as he slid his hands out of his pockets.

"Sure am," I replied, hoping my tone didn't give away how nervous I was. But the easy smile Nix gave me worked to ease my nerves, and I found myself relaxing in his company.

I locked up the apartment, and we headed down the stairs. He opened the door to the street and put his hand on the small of my back as we walked toward his truck.

He'd parked out front of the hardware store, and I tried not to look in the windows, knowing that Uncle Ed was working—and likely able to see us.

Nix opened the passenger door, holding it open for me so I

could climb in. He closed it once I was comfortably inside, walking around the front of his truck. My stomach growled when the scent of take-away hit my nostrils, and I glanced down at the boxes beside me as I buckled up my seat belt. Seeing The Hungry Hub logo stamped on the white boxes only made me hungrier.

I hadn't eaten much throughout the day, aside from a banana this morning while Daphne had eggs. My nerves were running high, so I didn't have an appetite. I'd been too focused on getting Daphne ready for her sleepover, dropping her off, and then talking to Nellie on video call while I panicked and tried to find something to wear. I hadn't had the time or focus to worry about food, but the scent from the take-away boxes made me regret that choice.

He opened his door, climbing into the cab with more ease than I'd managed, and sent me a crooked smile that made me feel all swoony with butterflies taking flight in my belly, replacing the hunger pangs.

"So...what do you have planned for us?" I asked him as he buckled his seat belt.

"You'll see." His smile turned to one of secrecy as he turned the key in the ignition, the truck roaring to life.

Nix checked his blind spots, then pulled out and drove down Main Street, turning left. We passed the historic, touristy shops and gas lamps that lined the side of the street.

We kept driving for a little while longer, out of town and down a private road, driving until we reached a gate with a padlock. "Okay, now I'm really curious...where are we headed?" I asked when Nix stopped the truck.

"I thought we'd have dinner on the beach—well, on the private beach," he said with a grin as he turned the engine off and took the keys. He disappeared long enough to unlock the padlock and open the gates before he climbed back into the truck and started the ignition, driving out onto the secluded beach.

Once we'd passed the gates, he hopped out and closed them before returning. Then he drove down the beach a little before turning so the bed of the truck faced the water, and the front of the truck faced the wooded area.

Nix cut the ignition and glanced across the cab at me. "Just let me set up, you hang tight for a minute," he instructed, smiling as he opened his door and climbed out.

"Okay...if you're sure. I don't mind helping."

"It won't take me long," he assured me before closing the door and walking to the back of the truck. I could hear him opening the tailgate. I turned my head, watching out the rear window as he arranged a bunch of blankets and pillows in the bed of his truck. "No peeking," he chided with a teasing grin.

I laughed, turning my head to allow him a moment to get everything set up. A few seconds later, he was opening my door, his kissable lips turned up in an excited grin.

"All right, it's finally ready for you," he said, holding his hand out for me to take. I took it, enjoying the feel of his warm, calloused palm against mine, and stepped onto the sand.

He released his hold on my hand so he could grab the take-away boxes, and I instantly felt bereft of his touch. He rectified that a moment later by putting the take-away boxes on the roof and placing his hand on the small of my back, guiding me toward the bed of his truck.

Nix had set up a comfortable-looking arrangement with the blankets and pillows. He'd even strung up string lights along the back of the cab for ambiance, and there was a wooden breakfast tray with a fancy-looking bottle in an ice bucket and two glass beer steins.

"Whoa, Nix...this is beautiful," I praised, taking it all in. It was such a sweet gesture and such a perfect idea for a first date.

I'd been growing more and more nervous as our date approached, worrying everyone would bear witness to it. But there wasn't a soul out on the private beach, just us and the beautiful lake.

Nix grinned as if my reaction was everything he'd hoped for and more. He climbed into the truck bed, holding his hand out so he could help me climb up too.

I took it, stepping on the hitch and allowing Nix's strength to pull me up. We got the food set up and got comfortable leaning with our backs against the cab, our faces turned toward the water. Our food was spread out on the wooden tray positioned at our knees.

"I hope you still like cheeseburgers," he said, handing me one of the take-away boxes.

"Oh, I'm a vegetarian..." I replied.

"Seriously? Shit." When he frowned in genuine concern, I burst out laughing.

"I'm kidding. A cheeseburger sounds great," I told him, opening the box and picking it up. I took a small bite, chewing it and swallowing.

"I mean, it wouldn't have been terrible if you *were* a vegetarian; I've got nothing against them. Or vegans," he added. "I just don't have a nonanimal option for tonight, so that would have sucked a little."

"Speaking of sucking...I hear vegans give good head." Nix whirled to look at me, his jaw slack with astonishment. "You know. Because they're used to eating nuts."

He stared at me for a beat, then started laughing, shaking his head. "Sage Whitaker, did you just crack a joke? And an inappropriate one at that?"

"I couldn't miss the opportunity." I smirked, satisfied I'd managed to surprise him a little. Judging by the grin on his face, he'd liked me surprising him.

"Well, I'm impressed," Nix admitted, picking up his own burger and taking a bite of it. He swallowed, then turned to look at me, and I knew by the glint in his eyes he had a joke. "What do you call a vegan guy who likes to pleasure himself?"

"I don't know, what?" I asked, trying to ignore the effect hearing him say *pleasure himself* had on me, or the accompanying visual.

"A nondairy creamer," Nix replied, and I laughed. "I could go all night, but we'll table the dirty jokes for now. We haven't even cracked open the beer yet."

"You got us beer?"

"Sure did. Do you want a glass now?" he asked, and I nodded. He twisted the cap off the bottle and poured the dark draft into the glasses. He handed me one, and I took it. "I hope you like it. It's from the Brewery in town. Apparently, it's really good. Parker recommended it. He said Tabitha loved it."

I lifted the glass to my lips, taking a sip. The crisp, rich flavour of the chocolate stout hit my taste buds. I held it in my mouth for a moment, trying to get a read on all the different flavours. "Mmm, this is delicious. I've never had a beer that's so...flavoursome."

Nix took a sip from his glass, letting it sit on his tongue for a moment, too, before swallowing. "Yeah, it's delicious. I think I taste chocolate, honey, and maybe even espresso. I'm impressed."

"All of this is really impressive," I told him, gesturing with my glass to the cute setup and the view of the water spread out in front of us. "Nobody's ever...done anything like this for me before," I admitted, taking another sip of the chocolate stout, wondering if I detected a hint of cinnamon and vanilla. *Interesting*, but not in a bad way...it was the best-tasting chocolate stout I'd ever had.

"Really? What's the most creative date you've been on?"

Nix asked, taking an onion ring from the take-away container he'd placed between us on the wooden tray.

I thought for a moment. "This one. All my other dates were just out to the movies, or for dinner, or sometimes a club. I've been on a few wedding dates—which, are those really dates or obligations?"

"Probably more of an obligation and less of a date, although you can still have fun with the right person," Nix replied.

"I guess that's true. What about you...what's the most creative date you've ever been on?"

Nix's cheeks turned a little rosy, and it was sweet to see him a little bashful. He brought his hand to the back of his head and scratched at his neck. "Well, I won't lie. I'm creative when it comes to the dating game. I had a great example with my dad and my mom. But this is hands-down one of my top-tier ideas. But personally, I think it's got more to do with the girl I'm trying to impress than my ability to plan a decent date." He winked. "But also...there's been no interruptions—yet, anyway —from nosey busybodies."

I peered around him, checking out the still-empty private beach. It was quiet, the crickets, grey tree frogs, and the waves lapping against the shoreline the only noises aside from our voices.

In my perusal of the beach, I realized the sun had begun its descent, the golden sphere touching the surface of the water and painting the sky in a beautiful array of orange, yellow, and pink. The clouds reflected those dazzling colours, too, reminding me of the beautiful bouquet Nix had brought me.

The colours changed minute by minute as the sun went down, almost appearing to sink deeper in the water. We finished our dinner and sipped at our beers as we watched it.

"It's stunning," I murmured, taking it all in. For a moment, I wished I'd brought my camera. But it would have been rude to pause our date to take pictures of it. My memory would just have to do.

"You're stunning," he said, and when I turned to look at him, he was watching me—not the sunset. The way he was looking at me sent an electrifying thrum throughout my body, and I got the sense I wouldn't be forgetting this sunset—or this moment—any time soon.

I bit my bottom lip, my eyes dropping to Nix's mouth. I wanted him to kiss me more than I wanted to breathe my next breath. I think he picked up on that desire because he moved a little closer, and I leaned in.

He brought his hand up to cup the side of my face, and then his lips were on mine. Tentatively, at first—as if he was making sure this is what I truly wanted. When I responded, my lips parting slightly, all bets were off.

He kissed me like he'd been wanting to do so for a long time. He kissed me like he needed to inhale me, and it was the most erotic first kiss I'd ever had. The way his mouth moved against mine had all my senses on fire and begging for more.

I let out a quiet moan, causing him to smile against my lips and then deepen the kiss as we moved even closer to one another. I don't know how long we sat like that, tangled up in each other's arms and kissing, but eventually, we had to come up for air.

Nix put his forehead against mine and let out a breath, the smile on his face mirroring my own.

CHAPTER EIGHTEEN

———————

Nix

"I'm really glad you moved back, Sage," I said, pulling back a little so I could gaze at her face before I continued. "I know it's probably not easy starting over...but I'm glad you're here. I always had the biggest crush on you," I confessed.

"Really?" she asked, sounding surprised.

"Really, really." I grinned when she nodded almost timidly. "I'm not sure how you couldn't tell before."

"Well, I can tell *now*," she joked, arching a brow pointedly toward the evidence of my arousal.

Unashamed, I leaned in for another kiss. The first one had merely solidified my desire for her. She kissed me back with just as much fervor, her hand gripping my shirt and pulling me closer.

Just when things were heating up, the sound of an ATV puttering down the beach had us pulling apart, and not a moment too soon. The headlights of the purple Commander washed over us.

Sage pulled away and lifted her hand to her eyes, shielding them from the bright light.

"Oh! It's Nix and Sage. Our apologies." Alice giggled, turning off the engine and the bright lights. It took a moment for my eyes to adjust, but when they finally did, I could see Alice, Dorothy, and Betty sitting in their purple ATV.

"We didn't mean to interrupt your...date. We weren't expecting to find anybody down here," Dorothy said, but the secretive smile she exchanged with the others belied their mischievous intentions.

"Here we were, thinking Damien Wood was finally coming around to us and left the padlock unlocked for us." Alice tutted, shaking her head.

"We like to drive along the trails and end our evening at the beach some nights. Brings back memories of when we were all young and in love," Dorothy explained.

"That's really sweet." Sage smiled, pulling her cardigan around her body more. I could tell she was uncomfortable.

"We're so sorry for intruding. You two carry on with your date now, we'll be on our way," Betty chimed in, tossing a stern look to her sisters.

They turned the Commander back on and reversed, retreating the way they came.

"Did you see? They had a bottle of Choco Temptation..." Dorothy could be heard saying as they drove away.

"Ooh! That'll do it," Betty replied before they were too far away to hear anymore.

Sage frowned, glancing at me. "What was that about?"

"I'm not all that sure, to be honest." I laughed. "The Hartley sisters often make cryptic remarks. I've learned to not take them too seriously, though."

She still looked unconvinced, and for a moment, I worried the sisters might have doused our date with a metaphorical bucket of cold water. She turned toward me, her hair spilling over her shoulder, and reached for the now-empty bottle of chocolate stout.

"Choco Temptation," she read the label, her brow furrowing. She turned it so she could read the back. "Contains chocolate, espresso, nutmeg, cinnamon, vanilla..." Her eyes shot to mine. "Wait, is this that ridiculous love elixir?"

I sat up, taking the bottle from her to read the ingredients, my stomach sinking with disappointment. "I don't know...it doesn't say so specifically." I looked at her and realized she did not look impressed. "If it is, I'm sorry. I had no clue."

Sage drew in a breath, as if trying to calm herself, her eyes going to mine. "Do you believe in it?"

"The love latte?" I asked. She nodded, worrying her bottom lip. "Not really. I mean, I know everyone in town's pretty much obsessed with it, and the tourists love it, but the jury's out for me."

"What's the story behind it anyway? Why's everyone so obsessed?"

"It's got a lot to do with the town's obsession with magic and witches," I explained. "Folklore has it the original witch who made the love elixir was the daughter of one of the towns founders, Augustus Hartley, and she crafted it to win the heart of Alexander Wood—the son of another founding family. Although Alexander was interested in Morgana, he was wary of her family's notoriety as witches, so apparently Morgana slipped him the love elixir. The recipe has been handed down from generation to generation. The Hartley triplets are descendants of Morgana Hartley. So are Evelyn, Delia, and Hazel Hartley. It's rumoured they are all witches too. Hazel runs the Sweet Indulgence chocolate shop along with her husband. Hazel's Spanish chocolate is included in the Tout de Sweets love latte, but I had no idea she'd also provided it to Klaus Bauer at the Brewery for the Choco Temptation stout."

"What about Delia?"

"Delia runs Elemental Echoes, a store that sells crystals and other...metaphysical items. It's located in the original Hartley homestead. The Hartley family really plays into the folklore, the tourists love it." I chuckled, shaking my head. "You should see this town in October."

"Do you believe in that kind of thing? Witches and love potions and...magic?" Sage wrinkled her nose.

I lifted a shoulder in a shrug. "I mean, I haven't seen anything proving it's real, but I've also not seen anything proving it's not real."

"Did you...drink the love latte with your ex?" she asked, peering at me with heavy emotion in her green eyes.

I thought back to my time with Lori—the early days when things were new and exciting between us. When I was...optimistic I'd found my person.

"Yeah, once. My ex had been somewhat new to town and heard about the folklore involving the love latte and really wanted to try it. We had it the one time. Obviously, its magic didn't work on us because our relationship didn't stand the test of time—or the allure of other men for Lori."

Sage nodded, processing my answer. She looked back down at the bottle. "If she hadn't cheated on you, would you still be with her?"

"I can't answer that," I replied honestly. "I was in love with the person I *thought* I knew, and the life I thought we had...but she had her secrets. I'm just glad they came out when they did."

She nodded again, relaxing as if my answer had soothed something in her. She put the bottle down and leaned back against the cab, sighing. "I guess that's the same for me. I thought Warren was someone he wasn't, and I thought we were building a certain kind of life together. I'm glad I found out who he really was before I married him."

"I'm a firm believer that your past brings you to your future. I'm not so sold on the love elixir thing, but I've heard it's only supposed to work on soulmates. It supposedly just gives them a push to let go of their fears and give in. Lori wasn't my soulmate..." I didn't say the *but* part, but Sage's eyes still came back to mine, probing and vulnerable. "I really am sorry. If I'd known, I would have left the chocolate stout off the menu..."

"It's not your fault. This town seems really sneaky about getting its inhabitants to take this so-called love elixir. I'm sure we would have been forced to drink or eat it at some point." Sage sighed, looking toward the water. "Even my aunt believes in it. She said she and Uncle Ed drank the love latte. Did your parents?" she asked, glancing back at me.

"Come to think of it...I've never asked them, and they've never said either way," I replied. "Parker and Tabitha got suckered into it, but they were really into each other before, so it's hard to know if it was the love latte or just their compatibility and chemistry."

Sage rested her head on the rear windshield and looked up at the sky, falling silent as she stared at the stars. "Great. Just great. Now I'm going to doubt if my feelings are authentic or just the result of some crazy love potion."

My lips quirked into a smile. "Well, how'd you feel about me *before* the chocolate stout?" I asked.

She looked at me, trying to suppress her smile while she studied me. "I've always thought you were attractive, and I've always liked you and spending time with you."

"So you were into me, then?" I flirted, and she laughed.

"I guess so," she admitted, her eyes shining with amusement.

"Then I don't think the love elixir has a bearing on...what

you're feeling right now. I can tell you honestly I wanted you before I cracked open that bottle, and I want you now too. We can take things as slow as you like, I'm in no hurry. All I know is…I want to see where this takes us."

Her eyes widened at my speech. She swallowed, the column of her throat working. Her tongue darted out to dampen her lips. "I'd like to see where this takes us, too…"

SAGE and I spent another couple of hours together in the bed of my truck. She lay with her head on my arm, her body against mine, but her face turned to the sky and all the stars above us. We talked about everything and anything that came to mind.

She shared a little about her childhood. About what it was like growing up with a mother who wasn't very maternal, who always seemed to pick the men in her life over her own daughter—and shared they weren't particularly close now as a result.

"That's why I'm so…hesitant to start this between us," she admitted to me near the end of the evening, her eyes moving from the dark sky above to rest on my face. "I'm worried Daphne will feel like I'm always looking for a man, any man. And that's not the case. If I didn't feel *something* for you, I wouldn't have said yes."

"I don't think she'll feel that way, but I understand. Like I said, we can take things as slow as you need. We don't even have to define things yet. But know that you're the only woman I'm interested in spending time with."

Her eyes brightened at that, like it'd been exactly what she'd needed to hear in the moment. She leaned over and kissed me, and we started making out, exploring each other's bodies over our clothes.

As our kisses grew more and more heated, our touches became more and more exploratory. My hand slid under her shirt, cupping her breast through her lacy bra while she palmed me over top of my jeans.

When we heard voices drifting down from somewhere nearby on the beach, we knew it was time to finally pack up and end the night...but neither of us really wanted to.

"Maybe we should...go somewhere more private?" she suggested, sounding a little vulnerable.

I swallowed hard. "If you want to, we can." Her gaze dropped down to my lips, and she bit her bottom lip, considering.

"I want to," she finally said with a decisive nod. "We could go back to my place if you'd like?"

The invitation sounded too good to resist. "Yeah, we could do that."

Sage helped me fold up the blankets and pillows, and I put them in the storage box along with the empty bottle of Choco Temptation and the folded-up tray. Once everything was tucked away, we collected the take-away boxes and wine glasses, then climbed into the cab.

We could see flashlights farther down on the beach. Figuring it was likely Damien or Noah coming out to check on things, I made sure to lock up the gates to the private beach before we left. Then I drove us back to her place.

"Can you park in the parking lot behind the hardware store?" she asked, and I nodded, doing so without complaint.

I didn't mind that she'd probably asked me to park there to make it less obvious to the townsfolk. I understood her desire to keep what we were doing on the down low. We were consenting adults, but that didn't mean the town wouldn't run amok with gossip if my truck was parked out front of Sage's apartment late at night.

There was more anonymity in parking in the lot behind the building, and I was happy to give that to her, especially after the whole love elixir mishap. I wanted her to know she could trust me, and I wanted her to set the pace. I was prepared to take it however slow—or fast—she wanted to go. If all she wanted was to continue kissing at her place, I was game for it.

Sage punched in the code to unlock the door and opened it, letting us into the back of the building. She glanced at me, her green eyes shining with desire and need, and slipped her left hand in mine, tugging me toward the stairs and leading me up them.

I held open the door at the top of the stairs, and she stepped into the hallway. Sage dropped my hand, bringing her finger to her lips to signal I needed to be quiet, gesturing with a tilt of her head to the other apartment door. I nodded, and we walked as soundlessly as we could down the hallway.

Once we were inside her apartment, Sage turned to me. "Do you want a glass of wine?" she asked as she removed her shoes.

"That sounds good," I told her, toeing my boots off and leaving them by the door while she went into the kitchen.

I watched her reach for two wine glasses from the top shelf of her cabinet, the bottom of her top rising to expose a little of her belly. I wanted to press my lips to that sliver of skin and see if she tasted as good there as she had everywhere else my lips had touched so far.

Instead, I moved behind her and brushed her hair aside, pressing a tender kiss to the side of her neck. She tilted her head, leaning her back against me and pushing her supple ass against my arousal as she poured the wine.

I tried not to thrust, but my hips moved involuntarily, and she spilled a bit of wine on the counter and giggled.

"Sorry," I murmured with a smile against the skin on her neck, reaching for the dishcloth in the sink to wipe it up for her, still pressing kisses to the side of her neck as I cleaned the mess I'd caused.

A soft sigh escaped her lips, and she picked up the wine glasses and turned around, her body still flush against mine. Sage offered one of the glasses to me. I took it from her and sipped it at the same time she sipped hers, but it wasn't what I wanted to drink in that moment.

She met my lustful gaze with her own, swallowing the wine and setting the half-full glass back down on the counter. I abandoned mine, too, my interest in wine evaporating as the heat of desire licked up my spine. She ran her hands up my torso, feeling the panes of muscles over my shirt.

My skin erupted into goosebumps as her hands explored me. I'd never wanted anybody more than I wanted her, never felt such pleasure from a woman's touches. I mean, I'd found pleasure before, obviously, but this...this was on a whole other level.

Then she was grabbing my shirt collar and tugging me even closer toward her. I cupped her face in my hands and kissed her, pouring all the pent-up desire I had for this woman into every stroke of my tongue against hers.

She ground her pelvis against my erection, and the sensational feeling had me pushing against her and deepening the kiss. I pulled away for just a moment, pulling back enough to catch her eyes. "Are you sure about this, Sage? We don't have to do this yet."

While I was talking, she slid one of her hands back down my chest, over my abdomen, and once she'd passed the hemline of my shirt, she unbuttoned my jeans and tugged the zipper down, slipping her hand into my boxers.

"I want to," she insisted, her hand wrapping around my hardness. I let out a low groan, my forehead falling to rest on hers as she stroked me.

"If you're sure..." I said, trailing off as her fingers tightened around me. She gave me a coy smile, and that was really all it took. My hands fell away from her face, gripping her hips as I ravished her mouth, kissing her like my life depended on it.

Sage pulled her hand free and started tugging my shirt up, breaking away long enough to pull it over my head. I lifted her tank top off too, tossing it to the floor with mine. Then our mouths collided again, frantic and searching. I lifted her on top of the island counter, gently pushing her legs aside so I could stand between them.

She slid her hands over my pectorals, still meeting each fevered kiss with one of her own. Kissing Sage was intoxicating, I could feel her becoming a willing addiction with the way my entire being responded to her. I had her, and yet I craved more and doubted I'd ever get enough of her signature taste.

With one hand, I unhooked her bra, freeing her breasts from entrapment. I took one of her nipples into my mouth, sucking on the pink peak until it hardened into a tight nub before I moved onto the other.

Sage seemed to really respond to the attention I lavished on her breasts, and I couldn't help but grin, dropping a hand down. I rolled my thumb over the seam of her jeans at the junction of her thighs, feeling her tremble with desire.

As I massaged her thighs, my fingers inched toward the button of her jeans. I pulled back enough to appraise her. I popped the button of her jeans, sliding the zipper down slowly as I looked into her eyes, watching for any sign of hesitation at all.

I found none. Sage's eyes burned with the same desire coursing through me. She nodded, biting on her bottom lip, and lifted her hips so I could drag her jeans off. I tossed them on the kitchen floor, my eyes going to the lacy pair of panties she wore. I rubbed her over the lace, feeling her heat and wetness through the thin material.

She moaned, arching her head back like she couldn't get enough of my touch. My mouth was watering for a taste. "Lie back," I instructed, my voice deep and affected.

Sage did as I asked, lying back against the island and spreading her legs for me. I lowered my mouth, breathing in her delectable scent. I sampled her over the lace, her flavour exploding on my tongue, and she let out a whispered plea.

I grinned at her, moving her panties aside so I could properly taste her. Within moments, I had her wavering on the counter, my free hand pressing down on her stomach to hold her in place.

Tired of her panties getting in the way, I tugged them down her legs and tossed them somewhere behind me. I cupped under her knees and dragged her forward, supporting her weight with my hands, I lowered my mouth to her and feasted.

She tasted like destiny. I didn't stop until I had her crying out my name, her juices dripping down my chin.

"Nix, I need you..." she panted, peering up at me with wide eyes, her cheeks and chest flushed. She looked like an entire meal, spread out for me to enjoy on her kitchen island. I'd been hoping for more restraint, maybe to take her to the bedroom and ease her into things, but I was acting on pure instinct and carnal drive.

My jeans were still on, so I reached into my back pocket for my wallet and pulled a condom out. Once I had the foil packet in hand, I discarded my jeans and boxers. Sage bit her lip, her eyes zeroing in on my erection. The woman made me absolutely mad with desire. It felt like I was harder than I'd ever been before.

She watched as I sheathed myself in latex and stepped toward her, my eyes raking over her body with appreciation.

I leaned over her, claiming her lips in a brief but heated kiss that spoke of promises and intent.

"The things I'm going to do to you, my flower," I murmured, my eyes on hers as I stroked my tip against her entrance. Sage's legs parted wider, inviting me in.

I took her in one quick, deep thrust, pushing in as far as she'd take me. Sage let out a whimper, and I stilled—worried I was hurting her. Then her thighs parted even more, and she rolled her hips, pulling me in deeper. She felt like pure ecstasy, her tight, velvety channels clamping down on me. It took everything in me to not embarrass myself then and there.

I pulled out slowly before slamming home, making her scoot forward on the island. Putting my hands under her knees, I pulled her back against me, and she moaned, her pleasure coating me more and more with each deep thrust. Watching her breasts move with each slam had my spine tingling, her whimpered cries spurring me on until I couldn't hold back anymore.

CHAPTER NINETEEN

Sage

My phone rang early the next morning, waking me up from the most comfortable sleep of my life. Nellie's name and picture flashed on the screen, along with the time of eight o'clock. I answered it before the shrill rings could wake Nix up too.

Slipping out of my bed and tiptoeing down the hallway in the oversized T-shirt and panties I'd put on before passing out, I spoke as quietly as I could so as not to disturb my sleeping guest. "Hello?"

"Tell me _all_ about it! How did it go?" Nellie's excited voice demanded. I knew she was just checking in to make sure it hadn't been a disaster. I was supposed to text her after to let her know how it went, but obviously, the date hadn't exactly ended.

"It went well. Really well...he's still here."

"No way." Nellie sounded shocked. "I'm impressed. I was hoping you'd bring him back for some fun. It's been a long time since you had any, and you're due for a little...attention."

"Gee, thanks for that," I deadpanned. "But yes, it was a lot of fun." I couldn't help the smile that graced my lips as I looked back over my shoulder down the hall. I could hear soft snores coming from my bedroom. "He's...*amazing*, and not just in bed—although he's incredible there too."

I'd never had a more attentive lover, and it took being with Nix to make me realize that. He made every touch—even the brush of his fingers against my thigh—a sensual experience.

Nellie's squeal of excitement almost broke my eardrums, and I had to pull the phone away from my ear. "This is *the best* news. Seriously."

"Why?" I asked, grabbing the coffee pot to put on some coffee.

"It just *is*. I can't wait to meet him when I come visit."

"You're getting a little ahead of yourself, aren't you?" I chuckled, filling the pot with water.

"I don't think I am," Nellie said, and I could almost hear her shrug over the line. "I have a good inkling about this, and you know my inklings are usually dead-on."

I didn't want to admit it, but she was right. Nellie's inklings had yet to be wrong. She'd ended up being right about Warren, even if it'd taken a few years for that truth to come out.

"When *are* you planning on coming out?" I asked, pouring the water into the reservoir before I went to grab the coffee from the cabinet. I blinked, spotting the lacy black thong I'd been wearing the night before on the cabinet handle. Nix must have tossed it there. I grabbed it, tossing it to the pile of yesterday's clothes on my kitchen floor with a blush rising to my cheeks. We hadn't made it very far into the apartment before taking things further.

"Closer to Halloween," Nellie informed me, interrupting my pleasant stroll down memory lane. "I tried to get some time off sooner, but Sal's being a bit of a jerk about things and claims he needs to hire someone else before he can grant me the time off. I told him he has until the last week of October. I'm used to going trick-or-treating with you and Daphne, and I can't miss it."

Nellie had joined Daphne and me every Halloween since we became friends, even after Warren and I were together. Warren didn't "get" Halloween and didn't want to participate in the dressing up and trick-or-treating. So Nellie happily continued accompanying us, wearing themed costumes and helping carry the extra pillowcase for Daphne's candy haul, which we'd always end up splitting with her.

"That's awesome. Daphne will be so excited," I told her as I put the filter in and hit brew. I heard footsteps in the hallway and turned my head, catching Nix as he disappeared into the bathroom. "He's up now, so I've gotta go...but I'll give you a call later, okay?" I whispered as the coffee started percolating.

"Fine, you better. I still need a play-by-play of your date," Nellie said.

Nix came out of the bathroom a few moments later and strolled into the kitchen wearing nothing but his boxers and the sexiest smile on his lips. His jeans and his T-shirt were still on my kitchen floor. "Hey, gorgeous," he said, pressing a kiss to my temple. "How'd you sleep?"

"Good, what about you?" I asked, feeling a little disappointed when he put his jeans on and pulled his T-shirt on over his head. He looked ready to head out. A wave of self-consciousness hit me, and I tugged the hem of my shirt down.

"Really good," he replied, his voice heavy with implication as his eyes dropped to my hemline. He stepped toward me, his hands cupping my rear as he tugged me against him. I wrapped my arms around the back of his neck. "Kind of hoped I'd wake up with you still in my arms, though."

"Sorry about that. Nellie called to make sure I was still alive."

"Still alive?" He cocked a brow at me in question.

"Back when I lived in Guelph, she'd go on dates with guys she met through online dating sites, and I'd always have her text me after to make sure she was safe. So...I guess she was returning the favour."

"She's a good friend," he said.

"She is." I nodded with agreement.

Nix brought his lips to mine, kissing me and effectively pushing my insecurities away. Things started to heat up again, and Nix had to pull back, resting his forehead on mine. He drew in a stabilizing breath as his gaze caught mine.

"As much as I really don't want to, I've got to head out soon. I promised my dad I'd help at the lumberyard. Now I'm seriously regretting that promise, but..." he glanced longingly down at my body, as if he really didn't want to let me go.

"Oh. I understand. Did you want a coffee before you go?" I asked.

"Sure." Nix gave my rear a little squeeze before he released me. I moved to the cabinet that had the mugs and grabbed two down. I fixed our coffees, and we moved to sit at the island, stealing glances at each other over our cups.

I know we'd talked the night before about taking things slow, but it didn't really *feel* like we were going slow, and I didn't know who to blame for that—or what. Was it just our chemistry, or did the love elixir have anything to do with this desire to be in his company?

I'd asked him to come home with me because I wasn't sure when I'd have the apartment to myself again. I didn't regret that decision, but now I felt uncertain on the next step for us.

"I had a lot of fun last night," I remarked, pausing to think about how to put to words the scrambled thoughts in my head.

Nix smiled, his eyes smoldering. "I did too."

"I'm not sure when we'll be able to...do something like this again," I said, gesturing between the two of us and my quiet, kid-free apartment.

His expression softened with understanding. "I know. It's probably a challenge for you to get away for dates, and I understand that completely. But I still want to spend more time with you...I still want to date you."

"I'd like that...I'd like to date you too," I confessed, smiling shyly. The fact we both couldn't stop smiling at each other had me smiling even more.

"How long of a lunch break do you usually get?" Nix asked.

"Half an hour. What about you?" I answered.

Nix set his half-full mug down. "I'm the boss, so I can take as long as I want," he said with a shrug. "I usually take about a half hour too, though. And I go to Candlelight at least once a week," he added, referring to the bistro beside the hardware store.

"So..."

"Let's have lunch this week. Whenever you want, just text me what day works best for you."

"I don't even have your phone number yet." I laughed, feeling a little embarrassed that I'd bedded the man twice before I'd even programmed his number into my phone. That wasn't like me—at least, I hadn't been that way with anyone else. Not even Warren. I'd made him wait months...

Of course, he'd probably been getting his fill elsewhere during that time, but I preferred not to think about that.

I told myself that wasn't the reason I'd given in to those urges with Nix so quickly. It had just felt right at the time, and it still felt right. I didn't regret my decision; I felt safe in his company. I felt like he held the key to unlock every part of me I'd kept fastened and sealed.

"What's your number?" he asked, pulling his phone out of his pocket. I told it to him, and he sent me a text message. My phone chimed on the other side of the kitchen with the text, and he beamed at me. "You've got it now."

"Good." I smiled back at him. The way his eyes swept over me, drinking me in, made the feeling of hope bloom in my chest like a flower in the sunlight. That's what Nix felt like—sunlight and warmth. Like his very presence *fed* my soul.

"Well, I've got to go now. I'll text you later, though," Nix said. Finished with his coffee, he stood up and pushed in the stool.

"Okay, that sounds good." I tried not to let my disappointment show. I had a busy day myself. I had to shower before I met up with Tabitha and Parker at the beach to pick up Daphne and do their family photo session.

Nix leaned forward, his hand framing the side of my face as he captured my lips in a kiss of unspoken promises. He pulled back; his eyes locked on mine.

"And for what it's worth, I honestly don't mind spending time with Daphne too. In fact, I'd like that a lot—she's a cool kid. There's a lot of fun stuff we can do around town, when you're ready to tell her about us," he told me, his eyes conveying his sincerity.

I nodded, absorbing his words and trying not to let those seeds burrow too deeply into my heart, but it was almost as if I didn't have a choice in the matter.

I walked Nix to the door, and he kissed me once more before leaving. Closing the door, I leaned against it and pressed a finger to my swollen lips.

CHAPTER TWENTY

Nix

"Some warning on what was in the Choco Temptation stout would have been nice," I said as I stormed into the garage and glared at my brother later that evening. It was the first time I'd seen him since Friday night.

I'd had a busy day at the lumberyard, and Parker had been tied up on a job. I found him in his garage working on a dresser, sanding it down and prepping it to be stained. He'd paused and looked up at me, almost appearing dumbfounded.

"What do you mean?" Parker asked, feigning innocence. But I could see right through it.

"Choco Temptation. The love elixir, really?" I huffed, aggravated. I'd spent the day thinking about how much that slip-up had *almost* cost me, and I wasn't impressed.

Sage had been so upset at first, and I couldn't blame her. For a moment, it'd felt like I betrayed her trust, but I honestly hadn't known the stout contained the love mixture.

"Oh crap, you got *that* one?" Parker's eyes widened. "Yeah, there's two kinds. The Midnight Malt, and the Choco Temptation Stout. The Choco Temptation is usually reserved for the couple packages at the Whimsical Woods Resort. I'm sorry, I didn't even think."

"I'm sure you are," I deadpanned.

"So you guys drank the love elixir, then? Guess that explains why you weren't home last night." He smirked.

I crossed my arms, giving him a look that said I clearly wasn't impressed. Even if I *did* end up having a great night with Sage, it could have easily been a disaster if she'd opted to get mad at me for unwittingly forcing her to drink the love elixir.

I mean, I hadn't forced her, per se...but I'd supplied the chocolate stout with the love elixir in it and poured it for her, which was almost the same thing.

"Yeah, well. No thanks to you guys."

"No, thanks to the *love elixir*. I told you, that stuff is potent." Parker nodded, convinced of it. "Did you guys have a good time, though?"

I sighed, letting my arms fall to my side. "Yeah, we did. Until the Hartley sisters showed up."

"They crashed your date?" Parker shook his head, a little shocked and a lot amused.

"Yeah, they did. Drove right up to us in their Commander. Then they made a comment as they drove off about how we'd had the Choco Temptation, and that's when Sage read the label on the bottle, and we found out we'd been drinking a new version of the love elixir."

Parker winced, the reality of how *not good* that situation must have been hitting him. "Dang, sorry to hear that. I'm glad it ended on a good note, though. Does she want to see you again?"

"She said she did," I replied, leaning against the work bench behind me. "But she also mentioned throughout the evening that she doesn't know if she can trust her feelings now, so that's great."

"Did you tell her that it only works if you are soulmates?"

"Yeah." I sighed. "Not sure how much of a comfort that was, though," I added. Who wanted to discuss the heaviness of soulmates on a first date? First dates were supposed to be casual and fun, about exploring one another and seeing if you even wanted that second date.

I mean, I'd known before the first date I wanted a second one, and a third, and a lifetime of dates with Sage Whitaker, but just because *I* was sure, didn't mean she had to be. Or that I should unload that on her. I'd meant it when I told her I'd take it as slow as she needed.

"I'll get Tabitha to talk to her if you want," Parker suggested.

"No, absolutely not. I'd rather you guys didn't involve your-selves in our dating life any further," I replied, sending him a stern look.

Parker lifted his hands in surrender. "Fine, fine. We'll keep our noses out of your business."

"Great. Now if only the rest of the town would too." I let out an aggravated breath.

"That's probably not going to happen." Parker smirked. "You know the residents of this town love following a good romance, and the Hartley sisters are relentless once they get an idea in their head..."

"Yeah, I know." I scratched the back of my neck and sighed again. The Hartley family's obsession with the love elixir and matchmaking *used* to be amusing and almost cute...when their attention *wasn't* focused on me, but I suppose this was my penance for the amusement I felt watching Parker go through it with Tabitha.

ON MY BREAK ON TUESDAY, I drove downtown to meet Sage for lunch at Candlelight Bistro. I found parking down the street and walked over.

Sage was just exiting the hardware store when I was almost at the bistro. Our eyes connected, and the smile she gave me had everything inside me shifting, realigning. Rightening.

"Hey, gorgeous," I said to her, crossing over to her and placing my hand on her hip. I kissed her on the temple. I would have preferred to capture her lips in a more demanding kiss, but the streets were busy, and I knew her uncle could probably see us from the window.

"Hey." She smiled, her cheeks flushing as she peered around. Nobody seemed to be paying attention, though. I dropped my hand to the small of her back as we started walking. "How's work been?" she asked me.

"Busy, but good. What about you?" I answered, opening the door to the bistro.

"Not so busy, but still good," she replied, walking through it. The bistro was busy—as it usually was at lunchtime. We waited in the lineup for our turn. "I'm not sure why Uncle Ed wanted to hire me. I feel like all he does is pay me to stand around."

"Yeah, but he's been able to go to his doctor appointments without having to close up, which probably helps him out a lot," I pointed out. She nodded thoughtfully. "Ed's busy season tends to be in the spring and summer, when all the summer tourists are making repairs on their cottages. It gets a little quiet during the fall and winter months."

"I guess that's true." Sage sighed. "I still feel guilty, though. It's like I'm needlessly costing him money."

"I don't think that's the case, but if you're worried, you could always ask him." She nodded, and the customer ahead of the person in front of us moved along. It was almost our turn. "Have you tried the shawarmas yet?"

"No, I've actually been trying to avoid this bistro." Sage chuckled. "I figured if I found out it was really good, I'd be in trouble—what with my apartment and place of work right here."

"Fair enough." I laughed. "This place really does make the best shawarmas. And the lavender rose lemonade is great too."

"Mmm, that does sound good," Sage remarked. "Okay, I'll try that."

The person ahead of us placed their order and moved on, leaving the counter free to us. We stepped forward, and Marvin Gauthier, the bistro owner and renowned chef, smiled. "Let me guess, beef shawarma panini?" Chef asked, giving me a knowing smile.

I placed my hand on the small of Sage's back, and Chef glanced at the contact, his smile growing. "Two of them, please, and two lavender rose lemonades," I replied. Like I'd told Sage earlier, I came to the bistro at least once a week, every week—specifically for their beef shawarma paninis.

"Coming right up," Chef said, typing our orders into the cash register. He handed me a number and offered Sage his hand with a welcoming smile. "Hi, I'm Chef Marvin. It's nice to meet you..."

"Sage Whitaker," she replied, shaking his hand.

"You're Ed and Emelia's niece," Chef exclaimed. "I've been meaning to pop over and introduce myself. We've been really busy the last few weeks, though." He chuckled, gesturing to the crowded bistro.

"That's okay; I could have come in sooner myself. It's nice to meet you," Sage replied.

"It's nice to meet you too. Welcome to Hartwood Creek," Chef beamed.

We let Chef get back to taking and fulfilling orders and found a free bistro table to sit at to wait for our paninis. We talked for a few more minutes, mostly about casual things like work and how she was a little nervous about the upcoming fundraiser.

"Tabitha showed me the photos you sent her; they're great, Sage. You've got a real talent," I told her. "You're going to do great."

"I hope so." She gave me a small smile. "It'd be nice to get some real business after...maybe do some more family sessions."

"I'm sure you'll be able to pull that off," I said with utter confidence. "Once they see what you're capable of, there will be no shortage of jobs coming your way." Sage appeared to blossom with that praise.

Before she could reply, Anya, the server, brought over our lavender rose lemonades, placing them in front of us with a flourish.

"Hi, Nix, who's your girlfriend?" she asked, looking at Sage with interest. Anya was my younger brothers' age, so I knew her through them—and from my frequent visits to the bistro.

Sage's eyebrow lifted, and I smiled at her. "Well, I'm not sure if she's ready for that label, though I'd like her to have it... this is Sage Whitaker. Sage, this is Anya Tillman. She's friends with my brothers, Preston and Paxton."

"Hi, Anya." Sage smiled at her.

"Hey, welcome to town," Anya said with a friendly grin before she turned to look at me. "How *are* your brothers these days? I haven't seen them around."

"They've been busy with their fishing tours and YouTube stuff," I said. "They'll be helping out at the fundraiser this Friday, though."

"Ooh! Are they running the dunk tank again?" Anya got a mischievous look in her eyes. At the last fundraiser, she'd spent nearly a hundred dollars trying to dunk them.

"Yup," I replied, and her smile widened.

"Excellent. I've been practicing my aim," she said gleefully. "I'll be back shortly with your paninis," she added before heading back to the service counter.

"It's so strange how everyone seems to know everyone else so well." Sage laughed awkwardly, tucking a strand of her hair behind her ear. "It wasn't like this in Guelph. I mean, people were nice, but not this nice. And they rarely remembered your name unless you were wearing a name tag. Everyone seems to know me sight unseen, though. Or they can tell I'm new here and want to know who I am, so they come up and straight up ask me."

"Yeah, I can see how that would be strange. But they mean no harm."

"Oh, I know that. Everyone's been so friendly and welcoming. I'm sure I'll get used to it...it's just definitely a different vibe. Takes some getting used to, I guess." Sage smiled softly.

CHAPTER TWENTY-ONE

The week passed quickly, and before I knew it, it was time for the Fall Fun Fundraiser.

It took me forever to decide on an outfit for the fundraiser, and in the end, I chose a pair of jeans and a frilly white top I paired with my olive-green jacket. I left my hair down and kept my makeup minimal, hoping I looked mature and professional.

I grabbed my camera bag and got my equipment ready. I'd left my batteries charging all day so they would have enough power, but I still triple-checked before putting them in the camera. Then I made sure I had a full memory card *and* a backup memory card—just in case. I had no idea how many people would want to use the photo booth, and I wanted to be prepared.

It was the first time I'd ever done anything remotely "professional" with my camera, and although it was a volunteer position, I'd be making a lot of connections, and I really didn't want to mess it up.

I'd gotten some practice in the Sunday before with

Tabitha's family session, but since I considered them friends, it was hard for me to count that experience as a qualified session. The resulting photos had been beautiful, though.

Tabitha cried when I delivered them, and she'd immediately given me permission to share some of them on my Instagram. Which had already accumulated more followers since I started sharing more of the photos I'd taken since moving.

My business cards arrived the day before, and I made sure I tucked a thick stack of them into my bag to hand out. Isla had done an amazing job on my new logo, and I was beginning to feel like a professional photographer. Minus the professional jobs, but I was hoping that tonight would lead to a few.

"Come on, Mommy. We're going to be late," Daphne called out, spurring me into action.

"All right, all right. Hold your horses." I grabbed my keys, and we headed out.

We arrived at Hartwood Creek Elementary School at a quarter to four, and the event started at five and ran until eight o'clock, although the photo booth would only be open for as long as the daylight lasted. I sat in my car for ten minutes, making Daphne sit with me. I was nervous, and my daughter could tell.

She leaned forward between the seats and wrapped her little arms around me in a hug. "It's going to be okay, Mommy. You'll do great."

"Thank you, Squirt." I bopped her nose. "Shall we do this, then?" Daphne nodded eagerly and opened the door, getting out of the car.

I got out, too, following my daughter toward the madness.

Volunteers were working hard to get everything ready. The vendor tables and games were being set up on the blacktop. She spotted the twins near the Hutchinsons' vendor table and took off to talk to them.

Auntie Em and Uncle Ed were there, too, chatting with Laurel Hutchinson and an elderly woman who must have been Nix's grandma. My aunt and uncle had agreed to come out and support the fundraiser and keep an eye on Daphne for me so I could focus on running the photo booth.

I followed, pausing at their table to say hello.

"Hello, Sage." Laurel smiled with warmth. "Gran, this is Sage Whitaker and her daughter, Daphne." She spoke to the elderly woman sitting beside her. The woman squinted, trying to see me better.

"So you're the one who's got my grandson tied up in knots," the elderly Mrs. Hutchinson said.

"Um, I guess so," I replied, my cheeks heating with embarrassment. Daphne was occupied with the twins and hadn't heard her, but I could feel my aunt's and uncle's eyes on me.

Although I hadn't come out and told them I was seeing Nix, I knew they probably had an idea there was something going on between the two of us. After all, Nix had shown up twice throughout the week on my lunch break to take me out for a quick date.

Nix's grandmother studied me for a moment longer, then nodded with satisfaction. "Well, it's nice to finally meet you."

"It's nice to meet you too, Mrs. Hutchinson."

"Call me Gran," the old woman insisted with a wave of her wrinkled hand and the knitting needle she held.

"Okay..." I trailed off, feeling a little awkward. But Gran had already gone back to her knitting. Daphne tugged on my coat, and I glanced down at her and smiled. "What's up, Squirt?"

"Can I have some money to buy things?" she asked. Nodding, I reached into my camera bag for the cash I'd pulled out from the bank earlier that day, handing her a few twenties.

"Don't forget to spend some of that on a new book," I reminded her.

"Okay, I will." Daphne nodded, folding up the bills and tucking them into her little jean pocket.

"We'll make sure she picks something out," Auntie Em promised.

"Thanks, Auntie Em." I smiled my appreciation before turning to Tabitha. "Have you seen Mr. Robertson? I'm not sure where I'm supposed to go."

"He's over by the fire truck," she replied, pointing in the direction. The fire department had their fire truck parked in the grass in front of the school, with Sparky the Fire Dog ready to greet kids and give out fire truck tours. Mr. Robertson was talking to a few of the firefighters. "I'll take you to him if you want?"

"No, that's all right. I'll just go over," I replied quickly. "I'll see you guys in a bit. Behave, Daph, and stick with Auntie Em and Uncle Ed. No wandering," I instructed, and she nodded solemnly.

"Good luck, love, you'll do great," Auntie Em told me, giving me a quick hug.

"I hope so." I hugged her back before I made my way over to Mr. Robertson to find out where the photo booth was.

"Hey, Sage! Glad you're here. Mr. Ashe and the high school students have set things up in front of the school," he said, walking me toward it.

"Oh," I said, trying not to look at the setup with disappointment, but the brick behind the photo booth setup wasn't doing it any favours. My gaze was pulled to the field beside the playground. "Is there any way we could move it to that field over there? I think the forest would make a better backdrop than the brick of the school..."

Mr. Robertson paused for half a beat, considering my

suggestion. "Huh, that's a great idea. I'm sure we can have them do that."

I helped Mr. Robertson, Mr. Ashe, and the high school students move the bench and the rest of the props over to where I wanted them. We'd just finished setting everything back up when the barista from the café, Jayden, arrived with another man carrying a bunch of beautiful flower arrangements.

"Hey, Sage. I want you to meet my handsome hubby, Ezra. He's the owner of Hartwood Creek Flowers," Jayden introduced us as he sat the arrangement he was carrying down.

They'd brought beautiful pots of orange and yellow mums, nestled with black-eyed Susans and a few other flowers I couldn't name.

Ezra's entire face lit up when Jayden said my name. "Oh! I've heard so much about you," he cooed, shaking my hand in earnest. "Welcome to Hartwood Creek, my dear."

"Thank you very much. And thank you for the beautiful bouquet you made. I love it. You're so talented," I replied, smiling.

"That is so kind of you to say," Ezra said with an appreciative smile, putting a hand to his heart as if my compliment had warmed it. "I'm glad you enjoyed them. I had a lot of fun making that arrangement." His eyes twinkled as he smiled at me, and I couldn't help but grin back.

Jayden and I chatted for a few more minutes while Ezra fussed over and arranged his floral display around the photo booth, making sure everything looked picture-perfect. Once he was finished, he stood back and appraised his work with a satisfied smile.

"All done," he exclaimed.

"Mind if I test my camera settings with a photo of you and Jayden?" I asked timidly.

"That would be amazing." Jayden grinned, taking Ezra's hand. They went over to the bench seat and sat down, wrapping their arms around each other. I snapped a few for them, catching Jayden throwing his head back and laughing at something Ezra whispered in his ear.

"Thank you so much for donating these, Ezra," Mr. Robertson said. He'd popped back over to check things out and hand me a clipboard to collect the names and emails so I could get their photos to them after the event.

"It's my pleasure," Ezra insisted. "Jayden and I are happy to help raise funds for the school."

After saying goodbye, the two men headed off in the direction of the vendors, and Mr. Robertson turned to me.

"You've got a little bit of time before the event starts if you wanted to have a walk around. It would be great if we could get some photos of the vendors, games, and volunteers, but no pressure at all if you'd like to just focus on the photo booth. We're thankful you volunteered your time," he said.

"Sure, I can do that. And really, I'm happy to help too," I assured him. I left the photo booth and started making my way around the school grounds.

There was a lot happening, so much so that it was almost overwhelming. Auntie Em had said this town didn't do things half-hatched, and that was very apparent from the amount of effort they'd put in for the school fundraiser.

I walked around, snapping pictures of the vendor tables and people as I explored.

The book fair was happening in the gym, and in the track field, a reptile company had set up with some of their exotic pets. They were planning on doing a presentation around six thirty.

There was also a fenced-off area for a small petting zoo,

with a couple of goats, a donkey, and a small pony in it munching on the hay.

There was a woman setting up stock of homemade gloves, hats, and crocheted amigurumi at one of the vendor tables. She had a brown alpaca with her—a real, live alpaca wearing an adorable red flannel bowtie. I just had to stop and take pictures of the woman and her furry friend.

"Hi, I'm Sage Whitaker. I'm running the photo booth," I introduced myself, pointing over my shoulder in the direction of the field and photo booth. "I wondered if I could get a few pictures of you and your furry friend?"

"Absolutely! I'm Hannah Albert, by the way. And this here is Chewpaca." She stood beside him and put her arm around his very long neck. The alpaca all but melted into her.

"Oh my gosh, he's so cute," I cooed, snapping their picture.

"Thank you! He's excited to be a part of the petting zoo but is unsure about the other animals. He's already broken out once, so I figured I'd let him hang out with me for a little bit. Klaus here is going to take him back over in a couple of minutes and make sure he doesn't break out again." She gestured to a serious-looking man lingering to the left of her table.

"Klaus Bauer." Klaus lifted his hand in greeting, his somber expression softening with the brief smile he gave me.

"Oh. The same Klaus who makes the Choco Temptation stout?" I asked, his name ringing a bell from my very recent... taste test.

"Sure am," he said proudly, his smile growing and warming his entire demeanor. "Have you tried it?"

"Yes, I have. It's very good." I managed to keep my smile in place because it was true—Klaus's chocolate stout *was* very good. I just hadn't been keen on the love elixir being snuck into it, although I suppose it wasn't exactly sneaking when he listed the ingredients on the label. It wasn't Klaus's fault I'd unwittingly consumed the elixir. It wasn't even Nix's fault—he'd seemed just as blindsided by it as I'd been.

After Nix had left Sunday morning, I'd called Nellie back and filled her in on every detail, including the love elixir consumption. She'd been confused at first, and then amused and told me I was being ridiculous. In the end, I'd resolved to put it behind me, because Nellie was right—I didn't even believe in the supposed magic of the love elixir, so why should it upset me that I'd consumed it with Nix?

"Thank you, I'm glad you enjoyed it," Klaus said almost humbly.

"I think it's almost time, Klaus," Hannah said, noticing the cars beginning to pull into the lot.

"All right. It was nice meeting you, Sage. Come on, Chewpaca, better get you back to the petting zoo," he said, tugging gently on the alpaca's lead.

I carried on with my exploring, stopping at Lilah's face-painting table. She was all set up and ready to go and finishing up practicing on Riley. She'd painted beautiful fairy wings on Riley's cheeks. "Hey, Lilah and Riley. Mind if I take your picture?"

"Sure," Lilah said, pausing to pose with her daughter. I took a couple of photos for them, then told Lilah we'd catch up later and continued making my way back to the photo booth.

Just past the vendor tables were the games, with a dunk tank positioned in the grass near the photo booth. I could spot Nix's younger twin brothers at the dunk tank, dressed in their swim trunks and matching T-shirts. I snapped some pictures of them horsing around before I walked onto the asphalt to check out the games.

Nix was at the ring toss table with Parker, all set up and ready to go. I made my way over, and Nix glanced up when I approached, his grin widening when he saw me. He stepped around the table and met me in front of it.

"Hey, beautiful," he said, putting his hand on my hip and pressing a kiss to my temple. It was the sweetest gesture and how he greeted me every time he saw me now. I loved it, melting into his touch almost as much as Chewpaca had with Hannah.

"Hey," I said, biting down on my bottom lip and peering up at him.

"I stopped by the photo booth earlier, but you weren't there. It looks great."

"Yeah, Mr. Robertson asked if I could walk around and take a few photos before the event started, so that's what I've been doing," I answered, glancing down at my watch. "Speaking of which, I should get back to the booth before anyone shows up. I'll see you after?"

"Definitely." Nix nodded. "Good luck."

___

CHAPTER TWENTY-TWO

Nix

"Is it just me, or was there, like, double the amount of people here than last year?" Parker asked later that night as we started packing up the booth.

We'd barely had a minute to talk all night. Our table, and every other game table, for that matter, had a lineup of people and kids wanting to play. Preston and Paxton's dunk tank was extra popular. They'd both been dunked several times throughout the night, much to their chagrin. Anya was able to get a dunk in and left grinning from ear to ear with satisfaction.

The ring toss table was positioned across from the dunk tank and beside the beanbag toss table my father ran. The field was in my line of view, so I was able to look up on occasion and see what Sage was up to.

For most of the evening, I hadn't been able to see much of anything but the crowd, but now that the crowd was beginning to thin out, I had a clearer view of the photo booth and the gorgeous blonde poised behind her camera, snapping pictures of a family. I couldn't help but grin with pride. It was neat, seeing her in her element from afar.

We were losing sunlight fast, though, and the event was coming to an end.

"Yeah, I think we've definitely seen more foot traffic this year," I agreed, my attention returning to my brother. He was grinning, having caught me watching Sage again for the umpteenth time that evening.

"Why don't you just go over and talk to her? I can handle getting things packed up here," Parker said, gesturing to the totes we'd brought to put the rings and stakes away.

"You sure?" I asked, and he nodded. "All right, fine," I relented with a grin. "I'll come back soon to help you load it into the truck."

"I can do it myself, and Sage probably needs more help than I do," Parker said, tipping his chin in her direction. I looked over my shoulder, taking in the line that had formed.

I left Parker to pack up the ring toss table and headed over to the photo booth. I wasn't sure how I could help her with the photo-taking aspect, but I could help take down the photo booth when the sun finally set.

By the time I arrived, Sage was photographing a different family, with about five or six left waiting. Most of the people waiting were volunteers and their families, who'd likely been too busy before to come over.

Lingering near the end of the lineup was a man wearing a business suit who seemed out of place. It wasn't just his attire, it was the way he was observing Sage with a deceitful, calculating look on his face.

I walked by him, and he didn't seem to register me at all, looking past me toward the front of the line. He had an aura of self-assurance, but the kind that came from an inflated ego and not genuine confidence. I didn't typically take an immense disliking to total strangers, but for some reason...something about this guy rubbed me the wrong way.

I approached her when she was checking her camera to see the latest set of photos she'd taken. "Hey, Parker thought you might need some help. What can I do?"

"Oh, hey," she blurted out, sounding relieved to see me. "Uh, if you could maybe get the rest of these people to fill out the form in advance, that might help speed things up a little. I want to try to get everyone in before we lose the sunlight. I think I have maybe ten or fifteen minutes left."

"I can do that." I nodded, and she handed me a pen and the clipboard she had set on the registration table.

"Thanks, Nix. You're the best," she said, stepping forward to take photos of the next family.

I approached the lineup, smiling at Damien Wood's twin daughters, Aria and Ronan. They were Tabitha's cousins, which meant they were related to my nieces and nephew too. "Hey, girls. Hey, Damien, how's it going?" I asked, passing the clipboard to him to fill out.

"Good, how about you?" Damien asked gruffly, taking the clipboard from me and passing it to his fiancée, Charlotte, who started filling out the information required.

"Can't complain," I said.

"Oh, I bet." Charlotte smirked, passing the clipboard back to me. "Word is you've got yourself a new girlfriend," she added, her eyes straying to Sage.

"Yeah." I glanced at the woman in question over my shoulder. She was directing the family sitting there, coaxing smiles out of the little ones. She snapped a few photos and straightened, thanking the family, and letting the parents know the photos would be available within the week.

Then it was Damien and Charlotte's turn. They headed over to the bench, taking the seat the other family had just vacated, and I moved on to the next people in line, getting them to fill out the form.

Sage worked quickly, and I kept up, having each family fill out the form ahead of time so they could walk on up to the bench and get their photos taken. I finally got to the guy in the business suit standing alone.

He had his arms crossed and an impatient look on his face.

I approached him, clipboard in hand. "Are you waiting for photos?" I asked, pulling his focus from Sage. He eyed me critically, taking in my attire—the plaid button-up, white T-shirt, and blue-jean look—and I could tell he found it lacking by the smirk he gave me.

"Nope, just waiting," the man said, returning his attention to where Sage stood.

I frowned, not liking the situation—or the man, for that matter—at all. My senses told me something was seriously off about him. The way he stared at Sage with deceitful intent had me wanting to protect her and knock him out.

I wasn't a violent person. In fact, out of all my brothers, I'd gotten into the least number of fights over the years. Most of my scuffles came from defending the people I cared about from people who had ill intentions of their own. The last time I'd gotten into a fight was outside of The Quarter Lounge in my early twenties, when a tourist got a little handsy with his girlfriend. I hadn't known his girlfriend, but I wasn't about to sit idly by and watch a man lay hands on a woman.

"Can I ask what you're waiting for?" I tried to keep my tone friendly and nonthreatening, I did, but for some inexplicable reason, my hackles were raised about the situation.

He turned his cold gaze to me. "That's my business."

I smiled, but it wasn't a friendly, kind smile. It was cautionary. "Well, you see. It kind of *is* my business because you're coming across as really creepy at a school fundraiser."

"I'm just standing here," the man shot back. He seemed pissed at the insinuation, but I didn't care—what he was doing and the way he was eyeing Sage *was* coming across as borderline predatory.

By this point, Sage had worked through the last of the families and had turned to see who was next in line, spotting me facing off with Suit. Her eyes widened with surprise when she looked at him, then flashed with anger.

She approached, her eyes still angry and her stance stiff with tension. Suit noticed her coming over, and his expression changed to contrite as if a switch had been flipped. "What are you doing here?" she demanded.

"I need to talk to you," Suit said beseechingly.

"I have no interest in talking to you, Warren," Sage replied. My eyes narrowed even more at him. So *this* was her ex-fiancé. I wasn't jealous, not by any means. If anything, I was even more concerned than when I'd thought he was just some random guy with a fixation on her.

"I came all this way, Sage," Warren said.

"Looks like you made the trip for nothing. You heard her, she doesn't want to talk to you," I replied. Warren's cold eyes slid to me.

"This doesn't concern you," he sneered.

"Oh, but it does," I replied, taking a step toward him. Sage placed her hand on my elbow, shaking her head slightly in warning. People were beginning to watch the situation unfold. When I immediately stilled at her touch, she let her hand drop to her side, and her unamused gaze went back to Warren.

"This is highly inappropriate. You need to leave, now," Sage insisted, frowning deeply and making her displeasure with him apparent.

My brothers, bless their intuition, sensed something was off with the situation and started heading over. When Warren saw three more sinewy guys were coming over, his bravery started to wane.

"Everything okay?" Parker asked. Preston and Paxton cracked their knuckles, wearing matching grins of menace. The Hutchinsons didn't routinely get into fights—our parents raised us better than that—but we all knew how to throw it down when the situation called for it.

Warren opted to ignore them, his calculating gaze zeroing in on Sage. "This isn't over. You and I *need* to talk."

"Absolutely not. I don't *need* to hear a thing you say. Go home, and don't come back," she replied forcefully.

With me and now my brothers backing her, Warren had no choice but to leave with his tail tucked between his legs, but the furious look he shot at us as he departed made me uneasy.

"Who was that?" Preston asked, looking from me to Sage, his expression growing concerned.

Sage took a deep breath, steadying herself before replying, "My ex. I don't know how he found me..." As soon as she said the words, her brow furrowed, as if she realized something. She brought her hand to her head and massaged her temple, sighing. "Actually, I have a good guess on that."

"Is he going to be a problem?" Paxton asked, glaring at Warren's retreating back as he stomped toward the road where a line of cars were parked.

"Honestly? I don't know," Sage admitted, sending me an apologetic look. I took her hand and squeezed it, letting her know it wasn't her fault. She hadn't asked him to show up, and she certainly hadn't looked pleased by his sudden reappearance.

"You let us know if he keeps bugging you," Preston told her, cracking his knuckles. "We'll handle it."

"Thanks, guys, but hopefully, that won't be necessary," Sage replied, watching warily as Warren climbed into his shiny black car and all but peeled away from the school, driving far too fast for a school zone. Parker scowled, evidently ticked about that.

"He looks like he's not done causing trouble," Parker remarked, crossing his arms and leveling a look at Sage. "Has he ever hurt you before?"

"No." She shook her head, frazzled. "He's never done anything like this before, either. I don't know what his deal is. I think maybe..." she trailed off, sparing me another apologetic look. "I think maybe my mother told him where to find me. She called me last week and said he had come looking for me at her house."

I was liking this situation less and less. My brothers exchanged a look with me. Before any of us could say anything further on the matter, Sage's aunt and uncle walked over with Daphne.

Spotting her daughter, Sage tried to hide her uneasiness with a smile.

"How did it go?" Emelia Alcott asked, seemingly unaware of the tension in the air.

"Looks like you had a lot of people wanting their photos taken," Ed added with a proud smile.

"Yeah, it went really well, I think. I'll know more when I start editing the photos later," Sage replied, tucking her hair behind her ear. "What about you, Squirt? Did you have fun?"

"Yeah! I played lots of games and got this book and this dragon," Daphne exclaimed, holding up a Pippi Longstocking book and a crocheted dragon for Sage to inspect.

"That's great!" Sage smiled at her.

"We were thinking we'd take Daphne home now. I know you guys still need to pack up, but your uncle's getting a little tired," Emelia explained.

"I told you, Em, I'm perfectly fine," Ed cut in, but he did look a little tired, and I knew Emelia worried about his heart.

"That sounds good. I can pick her up on my way home," Sage replied.

"Can't I sleep over at Auntie Em and Uncle Ed's again?" Daphne pleaded.

"I didn't pack you an overnight bag," Sage replied.

"That's all right, she can sleep in one of Uncle Ed's shirts." Emelia smiled. "Or if you're okay with it, we *do* have a spare key to the apartment. We could stop by and grab pajamas and pack some clothes for tomorrow."

Sage thought about it for a minute, considering her options. "All right, if that's what you want..."

"It is!" Daphne jumped up and down with excitement. "I love sleeping over at Auntie Em and Uncle Ed's."

CHAPTER TWENTY-THREE

I hadn't really wanted to send my daughter off again, especially not after Warren's bombardment, but I could tell she really wanted to have a sleepover. My aunt and uncle seemed perfectly fine with it, and it gave me the opportunity to stay late and help with the cleanup.

After all the vendors had packed up and left, it took another hour and a half for the remaining volunteers to clean up after the fundraiser. By the time we were finished, it was nearly ten at night.

"Who wants to go to The Quarter Lounge for some drinks? I think we all deserve it," Preston said in the parking lot as we were finally heading out. Preston, Paxton, Parker, Tabitha, Donavon, Nix, and I had all stayed to help Mr. Robertson and the other teachers clean up.

"Yes! Let's do that. Parker and I have a very rare kid-free night," Tabitha exclaimed. She'd gotten her parents to watch the baby, and Keith and Laurel had taken the twins home with them hours before.

"I'm probably going to call it a night," Mr. Robertson said, yawning. "I feel like I could sleep for the whole weekend and still wake up exhausted. But you guys have fun."

Nix had been watching me closely since the encounter with Warren. I could tell he wanted to talk about what happened, but I didn't know what more to say about the matter.

"What about you two?" Tabitha asked, looking at Nix and me.

"I don't know..." I trailed off, glancing at Nix. He lifted his shoulder in a shrug, leaving it up to me.

"Please, Sage?" Tabitha begged, her blue eyes wide. I don't think she'd been made aware of the situation with my ex showing up yet.

"I guess I could go for a couple of drinks," I replied. "I'm just going to drive home and ditch my car."

"I'll follow you," Nix said.

"Okay, we'll see you guys there," Parker said, holding open their minivan's door for Tabitha as Preston and Paxton climbed into the back seat.

Alone in my car for the brief ride home, I allowed my thoughts to drift to the situation with Warren earlier. I'd been surprised to see him there, and even more surprised to see the protective stance Nix had taken, even before knowing who he was.

I parked my car and grabbed my camera bag, my eyes surveying the parking lot for any sign of the black car I'd seen Warren get into earlier. I didn't see it, but I still waited until Nix pulled in to get out and lock my car.

Nix parked beside me and got out of his truck, strolling over with a concerned look on his handsome face. It was dark, and we were alone, so he pulled me into his arms, holding me close to him. "Are you okay?"

"Yeah, I'm fine. Just...that was really weird," I admitted,

leaning into his embrace and wrapping my arms around his lower back. I looked up at him, surprised to see him scanning the dark parking lot, as if he was looking for Warren's car too.

The uneasiness I'd felt at Warren's abrupt, unwanted reappearance into my life unsettled me. He hadn't tried very hard to convince me to stay when I caught him cheating. He'd placed the blame on me and let me pack up Daphne and my things. I'd been gone before a full twenty-four hours had passed after my discovery.

He hadn't tried to show up at Nellie's or my mom's while I stayed there. He hadn't tried to call—or at least, I didn't think he had. At the advice of Nellie, I blocked his number from contacting me. I'd thought it was a great idea at the time because I really wasn't interested in hearing what he had to say. He'd said enough after I caught him red-handed.

I still didn't care to hear what he had to say. As far as I was concerned, the relationship was over, and so was the need for me to listen to his drivel. It wouldn't change anything because I didn't want him back. He'd exposed his true self, and I'd found that person repulsive.

I had to drop off my camera gear before we could head out, so we started walking through the parking lot. I shook my head, still stewing about the situation.

"Are you sure it was your mom who told him?" Nix asked.

"Yeah, I'm positive." I sighed deeply. "Nellie's the only other person who knows where I am, and she'd sooner perform a root canal on herself than help him. She never liked him," I continued, opening the door to the apartment.

"Why would your mom do that?" Nix frowned, seeming to have difficulty with the concept of a mother putting her own child—and grandchild—at risk. I was just thankful Daphne hadn't been around to witness things. I didn't want her confused further by the situation.

I shrugged my shoulders as we started walking up the stairs. "She's team Warren. She thinks I should have forgiven him for cheating on me and worked harder to be a better partner to him." I rolled my eyes.

Nix's frown deepened. "You weren't to blame for any of his choices, Sage."

"I know. Honestly, I never listen to my mother's advice about relationships. She's the worst example." I laughed awkwardly, trying to hide my discomfort. I didn't like talking about my complicated relationship with my mother—or *why* it was so complicated.

I remember watching episodes of *Gilmore Girls* as a child, wishing for that connection and mother-daughter relationship that Lorelai and Rory seemed to have, but it never came. My mother was more interested in finding a man that would support her. Any "quality time" we had together was spent with her criticizing me on any perceived imperfection that would "make it difficult for me to land and keep a man." As if my worth was measured by that.

But to my mother, it really was. She measured her worth by who she was with or not with at the time. Appearances were just as important to her as they'd been to Warren, and I think that was why they hit it off. Warren turned out to be *exactly* like the men she constantly chose.

"I'm sorry to hear that," Nix said, leaning against the door-frame while I unlocked my apartment door.

"It's okay, I'm used to it. Luckily, I have Auntie Em for the maternal advice she lacks. My aunt just so happened to agree with me, and given that she's been in a healthy, happy marriage for three decades now, I'm more inclined to listen to her."

"Em is the best. Ed too," Nix remarked as we walked into the apartment, closing the door behind us. I nodded, walking over to the kitchen to set down my camera bag on the island, an exhausted sigh escaping my lips. "You sure you want to go to The Quarter Lounge tonight?" he asked, picking up on my mood.

"I told Tabitha we would..." I trailed off. I felt guilty for it, but I did want to bail. My social battery was drained, and I didn't really feel like drinking out in public.

"Parker and the twins have probably filled her in by now. She'll understand," Nix told me.

"I don't really want to be alone either." I looked up at him, hating the vulnerability I felt. He crossed over, wrapping me back up in his embrace.

"I'll keep you company." He smiled down at me, his calloused hand rubbing my lower back. "If you want me to."

"I do," I told him, letting myself surrender into his hold.

I WAITED until Nix left Saturday morning to make the dreaded phone call. I sat in the silence of my apartment at the island with a cup of coffee and dialed her number. It rang several times before my mother answered.

"Hello, darling," she sang, as if she hadn't sent someone I didn't want to see catapulting back into my life.

"Why did you tell Warren where he could find us?" I demanded, skipping the pleasantries.

"Oh! He showed up. How lovely," she replied, as if this news was the best she'd ever heard. My aggravation grew.

"No, Mom. It is *not* lovely, not at all. I don't want him in my life. I am not interested in what he has to say, and I cannot believe you've ignored everything I've said about the matter and told him where I am." My tone was biting, and I didn't care. She'd crossed a line, and this time, I wouldn't be forgiving her for it.

"You're being ridiculous, Sage," she scoffed. "Warren just wanted to talk to you."

"What part of 'I don't want to talk to him or see him ever again' are you not getting?" I said, enunciating every word. "There's a reason I blocked his number and left him. I am finished with him."

"I think you're making a mistake based off of hurt feelings—"

"I am not making a mistake, *Mother*," I cut her off, bringing my hand to my temple to massage the tension headache that had formed Friday night and hadn't let up since. "My feelings aren't hurt over the matter, and my mind is made up. I've moved on completely from him, and there is *never* a situation where I'd take him back."

"Sage—"

"He showed up at a school function, Mom, when I was volunteering my time and working. Do you know how inappropriate that is?"

"He just wanted to support the fundraiser. He told me he was going to donate to the school."

"I don't care. It wasn't appropriate, it was embarrassing," I replied.

"Well, I'm sorry you feel that way, but I think you're overreacting."

"And I think you're overstepping, and I also think you're being extremely toxic. I mean, you've always been toxic and manipulative, but this takes the cake," I said, probably a little harsher than I needed to, but my anger was still fresh.

"I am not toxic," my mother shouted with indignant outrage.

"But you are, though. You have harmed me so many times

over the years with the things you say to me and how you act. You've always prioritized the men in your life over our relationship, and this pattern has continued with you prioritizing more men over me. Warren should not have your undying support and sympathy; I should have had that." A tear escaped, rolling down my cheek. I wiped it away quickly, even though she couldn't see it. "But I don't, and I see that now. So I'm ending this call, and I'm stepping back to heal from the shit you've put me through."

I didn't give her a chance to say anything else before disconnecting the call.

I had a good cry while I showered, releasing emotions I'd kept bottled up for decades. Then I got ready to go to my aunt and uncle's to pick up my daughter.

When I walked into their house an hour later, Daphne was sitting at the kitchen table eating lunch with Uncle Ed. They looked up when I entered the room.

"Hey, guys, where's Auntie Em?"

"She's on the back porch, on the phone," Uncle Ed told me, giving me a sympathetic look as he stood up and walked his empty plate to the sink.

"Mimi called," Daphne informed me with a mouth full of the sandwich she was eating. "She was yelling at Auntie Em."

"I'm sorry," I said to Uncle Ed, and he smiled sadly.

"You don't need to apologize for your mother. Em knows how she is," Uncle Ed said. "I'm proud of you, kiddo. We both are."

My uncle's words brought a wave of emotion over me that made my eyes well up. Seeing the emotion, he wrapped me up in a hug.

"Thank you," I murmured, trying to blink the tears away before Daphne could notice them. "I should probably go see how she is," I added.

"Okay." He released me and placed his hand on my shoulder, making sure I'd meet his kind eyes. "But just know that you have nothing to feel guilty for. Nobody should ever feel guilty for setting boundaries."

I nodded, appreciating that more than I could articulate. I went to the patio door and peered through it, spotting Auntie Em sitting in a lounge chair and staring into her backyard with a contemplative look in her eyes, her phone resting on the table beside her.

I slid open the door and stepped out onto the porch to join her, and she looked over at me, her expression shifting from thoughtful to genuine affection. "How are you doing, sweetie?"

"I'm all right," I said, sitting down in the lounge chair beside her and turning my body toward her. "How are you?"

"I'm good." Auntie Em nodded, a soft smile gracing her lips. If she was upset about the call with my mother, she was trying not to show it.

"I heard my mother called you..."

"She did." She nodded again, the pursing of her lips the only indication she was upset. For a moment, I wondered if she was upset at me.

"Sorry about that. I set her off," I apologized, looking out over the backyard. Auntie Em leaned forward and reached for my hand, taking it in hers. I glanced back at her.

"Your mother has never liked hearing the truth of things if it doesn't fit her narrative," Auntie Em said wisely, her expression softening as she looked at me. "You had every right to be angry at her for disregarding your choices. I'm sorry she did that, and I'm sorry you had to put her in her place. It's not easy when we have to parent our parents."

Auntie Em's words and her loving touch unlocked the floodgates, and my eyes welled up with tears. I laughed awkwardly, wiping them away with embarrassment. "Well, I'm sorry she lashed out at you over it."

"I can take it," Auntie Em assured me with a wry grin. "I didn't know Warren showed up last night. Is that why the Hutchinson boys were all gathered around you like bodyguards?"

"Yeah, it all happened so fast." I sighed. "It's why I was so angry with her. I spoke to her last week and told her I had no desire to hear from or see him again, and she sent him straight to me."

"That wasn't fair of her, and I'm sorry she did that," Auntie Em said.

"Yeah, well. I shouldn't be surprised, and yet..." I sighed, looking back out over the backyard.

"Sometimes the past has to rear its ugly head to remind us to appreciate what we have now, and to look forward to the future," Auntie Em remarked.

I snorted. "I guess that's true."

Auntie Em laughed, too, giving me a secretive smile. "I'm happy to see you and Nix have...rekindled your friendship. He's a good man."

"He really is." I nodded in agreement, a smile lifting my lips. "He makes me feel...safe. Emotionally and physically." I thought back to the night before, how he held me in his arms and eased the hurt and betrayal I'd felt over my mother's actions with his mere presence.

"That's a good thing, sweetie. You deserve that," Auntie Em said, giving my hand a gentle squeeze.

"You don't think it's too soon?" I worried my lip, glancing at my aunt.

"I think it's not soon enough," Auntie Em winked. "There's always been a special connection between the two of you. I'm so happy you're finally exploring it."

CHAPTER TWENTY-FOUR

Nix

Sage had been really shaken up by her ex-fiancé's appearance at the school last night. She hadn't expected to see him and confessed she'd had no idea he was so interested in talking to her because she'd blocked his phone number. He'd also never tried to see her when she'd been in Guelph staying at her friend Nellie's place, and then her mom's.

She admitted it was only recently she'd heard from her mom that Warren was trying to get in touch.

We spent the evening talking about it and various other deeper topics. I held her in my arms, and we fell asleep that way after exhausting ourselves conversing. Although I would have liked to have made her forget about the whole thing in *other* ways, I knew she needed to talk about it, and I was happy to be that shoulder to help her process her thoughts.

I really hadn't wanted to leave Sage's apartment Saturday morning, but when I woke up, there were several missed text messages from my brothers. I knew Sage also had a phone call to make to her mother to find out why in the hell she'd given up her new address to someone Sage had explicitly said she was finished with.

Apparently, during their night out at The Quarter Lounge, my brothers and Tabitha had discovered our unwanted visitor was staying at the bed and breakfast Annalise's family owned. Now that I had that information, I decided to go to the bed and breakfast and face him myself.

The Galloway family had owned the bed and breakfast for a few generations, and Annalise worked as the innkeeper. I knew the information likely came from her—unofficially—and I didn't want to get her in trouble. She was in the main room dusting the library shelves when I walked in.

"Morning, Annalise." I smiled politely. "Is the dining room open today?"

"Yes...are you meeting someone?" Annalise asked, arching a brow in question.

"Sure am," I replied, walking past her and continuing toward the dining room.

She grabbed my elbow, tugging me back for a minute, a concerned look on her face. "Nix, you can't start anything here. This is a place of business."

"I promise I'm not going to start anything. I'm just going to have a friendly chat with the man over coffee."

Annalise's eyes narrowed like she didn't quite believe me. "I'm serious. No funny business."

"Scout's honour," I promised.

She sighed, glancing into the dining room with a look of aversion. It was evident she wasn't his biggest fan either. "Don't make me regret this," she warned, pointing her duster at me. I nodded, receiving the message loud and clear.

I continued my quest, walking into the dining room and spotting Warren sitting at one of the tables by himself, reading the newspaper with his breakfast almost untouched in front of him. He was in another fancy business suit, his hair slicked back and that aura of pomposity still lingering.

I sat down across from him, and he looked up, his expression going from annoyed at the interruption, to shocked at my appearance in front of him, to furious it was me crashing his morning.

"Hello again, Warren."

"What do you want? Other than more clothes, obviously," Warren sneered, staring at the clothes I'd been wearing yesterday while he folded up the newspaper in his hands and set it down beside him.

My smile widened. I wasn't about to tell him the only reason I was wearing the same clothes was because I'd spent the night at his ex-fiancée's. I wasn't there to goad the man.

"I just came by to make sure you were leaving today." I shrugged. He leaned back in his seat, appraising me.

"My business in Hartwood Creek isn't over yet, so no. I won't be leaving today," he jeered.

"If you're referring to the business with Sage, I can assure you—that's over."

"I wouldn't be so sure about that." He smirked.

I lifted a brow. "She wants nothing to do with you and has no desire to hear you out, so you're wasting your time there. She said as much yesterday, in front of the both of us. Frankly, your behaviour is concerning a lot of people who care about her."

"My behaviour?" He smirked, shaking his head. "There's nothing wrong with my behaviour. I have every right to talk to my fiancée—"

"*Ex*-fiancée," I corrected, cutting him off. "Or did you forget the part where she dumped your ass and left you?"

His eyes flashed with anger. "She only left because I let her."

"What a possessive, controlling thing to say." I laughed darkly, shaking my head. I leaned forward, my eyes full of intent. "She left because she wanted to. You cheated, and she realized she could do a hell of a lot better than you. She's moved on, and it's time for you to do the same. Pack your shit and get out of my town. I won't say it again."

"*Your* town?" he snipped.

"Yeah, *my* town. I live here. You don't. You're just here to stir up shit because your ego's bruised, and I'm here to tell you I'm not going to let you do that. Nor will anyone else in this town. Sage is one of us, and we protect our own."

I don't know if Warren registered the promise in my eyes and the sincerity in my voice, but the arrogant assurance he'd led with since showing up slipped away real quick.

He watched me wearily. "*You're* with her, aren't you?"

"Sure am, but even if I wasn't, what you're doing is wrong. When a lady tells you to back off, you back the hell off. You don't keep pursuing, and you certainly don't show up at her new town demanding she talks to you."

Warren listened, nodding slowly as if considering my words. "I'll admit, that wasn't my best move. Her mother made it seem like there was a possibility she'd hear me out if I showed up in person."

I shook my head, exhaling. "You thought you'd listen to the mother who barely knows what's right for herself, over the woman who's explicitly told you on more than one occasion it's over and she's done? She blocked your number. That should have been indication enough."

He looked like I was forcing him to swallow shards of glass —but I guess the truth tasted like that to some.

"Fair point," he managed. I kept my gaze on him, unyielding. He sighed. "Fine, I'll leave town."

Feeling like I'd gotten my point across, I stood and rapped

my knuckles on the table. "I hope you enjoy the rest of your *brief* stay in Hartwood Creek," I said, leveling a look at him.

Sage

Halfway through my workday on Monday, the door chimed, signaling the arrival of a customer. Uncle Ed was in the back office working on paperwork, leaving me to manage the cash register and help customers.

There hadn't been many people in, so when I heard the door chime, I looked up with a smile, ready to greet whoever walked in.

I wasn't expecting to see Warren—*again*. My smile immediately slipped. "What are you doing here?" I demanded.

Warren lifted his arms in surrender, approaching the counter as if he was dealing with a wild and potentially dangerous animal. "I mean no harm. I just came by to apologize before I head back to Guelph." He stopped in front of the counter.

I folded my arms across my chest, taking a defensive stance. "Well, you've apologized. Now leave."

Warren smiled, the same kind of lethargic, bemused smile he used to give me. It had zero effect on me now—I much preferred Nix's assortment of smiles, and how they made me swoon at the same time they showed his feelings and thoughts. I could always get a feel for what he was thinking by the way he was smiling at me.

"Don't worry, I know I'm not very...*welcome* here, and I'll leave as soon as I'm done saying this. But...how I handled myself the other night, and after...well, what happened between us, it was wrong, and I wanted to apologize for my behaviour. I deeply regret how I handled myself, both before our breakup and now after. I shouldn't have cheated on you, and I shouldn't have made you feel like it was your fault I did so. It wasn't. That was...all me."

"Okay..." I trailed off, my brows raising. "I'm not sure what you want me to say. That I forgive you? Because there's nothing to forgive. Not really, anyway. You weren't right for me, and I didn't realize it until you proved it. So thank you for proving it, I guess?"

Warren nodded, absorbing my answer. "I wanted to be right for you, I really did. I wanted to be the person you thought I was, but..."

"You weren't, and you aren't," I finished, my lips pursing.

He nodded again, this time in solemn agreement. "I am glad you've found that—glad you've found someone who cares about you as much as your plaid shirt guy seems to."

He was referring to Nix, and all I could do was stare at him, trying to figure out what his angle was. I didn't exactly trust his intentions, but he seemed sincere enough.

"I'm glad I've found him too," I finally said, because it was true—I was glad I'd found him and said yes to a date with him. After witnessing the protective stance he'd taken and the concern he'd shown when he thought I was threatened, I was glad I'd allowed him to comfort me.

The caring way he'd reassured me after I'd come to the realization my mother had betrayed my trust yet again had only emboldened the fact that he was the one for me.

Nix had carved his way into my heart, chiseling past my defenses. In that moment, I realized I was ready to let him in—let him stay there, where it truly felt like he belonged.

"You do seem a lot happier here," Warren concurred. "I'm...relieved to see that. I wish you all the best."

He went to leave, and I watched him go without saying anything else, my thoughts on Nix.

SOMEHOW, I made it to the end of the workday, my thoughts interlaced with my newly acknowledged deep feelings for Nix. Part of me had wanted to text him or call him and tell him I was ready to take things to the next step and make it official between us. We'd yet to do that, although I knew his intentions from the beginning.

But I also kind of felt like that was a conversation we should have in person, after I'd asked my daughter for *her* thoughts on the matter.

I wasn't sure what to do with all the noise in my head when I pulled up to Tabitha and Parker's house. Parker's truck was gone, and so was Nix's truck—both still at their respective jobs.

Tabitha and the kids were all in the backyard, taking advantage of the warm, sunny day. I opened the gate and walked through, waving at the girls as I made my way up to Tabitha, who was sitting on the deck using her foot to rock a sleeping Bryson in his car seat.

"Hey," she said softly, grinning as she set the paperback she'd been reading down on the table. "How was work?"

"Hey," I replied, sitting down across from her. "It was...interesting."

"How so?"

"Warren came by," I told her, and her smile immediately faded, a look of concern washing over her face. "He wanted to apologize for his behaviour at the fundraiser—and before. He also said he was glad I'd found someone who cares about me as much as 'plaid shirt guy' seems to care about me."

"Huh," Tabitha said thoughtfully, leaning back. "I'm assuming he's referring to Nix?"

"Probably. I'm sure that had something to do with the standoff they had at the fundraiser."

"Maybe," Tabitha said, trying to hold back a smile. I raised my brows, waiting for her to continue. "It might *also* have something to do with the private chat Nix had with him," she finished.

"What? When did Nix have a private chat with Warren?"

Tabitha bit down on her bottom lip, thinking. "Umm... Saturday morning, I think? When we were at The Quarter Lounge on Friday night, we found out Warren was staying at Annalise's bed and breakfast. I'm pretty sure the twins texted Nix. Annalise said he came by the next morning."

"What did he say?"

"You'll have to ask Nix for the full story. Annalise only overheard bits and pieces, but from the sounds of it, he gave Warren shit for not backing off and listening to you, and he made it clear he wouldn't tolerate any harassment toward you. He also *may* have told him to kick rocks because he wasn't welcome in our town."

I smiled, trying to picture Nix doing that. I'd never had someone rise to my defense so unquestionably before.

"He should be back soon if you want to hang around for him..." Tabitha suggested. I glanced out at the backyard, at my daughter playing happily with her girls. Aside from waving back when I first arrived, Daphne had been absorbed in their games.

"Well, she's in no rush." I laughed, shaking my head.

"If you want to, you and Daphne can stay for dinner. We were just going to order pizza from Pizza Picasso."

"That sounds good." I smiled.

CHAPTER TWENTY-FIVE

Nix

I pulled into the driveway way later than usual after being held up at the jobsite. Everything that could go wrong had gone wrong, and although I had hoped to get away long enough to surprise Sage for a quick lunch on my break, I hadn't managed it. Heck, I couldn't take a full break at all. Aside from the gut truck sandwich I'd managed to scarf down around three o'clock, I hadn't had much to eat.

Sage's car in the driveway was a welcoming sight. I wasn't expecting her to still be here, as she'd usually be long gone by now. I'd worried about her all day long, wondering if she was okay. Although she'd texted with me a few times on Sunday, I hadn't seen her since leaving her apartment Saturday morning. She had wanted to call and confront her mother about telling Warren where to find her.

I knew that conversation couldn't have been easy, but Sage had brushed it off in the text messages, assuring me she and everything else was fine. I wasn't sure how much of it was a front, though. Sage was very independent, and far too used to handling everything by herself. The betrayal in her eyes when she'd spoken about her mother had made *me* ache. All I wanted to do was fix it all for her and ease every hurt.

Which is probably what prompted my little chat with Warren. That was one situation I could rectify and had. Annalise texted to let me know that he'd checked out Monday morning. I hadn't expected him to leave the moment I'd threatened him—no, he was too stubborn for that—but Annalise had mentioned he hadn't left his room at the inn all Sunday. Knowing he was back in Guelph made me feel better.

My phone buzzed with a text message from Tabitha, letting me know they'd ordered enough pizza for me if I wanted to come join them. I stopped off at my apartment to change quickly before going into the main house, where I found everyone sitting around the dining room table.

Sage and Daphne were there, and the worried feeling I'd been carrying in my chest dissipated when I saw the contented look on Sage's face. She seemed lighter and happier than when I'd left her place on Saturday.

"Hey, everyone," I said when I walked in. Sage smiled softly at me, and everyone else said hello. Parker passed me a plate, and I started loading it up with slices of pizza and sat down across from them, between Parker and Brielle.

"Hey, Nix! Why did the old man fall in a well?" Daphne asked me, peering at me with her mother's beautiful shade of green eyes.

"I don't know, why?"

"Because he couldn't see that well, duh!" Daphne finished her joke, her smile wide and pleased when I laughed. "Uncle Ed told me that one. He's got funnier jokes than you."

"I'll have to get him to teach me a few." I chuckled, my gaze shifting to Sage. She watched us interact with a smile. The way

Sage was looking at me—like I hung the stars and the moon—made me feel weightless.

The evening carried on, conversations and laughter happening while we ate. When most of the pizza had been eaten and everyone was stuffed, I stood up to tidy the mess, grabbing the empty plates and carrying them over to the kitchen so I could load them in the dishwasher. It was something I tried to do anytime Tabitha or Parker extended an invitation to me to join them for a meal.

Sage got up, too, collecting the empty plates from their side of the table.

"Oh, you don't have to do that," Tabitha told her when she noticed. She'd been trying to wipe the pizza sauce from Bryson's face with a napkin.

"It's okay, I don't mind. Thank you again for dinner." Sage smiled, carrying the plates into the kitchen. "We'll probably get out of your hair now, since tomorrow is a school and workday."

"Aww!" came a chorus of voices from the table as all three girls voiced their displeasure.

Tabitha's lips twitched with a smile. "You'll see each other tomorrow at school," she reminded them.

"Yeah, but it's not the same. We sit at different desks, and we're only allowed to play and be silly at recess. That's not enough time, Mommy," Brielle complained.

Sage and I exchanged grins before she turned to look at her daughter. "You girls have fifteen minutes tops, then we have to go, Daph."

"Okay," they cheered, pushing back their chairs and scooting out of the dining room, heading for the family room to play.

"I'm going to give Mr. Bryson here a quick bath," Tabitha said, picking up a sauce-covered Bryson from his highchair and shooting Parker a look. "Come and help me?"

Parker went to argue, saw the expression on Tabitha's face, and got the hint. "Yeah, sure." He stood and followed Tabitha out of the kitchen, leaving Sage and me alone.

Sage started putting the dishes I'd rinsed into the dishwasher, and I helped. Once we'd loaded them all in, I closed it and took a step toward her, placing my hand on her hip and a kiss to her temple. I'd been wanting to do it since the moment I caught sight of her but hadn't wanted to be so familiar with her in front of Daphne.

"Hey, beautiful," I said.

"Hi," she said back, smiling at me shyly. She looked as if she had something on her mind.

"What's going on?" I asked, concerned.

"Nothing," she replied, and I gave her a look. "I was just thinking…"

"About what?" I asked, my curiosity growing.

"I know we only just started…seeing each other, so maybe it's crazy but…my heart, and my head…I feel…" She furrowed her brow and squinched up her face as if trying to organize her thoughts. I ran my hands up and down her arms, trying to soothe her, my lips tilting in a grin.

I'd felt her interest in me before. She'd made it very apparent she was into me, but I hadn't felt her walls come down until that moment when she'd looked at me across the table after Daphne told her joke.

Something had changed, and I could feel it in the air between us. I could *hear* it in the words she was struggling to get out.

"What are you trying to say, Sage?"

"I—I think I'm ready to make this official, if you still want that…" she trailed off, worrying her bottom lip as if she feared I'd changed my mind.

I grinned, tipping her chin up gently, my gaze locking on

hers. "Of course, I still want that," I assured her. "More than anything."

"Good," she murmured. She checked quickly to make sure nobody was around before standing on her tiptoes and pressing her lips to mine, her arms wrapping around my waist as she kissed me softly. I kissed her back with reverence.

After a couple of moments, she broke the kiss and rested her head against my chest. Nothing had ever felt more right.

"Does this make you my girlfriend now?" I asked, and she laughed lightly.

"Yes," she replied with zero hesitation, her eyes shining.

"How about for our first official date as a couple, I take you and Daphne somewhere together?"

"Really?" Sage looked surprised at my suggestion.

I nodded earnestly. "Yes, really. I meant it when I told you before, I don't mind spending time with Daphne too. There's a lot of fun stuff we can do in town."

"That sounds good. What are you thinking?"

"Maybe we'll go out for dinner and to Lakeview Mini Golf?" She nodded like she liked the sound of that. "Okay, how about Friday night?"

Sage

As I tucked my daughter into her bed later that night, my mind whirled with how to broach the topic of dating Nix. I didn't want to rush it, but I knew we had to have the chat before Nix took us out on Friday.

I'd said yes to officially being his girlfriend before I'd had the conversation with Daphne about it because I'd been so swept up in him, in the comfort and the anticipation of what he was offering.

He wanted to take the both of us out, together, and I knew it was heartfelt. As much as I didn't want to compare him to my ex, even Warren hadn't done that. He'd wanted to take me out on dates, sure, but never Daphne. He'd always been nice to her but also indifferent.

Nix wasn't aloof around her. He interacted with her the same way he connected to his nieces—as if she was a human he enjoyed being around.

But that didn't mean *she* would be into the suggestion. In fact, the very idea of me having another boyfriend might upset or confuse her, and that was the last thing I wanted to do.

"Did you have fun tonight?" I asked, pulling the blankets up to her chin.

"Yes. Did you?"

"I did." I smiled. "I enjoy hanging out with the Hutchinsons."

"And *Nix*?" she said his name teasingly, as if I had a crush on him and she knew it. She wasn't that far off, although I was pretty sure my crush had evolved into something so much more.

"Would it bother you if I...enjoyed hanging out with Nix?" I questioned, watching her closely for any telltales of sadness or doubt. But the grin that came to her face had me smiling too.

"No. Bella and Brielle say he has a crush on you. Do you have a crush on him?"

"A little bit," I admitted. Daphne gave me a look that suggested she wasn't buying my answer. "Okay, a lot. I like him a lot. He makes me feel happy."

"Good. I like Nix. He's nice! His jokes are a little lame, but we'll work on that. Maybe Uncle Ed can teach him some good ones."

"Maybe." My smile grew as I tucked a strand of her hair behind her ear.

"Is he honest, Mommy?" Daphne asked, her little face crinkling in concern.

I took a moment to reply, weighing what I knew about Nix from before and what I'd seen from him recently. Nix donned no mask; he was who he said he was. He wore his heart on his sleeve and was authentic in his words and actions.

It wasn't just in what I knew and felt—the whole town seemed to love him. He had the approval of the Hartley sisters, and as much as I tried to deny the magic of the love elixir, I had to admit the sisters seemed to have a pretty good read on people.

"Yes, I think he is."

"Good." She seemed satisfied with my answer.

"He wants to take us out on a date Friday night," I told her.

"Both of us?" Her eyes widened with bewilderment.

"Yes, both of us. Would you like that?"

Daphne thought about it for a few moments, and then she nodded. "Yes."

"All right, good. I'll tell him we can go." Leaning forward, I kissed her on the cheek. "Goodnight, Squirt."

"Goodnight, Mommy." I had almost made it to the door when she spoke again. "Mommy? If you marry Nix one day, will I be Bella and Brielle's sister?"

"Marriage is a long way off," I replied, growing a little concerned. "Like, a *long* way off. Right now, we're just... boyfriend and girlfriend."

"Oh, I know that. But...if you *did* marry him one day, *would* I be their sister?"

"No, but you'd be cousins."

"Okay." She nodded, accepting that answer. She wiggled in

her bed, getting comfortable, and closed her eyes, a peaceful expression settling over her face.

I flicked out her light and closed the door softly, standing outside of it for a moment. I was surprised at how easy the conversation had gone, but then again...I hadn't serial dated throughout her life. Warren was the only serious relationship I'd had, so she had some memories of me dating, but nothing like the memories I had of my mother.

Nix

On Friday night, I showed up at five thirty with another beautiful custom bouquet of flowers from Hartwood Creek Flowers for Sage, and a matching, slightly smaller one for Daphne. I knocked on their apartment door and waited.

A few moments later, Sage's door swung open to reveal a dressed-up Daphne.

"Mommy's still getting ready, but she said you could come in," she informed me. She spotted the bouquets in my hand. "Are those flowers?" she asked, wide-eyed.

"Of course they are. Can't take a girl out on a date without bringing her flowers," I replied. "These are for you." I handed Daphne her bouquet.

"For *me*?" she exclaimed, excitedly taking the bouquet from me. "They're beautiful. Mommy, look what Nix brought me," she shouted, whirling around and running down the hallway toward Sage's bedroom.

Sage stepped out of her room, meeting her daughter in the living room. "Ooh, very pretty!" she complimented, her eyes rising to meet mine. She was wearing a sundress and a pair of white tennis shoes, her hair curled around her shoulders.

Daphne was in similar attire—a sundress and white tennis shoes, although her hair was braided in two thick braids down her back.

"You both look beautiful," I told them, grinning. "Are you ready for our date?"

"Where are we going?" Daphne asked, practically bouncing on her tiptoes with excitement.

"I figured we'd grab something to eat, then go check out Lakeview Mini Golf."

"That sounds fun, doesn't it, Daph?" Sage asked, and Daphne nodded eagerly.

"I've never played mini golf before," she exclaimed.

"Let's go put those flowers in some water, and then we'll go," Sage said. They came into the kitchen, and as Sage passed me, she noticed the other bouquet in my hands.

"These are for you," I told her, pressing a kiss to her temple.

"Thank you." She smiled, taking them from me and bringing them to her nose to sniff. "These are beautiful. We love them...don't we, Daph?"

"Yes!" Daphne nodded her agreement. Sage put their flowers in water, leaving them on the island, and grabbed her purse off the stool.

"I guess we should probably take my car...for Daphne's car seat?" She looked at me with uncertainty.

"Yeah, that'd probably be best. Mind if I drive?" I asked. Sage nodded, grabbing her keys. We waited for her to lock the apartment up, then the three of us headed down to the parking lot to get into Sage's car.

I moved the seat back to accommodate my longer legs, grinning when I met Daphne's excited eyes in the rear-view mirror. The kid was grinning from ear to ear. "Who's hungry?" I asked.

"I'm *starving*," Daphne said, buckling her seat belt. I pulled out of the parking lot, driving us to the Mexican restaurant.

Juan in a Million was owned by the Lopez family, and they were known to have the most amazing chimichangas and enchiladas in three counties. It was another gem of a spot in Hartwood Creek I was excited to introduce Sage—and Daphne—to. And I was glad I had. They both *loved* the restaurant and the renowned enchilada sauce.

After finishing our meal, we headed to the zone to play a round of mini golf. Daphne loved the nautical theme. The mini golf course holes had running water, shipwrecks, and caves, each hole more of a challenge than the last. But to Daphne's delight, she beat both Sage and me at every round.

"Are you *sure* she's never played mini golf before?" I asked, eyeing the six-year-old with suspicion as she sent the golf ball directly through the lighthouse on the last course, effectively winning the round.

"No." Sage laughed. "But she picks up on things fast." She looked at her daughter with pride.

"She gets it from you," I remarked, and Sage turned to look at me with an appreciative smile.

"Thank you for including her. It means a lot to us both."

I put my arm around her waist, tugging her close. "Get used to it. I'm just as serious about her as I am about you...and I'm really serious about you."

"Most guys say they're serious, but they don't want the added aggravation of accommodating a kid or including them on date nights," Sage pointed out.

"Well, I'm not most guys. And if I'm going to make her mother fall in love with me, I better make sure she does too."

"You won't have to try very hard to make me fall in love with you. I'm already there. As for Daphne, I'm sure you could win her heart by continuing to make her feel important."

I gazed at her with adoration before leaning in, sealing my promises and intentions with a kiss.

WHEN WE GOT BACK to Sage's house later that night, I stuck around until after Daphne went to bed. I had a little gift for Sage I'd wanted to give her that had burnt a metaphorical hole in my pocket all night.

Once Sage returned from tucking Daphne in, she poured two glasses of wine and we curled up on her couch. I wrapped my arm around her shoulder, and she leaned into me.

"I had an amazing time tonight, Nix. So did Daph. Thank you for taking us out," she told me, resting her head on my shoulder.

"Honestly, I had a great time too. We'll do it again sometime soon. Maybe we could check out the Fall Fair together next weekend?"

Sage lifted her head, glancing at me. "That would be great. Daphne loves fairs."

"What kid doesn't." I grinned. "Heck, I love them too. Can't beat the cotton candy and the food trucks."

"It's a date, then." Sage grinned at me, her eyes dropping to my mouth. Her tongue darted out, licking the seam of her lips. I couldn't resist the pull, leaning in to kiss her how I'd wanted to all evening. My other hand framing the side of her face, I poured everything into the kiss, letting her know exactly what I felt about her.

When she pulled away to catch her breath, her eyes were smouldering. "Did you want to stay a little later?" She arched a delicate brow suggestively.

"Damn right I do, but first...I have something to give you," I said, reaching into my pocket.

"Oh, you didn't have to get me anything," Sage exclaimed.

"It's just a little something I made for you," I told her, handing it to her. She looked at it, her eyes widening as she took in the intricate hand-carved Celtic love knot pendant. It was made up of two interlacing knots forming the shape of a heart.

The knots weaved between each other to make one heart facing downward and the other facing upward, and was made of one continuous line.

I'd carved it from walnut hardwood and sanded it with a high grit sandpaper for the smooth, shiny, even surface. I oiled it twice and rubbed it with natural beeswax paste to protect it from humidity before looping it through a black leather cord.

"Oh, Nix. It's beautiful!" Sage whispered, running her finger over its smooth surface.

"You're beautiful," I told her, rubbing her shoulder with my fingers. She looked at me, like she couldn't believe her luck. In reality, I couldn't believe *mine*. That this incredible woman had agreed to trust me with her heart. I would spend all of eternity happily proving to her I was worth that trust.

"What does it mean?" Sage asked, glancing back down at the pendant.

I swallowed, preparing myself. "It represents two people joined together in love. The continuous line represents the eternity of love. Sage, I know we're just starting out on this path together...but I'd be lying if I said I haven't had strong feelings for you for a while now. I'm so head over heels in love with you."

"I—I—" She seemed to be at a loss for words. Her eyes glistened with unshed tears, although they didn't appear to be sad tears. Unable to formulate a sentence, Sage leaned in and kissed me, conveying all she couldn't verbalize with her lips. She pulled back, drawing in a stabilizing breath. It was like she was still trying to figure out what to say.

I framed her face, running my thumb along her jaw and urging her to meet my eyes. "You don't have to say anything, I just wanted you to have this—and I wanted you to know how I feel about you," I assured her.

She shook her head, smiling. "I love it, Nix. And...I love

you. I think I've been in love with you for a long time too. There's always been something about your soul that's called to mine, and I'm ready to answer that call."

I grinned as I helped her put the pendant on, and she admired it for a moment before climbing onto my lap and kissing me deeply. Her hands trailed over my shoulders, running down my chest to toy with my abdomen, making my muscles tighten in anticipation.

EPILOGUE

Sage

Daphne skipped ahead, her plastic jack-o-lantern bucket bouncing around with each step she took. "Come on! We're going to be late," she called out, looking back over her shoulder at us with impatience.

We were on our way to the Tout de Sweets to meet Nix's family for the Halloween Spook costume contest. The Halloween Spook was the big celebration the town put on, and the costume contest was one Daphne had been looking forward to most. The shops put on spooktacular sales and vendors offered psychic readings and seances. Visitors and tourists could also learn about the original Hartley sisters and the lore of the love elixir.

Every local and tourist in attendance wore costumes, even the pets got in on it. Earlier that afternoon, there had been a pet parade where locals dressed their pets up in costumes and walked the streets. Hannah Albert and Klaus Bauer had dressed up Chewpacca as his namesake, wearing a bandolier and a fake bowcaster while they dressed up as Princess Leia and Hans Solo. Daphne had *loved* that event, and immediately started asking for a puppy so she could enter next year's pet parade.

Nix had warned me the town of Hartwood Creek really went to the extremes at Halloween, but I'd still been surprised. They'd spared no expense, every single shop in the downtown core was decorated. There were elaborate fall arrangements from Hartwood Creek Flowers with skeletons peeking out hanging from every streetlamp. Each store participated in the pumpkin carving contest, displaying their carved pumpkins outside.

There was a giant pumpkin weighing 2,560 pounds in Hartwood Park that had been painstakingly carved in the original Hartley triplet's likeness, with a witchy spin. According to the local newspaper, it had taken eleven hours to carve.

Hartwood Creek put on a lot of town events, but I had to admit—this one was shaping up to be my favourite.

Nix held my hand as we walked, to Nellie's absolute delight.

Nellie had come out the day before to join us, and she absolutely adored Nix. She'd given him the stamp of her approval within twenty minutes of meeting him. "I get a good vibe off him," she'd told me with the biggest grin on her face. That approval had only grown when Nix showed up to pick us up dressed in full costume.

We'd all dressed as monsters from the "Monster Mash" song—Nellie's grand idea, of course. She always came up with the best costume themes, and although she originally balked at the number of people she'd have to coordinate this year, she'd managed to pull off a great idea that everyone had been on board for.

Nix was Gillman, the fish monster, while I was dressed as a mummy with bandages wrapped all around my body, including my face. Daphne was a witch, and Nellie was Dr. Jekyll and Mr. Hyde, her costume a perfect split of both characters. Her makeup was incredible—it was so good she'd made Daphne gasp in horror when she first walked out of my bathroom.

"Is that them?" Nellie asked, squinting toward the boardwalk at the group gathered there. The Bride of Frankenstein waved frantically to get our attention, a megawatt smile on her face, while Frankenstein looked a little less enthused.

Tabitha was holding Bryson in her arms; he was a baby Frankenstein. Bella and Brielle were dressed as zombies, while Preston and Paxton had gone all out with their costumes. Preston was Igor, and Paxton was the Mad Scientist.

Even Laurel and Keith had shown up in costumes, both wearing matching skeleton onesies.

"Wow, the whole family got in on it," I remarked, impressed. They'd taken Nellie's idea and ran with it.

"My family rarely does anything half-assed," Nix replied, his voice a little muffled behind his Gillman mask. I giggled because he sounded so ridiculous and squeezed his hand.

Daphne spotted the twins and raced toward them, her bucket swinging out behind her. We joined them all, and Nix introduced Nellie to his family, pointing out who everyone was.

"Whoa! Uncle Nix, is that you?" Bella asked, her zombified eyes widening.

"Yup! My mom's a mummy, and Nellie's Dr. Cackle and Mr. Hyde," Daphne informed them proudly.

"It's Dr. Jekyll and Mr. Hyde," I corrected with a smile.

"We're going to win the group costume *for sure*," Brielle declared. It had been the kids' idea to enter the Halloween costume contest at Tout de Sweets. The girls took off toward the action, forcing the adults to follow.

We hit up every shop along the way to the café, watching as

the girls collected candy and the townsfolk fussed over their costumes—and ours.

We finally made it to Tout de Sweets just as the Hartley triplets were calling everyone who wanted to participate in the contest forward. They were dressed as the Sanderson sisters from *Hocus Pocus*. Dorothy's hair was styled up in two curly buns and sprayed red like Winifred Sanderson, while Betty was rocking a black wig with purple streaks like Mary. Alice had an arm of bangles and a long blond wig, which she kept tossing over her shoulders.

The Hartley sisters shared a microphone between the three of them, and Dorothy was speaking into it, explaining the rules. "We'll be choosing winners in three separate categories: Best Individual Costume, followed by Best Couples Costume, and finally...the Best Group Costume."

"Please stay where you are and allow the three of us to come around and check out your wonderful costumes. Then we'll pick the winners," Betty added, and the sisters started their rounds.

The kids munched on candy as patiently as their excitement allowed them, while the adults in our group chatted amongst themselves. Tabitha and Parker were trying to keep Bryson entertained, who was beginning to get restless in his costume, while Preston and Paxton were both hitting on Nellie. From the sounds of it, they were trying to see which one she'd prefer—which was hysterical, considering they both looked ridiculous in their costumes. Nellie seemed to enjoy the attention, though.

Keith and Laurel were chatting with Auntie Em and Uncle Ed, who'd surprised us all and shown up in costumes that fit the theme too. Uncle Ed was a werewolf, while Auntie Em had dressed up as Dracula. She'd even worn her hair pulled back in a braid and done a fake widow's peak.

Daphne was ecstatic they'd shown up, and when the Hartley sisters approached us to find out the inspiration for our costume, she happily informed them we were "from the 'Monster Mash' song."

Dorothy, Betty, and Alice had all exchanged impressed looks with each other before moving on to judge the rest of the costumes.

My cheeks hurt from smiling, and my heart practically burst with happiness to see my daughter surrounded by so many people who cared about her. And not just her, either... but me as well.

This town and the people in it had embraced me as one of their own the moment I'd relocated here, and I couldn't be more grateful for it. It felt like my own personal Stars Hollow; only instead of a grumpy diner owner, I'd fallen in love with an affectionate, compassionate carpenter who knew how to keep me laughing.

Nix put his arm around me, pulling me close to him, and brought his fish-mask-covered face close to my ear. "These costumes were a great idea. I can't wait to unwrap those bandages later," he murmured, tugging at one of the loose ones.

I laughed, trying to push him away a little. "You're lucky I love you." I shook my head.

Nix pulled his mask up, revealing his face and the euphoric grin on it. "I'm sorry, I didn't catch that?"

"I said—" I turned toward him, wrapping my arms around his waist and peering up into his warm brown eyes. "You're lucky I love you."

"I really am," he said, lowering his lips to mine. He gave me a soft kiss with the promise of more to come. His tongue ran along the seam of my lips for a fleeting moment that weakened my knees. All too soon, he was pulling back, his eyes shining with devotion. "I love you too, Sage. So very much. You are my entire future."

"Ehem!" Alice cleared her throat, back at the front of the shop. Her eyes twinkled as she took in the crowd. "We have decided on our winners. For Best Individual Costume, the honour goes to Elena Rodriguez, come on up here, honey!"

A young woman made her way to the front of the shop to accept her trophy and a little gift bag from the Hartley sisters. She was dressed as the Queen of Hearts from *Alice in Wonderland,* her makeup elaborately done so her entire right eye was covered with a sparkling red heart. Her lips were also painted the same, sparkling red colour.

"For Best Couples Costume, we have Marvin and Donna Gauthier," Betty announced. Marvin Gauthier was wearing a chef costume and his wife, Donna, was dressed as a rat. If I had to take a guess, they'd drawn inspiration from the *Ratatouille* movie. They approached the front, and Betty passed them their trophy and gift bag before motioning for them to go stand beside Elena Rodriguez.

"And finally...for Best Group Costume, we have the group that dressed up as the 'Monster Mash' song! I believe it's the Hutchinsons, the Alcotts, the Whitakers and Co," Alice announced, smiling wide. "Very impressive group effort!"

"I don't think we've ever had a group entry this big before," Betty added, chuckling.

Daphne, Bella, and Brielle all let out a cheer and took off as fast as they could to the front of the shop. The crowd parted for the rest of us, and soon all fifteen of us gathered around the Hartley triplets for our trophy and a gift bag.

The trophy was of a pumpkin that said '*Hartwood Creek's Halloween Spook, Best Group Costume*' with the date. In the gift bag were a bunch of coupons and gift cards to local shops, and small chocolates from Sweet Indulgence.

Betty, Alice, and Dorothy took to the stage again to congratulate all the winners and offer free beverages. "And don't forget, tonight is the Witches' Ball at the Hartwood Creek Inn! Adults only!"

Daphne, Bella, and Brielle all groaned with disappointment. Auntie Em put her arms around their shoulders. "Cheer up girls, we'll have our own ball!"

I'd been on the fence about going to the Witches' Ball, but Auntie Em and Uncle Ed had successfully talked me into it, mostly by inviting Daphne, Brielle, and Bella over for a sleepover. Laurel and Keith had offered to take Bryson for the night so Parker and Tabitha could join us.

Nellie was ecstatic to attend. "Oh, we are *so* doing that! I've never been to a town ball before," she'd said when I broached the idea to her. I'd never been either, and I was more than a little curious. As the leaves had started to change colour, the Witches' Ball was the talk of the town.

Apparently, it was a long-standing tradition in Hartwood Creek. Babysitters were booked months in advance for the occasion. They started selling tickets for the Witches' Ball at the Fall Fair in September, and by the end of the month... tickets were sold out. You couldn't just randomly show up.

The town allotted a small chunk of tickets for out-of-towners, but the majority of attendees were residents of Hartwood Creek, and the out-of-towner tickets sold fast. I'd managed to score one for Nellie from Tabitha, who ensured Annalise set one aside for her when she realized one of the reasons I was hesitating was my friend would be in town.

"See you girls soon," Auntie Em said, pressing a kiss to Daphne's forehead before she pulled me in for a hug. We had to get the girls something to eat beforehand, and we had to stop off at the apartment to pick up Daphne's overnight bag.

"Yes! Get the popcorn ready!" Daphne instructed with a toothy grin.

"Of course!" Uncle Ed winked, and the two of them headed out.

Tabitha handed a squirming Bryson over to Laurel while Keith took the diaper bag from Parker, shouldering it and tickling under Bryson's chin to make him giggle. "Thanks again for taking him overnight. I didn't want to overwhelm the Alcotts too much. They'll have their hands full with the girls," Tabitha remarked.

"It's our pleasure," Laurel said while Bryson snuggled into her and blinked sleepily. She practically melted, pressing a kiss on his forehead. "Oh, how I miss this age. Don't you, Keith?"

"Sometimes," Keith admitted, sending a warm smile to his grandson. "But having grandkids is pretty neat. We can send them back when we get tired."

Parker followed Laurel and Keith out to transfer Bryson's car seat while the rest of us debated on where to grab dinner.

"We could pick up a pizza on our way back to the apartment," Nix suggested. He'd pulled up his fish mask so he could breathe.

"Catch you guys later at the ball!" Paxton said, waving his gloved hand at us as he dragged Preston out. Once Parker returned, we made our way back to my apartment, stopping briefly at Pizza Picasso to pick up dinner.

After everyone ate, Parker drove the girls over to Auntie Em and Uncle Ed's before returning to grab the rest of us.

Finding parking at the inn was almost impossible, but Parker and Tabitha lived a few blocks away, so we parked at their house and walked over.

The Hartwood Creek Inn looked spooky with all the elaborate Halloween decorations. The inn was covered in fake-but-realistic looking spiderwebs with massive creepy spiders.

Hundreds, if not thousands, of pumpkins in varying sizes lined the walkway leading to the front door. Gravestones were scattered throughout the front yard to make an old-timey looking cemetery, with skeletons bursting out of graves. Ghosts and ghouls hung from the tree branches, and the upper windows facing the street had a projection display of zombies trying to break out.

The eerie green and purple light show happening from within made everything creepier. Music was pumping, and people dressed up in costumes were coming from every which way, walking up the sidewalks toward the inn.

"You guys are going to *love this!*" Tabitha squealed with excitement, practically skipping ahead of us and dragging Parker behind her. "If you think the town went all out for the Halloween Spook, just you wait!"

Nix took my hand, sending me a wink before he pulled his Gillman mask down over his face.

We followed the trail of people inside, stopping long enough to give our tickets to the tall burly man dressed as Lurch. He stamped our hands with an exaggerated moan, and we continued inside.

Each room had a spooky theme. Tabitha led the way to the bar. The extensive drink menu boosted Halloween Sangria, Bloody Mary Syringes, Black Magic Margaritas, Frankenpunch, Jekyll & Gin, Witches' Brew Lemonade, Sweet Poison Cocktails, Black Magic Jell-O Shots, the Zombie Cocktail, Pumpkin Spice White Russians, Salted Caramel-Apple Cider, and Fireball Sangria to name a few.

Overwhelmed, I let Tabitha order. She insisted we try the Halloween Sangria first. "Although, the night is young and you have to sample like, all of them," she insisted, passing it to me. Nix and Parker ordered Fireball Sangrias, then the five of us made our way to the dance floor.

Annalise had told me they'd cleared out a lot of furniture to create a makeshift dance floor in the front room, living room, and dining room. There was a live DJ set up, with speakers throughout the main floor. A long table was pushed against the far wall in the dining room full of hor d'oeuvres and other Halloween themed finger foods.

I sipped at my drink, taking in the sights with wide eyes. It was impressive and intimidating all at once. Nix wrapped his arm around my waist, keeping close to me as if he sensed it was overwhelming for me.

Preston and Paxton found us a few drinks later, when I'd relaxed enough to allow the others to drag me off to the dance floor. Lilah, Annalise, Ophelia, Isla and her husband appeared. Lilah came as Medusa, Annalise was dressed as Cleopatra, Ophelia as a Shield Maiden, and Isla and her husband were dressed as Ariel and Prince Eric.

I complimented Annalise on the amazing setup, and she grinned from ear to ear. "Thank you! I'm glad you're enjoying yourself. It's a lot to pull off every year, but it's worth it!" she yelled into my ear over the music.

Soon, Igor and the Mad Scientist were joining our dance circle and pulling some elaborate dance moves that made us all burst into laughter.

I was a little shocked Nix seemed to love dancing with me, but the Hutchinson brothers didn't seem to shy away from the dance floor. Even Parker embraced it as he danced with Tabitha. Parker and Nix's moves weren't as ridiculous as Preston's and Paxton's, but they were all having fun.

We were later joined by three more of Nix and Parker's friends, Noah Wood—who'd dressed as the Witcher, Donovan Ashe—who wore a VooDoo Man costume, and Mr. Robertson —who'd dressed up as Hercules.

A witch carrying a tray of Sour Patch Jell-O shots stopped

and asked us if we wanted any. Nellie insisted on taking half the tray, passing them out to our group. She even forced one in an unwilling Parker's hand, who shivered after downing it and insisted it was too sweet for him and that he'd stick to the Fireball Sangria.

Nix's hands on my waist grounded me, and the presence of all our friends and Nix's brothers made me feel safe and carefree.

Around eleven o'clock, Nellie tried to drag me upstairs to check out the psychic reading provided by Delia Hartley. I didn't buy into that kind of thing, even though Nellie tried to entice me by reminding me that it was Halloween. I declined, preferring to stay on the dance floor in Nix's arms. I didn't need a psychic reading to know I'd found my destiny.

Annalise happily took her up, and they returned sometime later with Nellie looking more than a little perplexed.

"Everything okay?" I shouted into her ear.

"Yeah, things are great. Awesome," Nellie replied, grabbing one of the Black Magic Jell-O shots from the tray a woman dressed as a serving wench was carrying. She tossed it back and grabbed two more, passing one to me while downing the other.

The drinks kept flowing, and we all kept laughing and dancing, having a great time. Nellie was flirting it up, enjoying all the attention her out-of-towner status brought. Noah, Preston, and Paxton were in serious competition, trying to garner her affections. Annalise and Ophelia were dancing with each other, Donovan was hitting on the serving wench, and it looked like Lilah was getting more than a little cozy with Mr. Robertson.

At some point during the night, we'd made our way over to the selfie station to take a few massive group photos.

By last call at one o'clock, we were all feeling no pain as we stumbled out of the inn, following the hordes of leaving people.

Shuttles had been arranged by the Galloway's to provide rides to party-goers, ensuring everyone got home safely.

Parker, Tabitha, Nix, Nellie and I planned on walking back to Parker and Tabitha's place, but Nellie threw her arms around me on the sidewalk.

"I'm gonna go with Noah back to his place," Nellie told me, hiccupping.

"You sure about that?" I asked, sending a wary glance at Noah Wood.

"Positive," Nellie nodded seriously. "I need a good dicking, and he looks like he can provide a fun little romp or two."

"Heard that, and yes I absolutely can." Noah grinned.

"How are you getting home?" Nix asked, his tone slightly parental. He'd long since lost his Gillman mask after setting it down somewhere inside.

"One of the shuttles will take us to my place. I got dropped off by Damien, so I can drive Nellie back tomorrow...at some point," Noah promised, smirking down at Nellie.

Once Nellie and Noah joined the shuttle line, Tabitha, Parker, Nix, and I started walking. I yawned, not used to staying out so late or partying. Tabitha seemed to be in worse shape, Parker had to keep his arm around her waist to keep her walking in a straight line—but she giggled the whole time like she thought it was the funniest thing.

When we got back, we went our separate ways—Tabitha and Parker went into their house, and Nix led the way up to his apartment over the garage.

I'd been in Nix's apartment a few times before, but we hadn't spent a lot of time there as he usually came to my place.

I didn't have a lot of time to explore; as soon as the door closed behind us, Nix was kissing me, his hands peeling off my costume just like he'd promised earlier. The layers fell away easily, but his costume was a little harder to get off. As soon as we'd gotten rid of our pesky costumes, we fell onto Nix's couch, all heated hands and searing kisses.

Nix normally took his time with me, but we were both too desperate after spending the entire night touching and teasing each other over clothes, dancing closely and grinding to music. The alcohol made us both even more frantic. He entered me in one quick, impatient thrust, and I welcomed him—fully ready and aching for more.

He filled me almost to the point of pain—but sweet pain that quickly faded into a throbbing pleasure. He pumped in and out in rhythmic, deep thrusts that hit every sweet spot within me until I was clawing at his back and shattering around him, the orgasm hitting me hard and dragging out.

Nix followed shortly after; he pounded into me a few more times, then he stiffened, his corded muscles tense as he came. "My flower. You always feel so good," he murmured against my neck, his arms pulling me closer.

He'd taken to calling me his flower as a term of endearment shortly after we made things official, and every time, it made me melt. His lips found mine again, giving me a slow, deep kiss before he pulled out and stood up.

"Uh, Nix?" I bit my lip, the alcoholic haze lifting enough. "We forgot to..." I looked pointedly at the erection he was still sporting with no condom in sight.

"Crap," Nix's brow furrowed. "I'm sorry, Sage. I got carried away," he added, sheepishly running a hand through his mused hair.

"We both got carried away," I corrected, sitting up.

"I've had STI testing between my last partner and you, and the results were negative, I swear, but..." he trailed off, his hand going to the back of his neck. "Hutchinson men are pretty damn fertile."

"I'm negative for STIs too," I assured him. I'd gotten tested shortly after finding out about Warren's cheating ways. "But the one and only time I had a whoops, nine months later Daphne was born..." I trailed off, thinking about how panicked I'd been when I realized the condom had broken.

Inwardly, I wasn't panicking like I probably should have been. I wasn't on any form of contraception—birth control pills made me hormonal and crazy, and as a teen I'd had a terrible experience with an IUD. I mainly just tracked my cycles and avoided being intimate without a condom. Nix knew this, and usually we were both a lot smarter about wrapping it before engaging but—I hadn't thought once about it during our quick rendezvous. I'd been too desperate to have him inside me.

"Damn, this is a heavy conversation to have while still a little drunk." Nix laughed, shaking his head. He sat down beside me, turning his body toward me, and taking my hand in his. "We haven't even really talked about that. About whether you want more kids or not."

"I do...definitely I do, in the future...I'm just not so sure about right now." I bit my lip, hoping I wasn't hurting his feelings.

Nix nodded, absorbing my answer, his lips lifting into a grin. "I want more kids too, one day. Especially with you." The way he'd said *more* kids, as if he'd included Daphne as his own and wanted more to follow, had my heartbeat skipping in my chest. "But I know things are early still, so if you want me to take you to get Plan B before we go for breakfast in the morning, we can do that for sure. I support you in whatever you want to do."

My eyes welled up with tears at his words, at his unwavering support and understanding. Being with Nix was so easy, so right. It was like the answer to every question I ever had, and every question I never knew I had.

"I think that would be best...for now. I kind of want to do things in the right order with you."

He pulled me into his arms, leaning back on the couch. "Sage, no matter what order things happen in—they're the right order for us. Trust me when I say, I'll happily walk whatever path you want to take holding your hand—and Daphne's. We will build our life together one step at a time."

18. Good Place – Mitchell Tenpenny
19. Lavender Haze – Taylor Swift

OTHER BOOKS BY J.C. HANNIGAN

Hartwood Creek Romance

Wood You Knot

Last Resort

ABOUT THE AUTHOR

J.C. Hannigan lives in Ontario, Canada with her husband, their two sons, and their dogs. She writes contemporary new adult romance and suspense. Her novels focus on relationships, mental health, social issues, and other life challenges.

Facebook: www.facebook.com/authorjchannigan
Threads: www.threads.com/@authorjchannigan
Instagram: www.instagram.com/authorjchannigan
Website: www.jchannigan.com
Goodreads: http://bit.ly/jchannigangr

If you enjoyed this story (or if you didn't), please take a moment to **post a review** on Goodreads, your blog, or whichever platform you use. Reviews help other readers find books, and I appreciate any and all reviews!

Sign up for my newsletter to receive exclusive stories, sneak peeks, and updates:
https://jchannigan.myflodesk.com/g343nxhzay

And if you like shenanigans, join my readers group FANnigans! There are exclusive giveaways, monthly live video events, and tons of other perks of becoming a FANnigan!
https://www.facebook.com/groups/FANnigans/